The PUFFIN TREASURY *of* CLASSICS

The
PUFFIN
TREASURY
of
CLASSICS

TED SMART

VIKING/PUFFIN

Published by the Penguin Group
Penguin Books Ltd, 27 Wrights Lane, London W8 5TZ, England
Penguin Books USA Inc., 375 Hudson Street, New York, New York 10014, USA
Penguin Books Australia Ltd, Ringwood, Victoria, Australia
Penguin Books Canada Ltd, 10 Alcorn Avenue, Toronto, Ontario, Canada M4V 3B2
Penguin Books (NZ) Ltd, 182–190 Wairau Road, Auckland 10, New Zealand

Penguin Books Ltd, Registered Offices: Harmondsworth, Middlesex, England

First published 1997
1 3 5 7 9 10 8 6 4 2

Printed in Italy by L.E.G.O.

British Library Cataloguing in Publication Data
A CIP catalogue record for this book is available from the British Library

ISBN 0–670–87847–2

This edition produced for The Book People Ltd, Hall Wood Avenue,
Haydock, St Helens WA11 9UL

CONTENTS

FOREWORD

Puffin's aim is, and always has been, to publish the best for children. This means not only seeking out the best contemporary work, but also preserving the literature and heritage of the past. Puffin Classics, with over one hundred and twenty titles in print, is the largest collection of paperback English-language children's classics in the world.

This treasury is an introduction to the world of children's classics. It draws on an exceptionally rich diversity of stories and verse from across the centuries. Some of these were never originally intended for children, but all have gained an unforgettable place in our tradition, and found their way into the hearts and minds of generations.

Whether this book is a first experience of the classics or a rediscovery of old favourites, we hope it will be enjoyed by everyone, and treasured for a lifetime.

PHILIPPA MILNES-SMITH
Publisher

Sabrina fair,
Listen where thou art sitting
Under the glassy, cool, translucent wave,
In twisted braids of lilies knitting
The loose train of thy amber-dropping hair;
Listen for dear honour's sake,
Goddess of the silver lake,
Listen and save.

JOHN MILTON
from COMUS

Hans Christian Andersen

from THE SNOW QUEEN

FROM
HANS ANDERSEN'S FAIRY TALES
Retold by Naomi Lewis

Illustrated by Alison Jay

One day Kay and Gerda were sitting looking at a picture book of birds and animals, and then – just as the clock in the great church tower began to strike five – Kay said, 'Oh! Something pricked me in my heart! Oh! Now I've got something in my eye!'

The little girl put her arm round his neck, and he blinked his eyes. But no, there was nothing to be seen.

'I think it's gone,' he said. But it hadn't. It was one of those tiny splinters from the demon's looking-glass – I'm sure you remember it. Poor Kay! He had got another piece right in his heart, which would soon be like a lump of ice. He didn't feel it hurting now, but it was there all right.

'Why are you crying?' he asked. 'It makes you look horribly ugly. There's nothing the matter with me. Ugh!' he cried suddenly. 'That rose has a worm in it. And look at that one – it's crooked.

They're rotten, all of them. So are the boxes, too.' And then he kicked the box hard, and tore off the two roses.

'Kay, what are you doing?' cried the little girl. And when he saw how frightened she was, he tore off a third rose, and ran in at his window, away from his little friend Gerda.

After that, when she brought out the picture book, he said that it was baby-stuff. When the grandmother told them stories, he would always find fault, and argue. He would even walk close behind her, put on spectacles, and mimic her way of talking. It was so well done that it made the people laugh. Soon he could mimic the ways of everyone in the street, especially if they were odd or unpleasant. People used to say, 'Oh, he's clever, that boy!' But all this came from the splinters of glass in his eye and in his heart; they made him tease even little Gerda, who loved him more than anything in the world.

His games had become quite different now; they were so scientific and practical. One winter's day, as the snowflakes drifted down, he brought out a magnifying glass, then held out the corner of his blue jacket to catch some falling flakes.

'Now look through the glass, Gerda,' he said. And she saw that every flake was very much larger, and looked like a splendid flower or a ten-pointed star. It was certainly a wonderful sight. 'Look at that pattern – isn't it marvellous!' said Kay. 'These are much more interesting than real flowers – and there isn't a single fault in them. They're perfect – if only they didn't melt.'

A little later Kay came back wearing big gloves and carrying his sledge on his back. He shouted into Gerda's ear: 'They're letting me go tobogganing in the town square where the others are playing!' And away he went.

Out in the square the boldest boys could often tie their sledges to farmers' carts, and so be pulled along for quite a ride. It was enormous fun. This time, while their games were in full swing, a very large sledge arrived; it was painted white all over, and in it sat a figure muffled up in a white fur cloak and wearing a white fur hat. This sledge drove twice round the square; but, moving quickly, Kay managed to fix his own sledge behind it, and a swift ride began. The big sledge went faster and faster, then turned off into the next street. The driver looked round and nodded to Kay in the friendliest fashion, just as if they had always known each other. Every time that Kay thought of unfastening his sledge, the driver would turn and nod to him again, so he kept still. On they drove, straight out of the city gates. And now the snow began to fall so thick and fast that the little boy couldn't even see his hand in front of him as they rushed along. At last he *did* manage to untie the rope but it was of no use; his little sledge still clung to the big one, and they sped along like the wind. He cried out at the top of his voice, but no one heard him; the snow fell, and the sledge raced on. From time to time it seemed to jump, as if they were going over dykes and hedges. Terror seized him; he tried to say the Lord's Prayer, but all he could remember was the multiplication table.

The snowflakes grew bigger and bigger, until at last they looked like great white birds. All at once they swerved to one side; the sledge came to a halt, and the driver stood up. The white fur cloak and cap were all of snow and the driver – ah, she was a lady, tall and slender, dazzlingly white! She was the Snow Queen herself.

'We've come far and fast,' she said. 'But you must be frozen. Creep under my bearskin cloak.' She put him beside her in the sledge and wrapped the cloak around him; he felt as if he were sinking into a snowdrift. 'Are you still cold?' she asked, and she kissed him on the forehead. Ah-h-h! Her kiss was colder than ice; it went straight to his heart, which was already half way to being a lump of ice. He felt

as if he were dying, but only for a moment. Then he felt perfectly well, and no longer noticed the cold.

'My sledge! Don't forget my sledge!' That was the first thought that came to him. So it was tied to one of the big white birds, which flew along with the little sledge at its back. The Snow Queen kissed Kay once again, and after that he had no memory of Gerda and grandmother, nor of anyone at home.

'Now I must give you no more kisses,' said the Snow Queen, 'or you will be kissed to death.'

Kay looked at her. She was so beautiful; he could not imagine a wiser, lovelier face. She no longer seemed to him to be made of ice, as she once had seemed when she came to the attic window and waved

4

to him. Now in his eyes she was perfect, and he felt no fear. He told her that he could do mental arithmetic, and fractions too; that he knew the square miles of all the principal countries, and the number of inhabitants. As he talked she smiled at him, until he began to think that what he knew was, after all, not quite so much. And he looked up into the vast expanse of the sky, as they rose up high, and she flew with him over the dark clouds, while the storm-wind whistled and raved, making him think of ballads of olden time. Over forest and lake they flew, over sea and land; beneath them screamed the icy blast; the wolves howled, the snow glittered; the black crows soared across the plains, cawing as they went. But high over all shone the great clear silver moon, and Kay gazed up at it all through the long long winter night. During the day he slept at the Snow Queen's feet.

J. M. Barrie

FROM
PETER PAN

Illustrated by Paul Howard

When Peter flies into the home of the Darling children it is only the beginning of their magical adventures with Peter, the fairy Tinker Bell, and the evil Captain Hook.

'Second to the right, and straight on till morning.'

That, Peter had told Wendy, was the way to the Neverland; but even birds, carrying maps and consulting them at windy corners, could not have sighted it with these instructions. Peter, you see, just said anything that came into his head.

At first his companions trusted him implicitly, and so great were the delights of flying that they wasted time circling round church spires or any other tall objects on the way that took their fancy.

John and Michael raced, Michael getting a start.

They recalled with contempt that not so long ago they had thought themselves fine fellows for being able to fly round a room.

Not so long ago. But how long ago? They were flying over the sea before this thought began to disturb Wendy seriously. John thought it was their second sea and their third night.

Sometimes it was dark and sometimes light, and now they were very

cold and again too warm. Did they really feel hungry at times, or were they merely pretending because Peter had such a jolly new way of feeding them? His way was to pursue birds who had food in their mouths suitable for humans and snatch it from them; then the birds would follow and snatch it back; and they would all go chasing each other gaily for miles, parting at last with mutual expressions of good-will. But Wendy noticed with gentle concern that Peter did not seem to know that this was rather an odd way of getting your bread and butter, nor even that there are other ways.

Certainly they did not pretend to be sleepy, they were sleepy; and that was a danger, for the moment they popped off, down they fell. The awful thing was that Peter thought this funny.

'There he goes again!' he would cry gleefully, as Michael suddenly dropped like a stone.

'Save him, save him!' cried Wendy, looking with horror at the cruel sea far below. Eventually Peter would dive through the air, and catch Michael just before he could strike the sea, and it was lovely the way he did it; but he always waited till the last moment, and you felt it was his cleverness that interested him and not the saving of human life. Also he was fond of variety, and the sport that engrossed him one moment would suddenly cease to engage him, so there was always the possibility that the next time you fell he would let you go.

He could sleep in the air without falling, by merely lying on his back and floating, but this was, partly at least, because he was so light that if you got behind him and blew he went faster.

'Do be more polite to him,' Wendy whispered to John, when they were playing 'Follow my Leader'.

'Then tell him to stop showing off,' said John.

When playing Follow my Leader, Peter would fly close to the water and touch each shark's tail in passing, just as in the street you may run your finger along an iron railing. They could not follow him in this with much success, so perhaps it was rather like showing off, especially as he kept looking behind to see how many tails they missed.

'You must be nice to him,' Wendy impressed on her brothers. 'What would we do if he were to leave us?'

'We could go back,' Michael said.

'How could we ever find our way back without him?'

'Well, then, we could go on,' said John.

'That is the awful thing, John. We should have to go on, for we don't know how to stop.'

This was true; Peter had forgotten to show them how to stop.

John said that if the worst came to the worst, all they had to do was to go straight on, for the world was round, and so in time they must come back to their own window.

'And who is to get food for us, John?'

'I nipped a bit out of that eagle's mouth pretty neatly, Wendy.'

'After the twentieth try,' Wendy reminded him. 'And even though we became good at picking up food, see how we bump against clouds and things if he is not near to give us a hand.'

Indeed they were constantly bumping. They could now fly strongly, though they still kicked far too much; but if they saw a cloud in front of them, the more they tried to avoid it, the more certainly did they bump into it. If Nana had been with them she would have had a bandage round Michael's forehead by this time.

Peter was not with them for the moment, and they felt rather lonely up there by themselves. He could go so much faster than they that he would suddenly shoot out of sight, to have some adventure in which they had no share. He would come down laughing over something fearfully funny he had been saying to a star, but he had already forgotten what it was, or he would come up with mermaid scales still sticking to him, and yet not be able to say for certain what had been happening. It was really rather irritating to children who had never seen a mermaid.

'And if he forgets them so quickly,' Wendy argued, 'how can we expect that he will go on remembering us?'

Indeed, sometimes when he returned he did not remember them, at least not well. Wendy was sure of it. She saw recognition come into his eyes as he was about to pass them the time of day and go on; once even she had to tell him her name.

'I'm Wendy,' she said agitatedly.

He was very sorry. 'I say, Wendy,' he whispered to her, 'always if you see me forgetting you, just keep on saying "I'm Wendy", and then I'll remember.'

Of course this was rather unsatisfactory. However, to make amends he showed them how to lie out flat on a strong wind that was going their way, and this was such a pleasant change that they tried it several times and found they could sleep thus with security. Indeed they would have slept longer, but Peter tired quickly of sleeping, and soon he would cry in his captain voice, 'We get off here.' So with occasional tiffs, but on the whole rollicking, they drew near the Neverland; for after many moons they did reach it, and, what is more, they had been going pretty straight all the time, not perhaps so much owing to the guidance of Peter or Tink as because the island was out looking for them. It is only thus that anyone may sight those magic shores.

'There it is,' said Peter calmly.

'Where, where?'

'Where all the arrows are pointing.'

Indeed a million golden arrows were pointing out the island to the children, all directed by their friend the sun, who wanted them to be sure of their way before leaving them for the night.

Wendy and John and Michael stood on tiptoe in the air to get their first sight of the island. Strange to say, they all recognized it at once, and until fear fell upon them they hailed it, not as something long dreamt of and seen at last

but as a familiar friend to whom they were returning home for the holidays.

'John, there's the lagoon.'

'Wendy, look at the turtles burying their eggs in the sand.'

'I say, John, I see your flamingo with the broken leg.'

'Look, Michael, there's your cave.'

'John, what's that in the brushwood?'

'It's a wolf with her whelps. Wendy, I do believe that's your little whelp.'

'There's my boat, John, with her sides stove in.'

'No, it isn't. Why, we burned your boat.'

'That's her, at any rate. I say, John, I see the smoke of the redskin camp.'

'Where? Show me, and I'll tell you by the way the smoke curls whether they are on the war-path.'

'There, just across the Mysterious River.'

'I see now. Yes, they are on the war-path right enough.'

Peter was a little annoyed with them for knowing so much; but if he wanted to lord it over them his triumph was at hand, for have I not told you that anon fear fell upon them?

It came as the arrows went, leaving the island in gloom.

In the old days at home the Neverland had always begun to look a little dark and threatening by bedtime. Then unexplored patches arose in it and spread; black shadows moved about in them; the roar of the beasts of prey was quite different now, and above all, you lost the certainty that you would win. You were quite glad that the night-lights were on. You even liked Nana to say that this was just the mantelpiece over here, and that the Neverland was all make-believe.

Of course the Neverland had been make-believe in those days; but it was real now, and there were no night-lights, and it was getting darker every moment, and where was Nana?

They had been flying apart, but they huddled close to Peter now. His careless manner had gone at last, his eyes were sparkling, a tingle went through them every time they touched his body. They were now over the fearsome island, flying so low that sometimes a tree grazed their face. Nothing horrid was visible in the air, yet their progress had become slow and laboured, exactly as if they were pushing their way through hostile forces. Sometimes they hung in the air until Peter had beaten on it with his fists.

'They don't want us to land,' he explained.

'Who are they?' Wendy whispered, shuddering.

But he could not or would not say. Tinker Bell had been asleep on his shoulder, but now he wakened her and sent her on in front.

Sometimes he poised himself in the air, listening intently with his hand to his ear, and again he would stare down with eyes so bright that they seemed to bore two holes to earth. Having done these things, he went on again.

His courage was almost appalling. 'Do you want an adventure now,' he said casually to John, 'or would you like to have your tea first?'

Wendy said 'tea first' quickly, and Michael pressed her hand in gratitude, but the braver John hesitated.

'What kind of adventure?' he asked cautiously.

'There's a pirate asleep in the pampas just beneath us,' Peter told him. 'If you like, we'll go down and kill him.'

'I don't see him,' John said after a long pause.

'I do.'

'Suppose,' John said a little huskily, 'he were to wake up.'

Peter spoke indignantly. 'You don't think I would kill him while he was sleeping! I would wake him first, and then kill him. That's the way I always do.'

'I say! Do you kill many?'

'Tons.'

John said 'how ripping', but decided to have tea first. He asked if there were many pirates on the island just now, and Peter said he had never known so many.

'Who is captain now?'

'Hook,' answered Peter; and his face became very stern as he said that hated word.

'Jas. Hook?'

'Aye.'

Then indeed Michael began to cry, and even John could speak in gulps only, for they knew Hook's reputation.

'He was Blackbeard's bo'sun,' John whispered huskily. 'He is the worst of them all. He is the only man of whom Barbecue was afraid.'

'That's him,' said Peter.

'What is he like? Is he big?'

'He is not so big as he was.'

'How do you mean?'

'I cut off a bit of him.'

'You!'

'Yes, me,' said Peter sharply.

'I wasn't meaning to be disrespectful.'

'Oh, all right.'

'But, I say, what bit?'

'His right hand.'

'Then he can't fight now?'

'Oh, can't he just!'

'Left-hander?'

'He has an iron hook instead of a right hand, and he claws with it.'

'Claws!'

'I say, John,' said Peter.

'Yes.'

'Say, "Aye, aye, sir." '

'Aye, aye, sir.'

'There is one thing,' Peter continued, 'that every boy who serves under me had to promise, and so must you.'

John paled.

'It is this, if we meet Hook in open fight, you must leave him to me.'

'I promise,' John said loyally.

William Allingham

THE FAIRIES

Illustrated by James Marsh

Up the airy mountain,
  Down the rushy glen,
We daren't go a-hunting
  For fear of little men;
Wee folk, good folk,
  Trooping all together;
Green jacket, red cap,
And white owl's feather!

Down along the rocky shore
  Some make their home;
They live on crispy pancakes
  Of yellow tide-foam;
Some in the reeds
  Of the black mountain lake,
With frogs for their watch-dogs,
  All night awake.

High on the hill-top
  The old King sits;
He is now so old and grey
  He's nigh lost his wits.
With a bridge of white mist
  Columbkill he crosses,
On his stately journeys
  From Slieveleague to Rosses;
Or going up with music
  On cold starry nights,
To sup with the Queen
  Of the gay Northern Lights.

They stole little Bridget
  For seven years long;
When she came down again,
  Her friends were all gone.
They took her lightly back,
  Between the night and morrow,
They thought that she was fast asleep,
  But she was dead with sorrow.
They have kept her ever since
  Deep within the lake,
On a bed of flag-leaves,
  Watching till she wake.

By the craggy hill-side,
  Through the mosses bare,
They have planted thorn-trees
  For pleasure here and there.
Is any man so daring
  As dig them up in spite,
He shall find the thornies set
  In his bed at night.

Up the airy mountain,
  Down the rushy glen,
We daren't go a-hunting
  For fear of little men;
Wee folk, good folk,
  Trooping all together;
Green jacket, red cap,
  And white owl's feather!

E. Nesbit

FROM

FIVE CHILDREN AND IT

Illustrated by Emma Chichester Clark

'It' is a Sand-fairy the children find one day in a sand-pit.
It grants them one wish a day, lasting until sunset.

Anthea was late for breakfast. It was Robert who quietly poured a spoonful of treacle down the Lamb's frock, so that he had to be taken away and washed thoroughly directly after breakfast. And it was of course a very naughty thing to do; yet it served two purposes – it delighted the Lamb, who loved above all things to be completely sticky, and it engaged Martha's attention so that the others could slip away to the sand-pit without the Lamb.

They did it, and in the lane Anthea, breathless from the scurry of that slipping, panted out –

'I want to propose we take turns to wish. Only, nobody's to have a wish if the others don't think it's a nice wish. Do you agree?'

'Who's to have first wish?' asked Robert cautiously.

'Me, if you don't mind,' said Anthea apologetically. 'And I've thought about it – and it's wings.'

There was a silence. The others rather wanted to find fault, but it was hard, because the word 'wings' raised a flutter of joyous excitement in every breast.

'Not so dusty,' said Cyril generously; and Robert added, 'Really, Panther, you're not quite such a fool as you look.'

Jane said, 'I think it would be perfectly lovely. It's like a bright dream of delirium.'

They found the Sand-fairy easily. Anthea said:

'I wish we all had beautiful wings to fly with.'

The Sand-fairy blew himself out, and next moment each child felt a funny feeling, half heaviness and half lightness, on its shoulders. The Psammead put its head on one side and turned its snail's eyes from one to the other.

'Not so dusty,' it said dreamily. 'But really, Robert, you're not quite such an angel as you look.' Robert almost blushed.

The wings were very big, and more beautiful than you can possibly imagine – for they were soft and smooth, and every feather lay neatly in its place. And the feathers were of the most lovely mixed changing colours, like the rainbow, or iridescent glass, or the beautiful scum that sometimes floats on water that is not at all nice to drink.

'Oh – but can we fly?' Jane said, standing anxiously first on one foot and then on the other.

'Look out!' said Cyril; 'you're treading on my wing.'

'Does it hurt?' asked Anthea with interest; but no one answered, for Robert had spread his wings and jumped up, and now he was slowly rising in the air. He looked very awkward in his knickerbocker suit – his boots in particular hung helplessly, and seemed much larger than when he was standing in them. But the others cared but little how he looked – or how they looked, for that matter.

For now they all spread out their wings and rose in the air. Of course you all know what flying feels like, because everyone has dreamed about flying, and it seems so beautifully easy – only, you can never rcmember how you did it; and as a rule you have to do it without wings, in your dreams, which is more clever and uncommon, but not so easy to remember the rule for. Now the four children rose flapping from the ground, and you can't think how good the air felt running against their faces. Their wings were tremendously wide when they were spread out, and they had to fly quite a long way apart so as not to get in each other's way. But little things like this are easily lcarned.

All the words in the English Dictionary, and in the Greek Lexicon as well, are, I find, of no use at all to tell you exactly what it feels like to be flying, so I will not try. But I will say that to look *down* on the fields and woods, instead of *along* at them, is something like looking at a beautiful live map, where, instead of silly colours on paper, you have real moving sunny woods and green fields laid out onc after the other. As Cyril said, and I can't think where he got hold of such a strange expression, 'It does you a fair treat!' It was most wonderful and more like real magic than any wish the children had had yet. They flapped and flew and sailed on their great rainbow wings, between green earth and blue sky; and they flew right over Rochester and then swerved round towards Maidstone, and presently they all began to feel extremely hungry. Curiously enough, this happened when they were flying rather low, and just as they were

21

crossing an orchard where some early plums shone red and ripe.

They paused on their wings. I cannot explain to you how this is done, but it is something like treading water when you are swimming, and hawks do it extremely well.

'Yes, I daresay,' said Cyril, though no one had spoken. 'But stealing is stealing even if you've got wings.'

'Do you really think so?' said Jane briskly. 'If you've got wings you're a bird, and no one minds birds breaking the commandments. At least, they may *mind,* but the birds always do it, and no one scolds them or sends them to prison.'

It was not so easy to perch on a plum-tree as you might think, because the rainbow wings were so *very* large; but somehow they all managed to do it, and the plums were certainly very sweet and juicy.

Fortunately, it was not till they had all had quite as many plums as were good for them that they saw a stout man, who looked exactly as though he owned the plum-trees, come hurrying through the orchard gate with a thick stick, and with one accord they disentangled their wings from the plum-laden branches and began to fly.

The man stopped short, with his mouth open. For he had seen the boughs of his trees moving and twitching, and he had said to himself, 'Them young varmints – at it again!' And he had come out at once, for the lads of the village had taught him in past seasons that plums want looking after. But when he saw the rainbow wings flutter up out of the plum-tree he felt that he must have gone quite mad, and he did not like the feeling at all. And when Anthea looked down and saw his mouth go slowly open, and stay so, and his face become green and mauve in patches, she called out:

'Don't be frightened,' and felt hastily in her pocket for a three penny-bit with a hole in it, which she had meant to hang on a ribbon round her neck, for luck. She hovered round the unfortunate plum-owner, and said, 'We have had some of your plums; we thought it wasn't stealing, but now I am not so sure. So here's some money to pay for them.'

She swooped down towards the terror-stricken grower of plums, and

slipped the coin into the pocket of his jacket, and in a few flaps she had rejoined the others.

The farmer sat down on the grass, suddenly and heavily.

'Well – I'm blessed!' he said. 'This here is what they call delusions, I suppose. But this here three-penny' – he had pulled it out and bitten it – '*that's* real enough. Well, from this day forth I'll be a better man. It's the kind of thing to sober a chap for life, this is. I'm glad it was only wings, though. I'd rather see birds as aren't there, and couldn't be, even if they pretend to talk, than some things as I could name.'

He got up slowly and heavily, and went indoors, and he was so nice to his wife that day that she felt quite happy, and said to herself, 'Law, whatever have a-come to the man!' and smartened herself up and put a blue ribbon bow at the place where her collar fastened on, and looked so pretty that he was kinder than ever. So perhaps the winged children really did do one good thing that day. If so, it was the only one; for really there is nothing like wings for getting you into trouble. But, on the other hand, if you are in trouble, there is nothing like wings for getting you out of it.

William Shakespeare

WHEN ICICLES HANG BY THE WALL

FROM

LOVE'S LABOUR'S LOST

Illustrated by Paul Birkbeck

When icicles hang by the wall,
  And Dick the shepherd blows his nail;
When Tom bears logs into the hall,
  And milk comes frozen home in pail;
When blood is nipped, and ways be foul,
– Then nightly sings the staring owl:
  To-who,
To-whit, To-who – a merry note,
While greasy Joan doth keel the pot.

When all aloud the wind doth blow,
  And coughing drowns the parson's saw,
And birds sit brooding in the snow,
  And Marian's nose looks red and raw;
When roasted crabs hiss in the bowl,
– Then nightly sings the staring owl:
  To-who,
To-whit, To-who – a merry note,
While greasy Joan doth keel the pot.

Robert Browning

THE PIED PIPER OF HAMELIN

Illustrated by Siân Bailey

Once more he stepped into the street
  And to his lips again
  Laid his long pipe of smooth straight cane;
And ere he blew three notes (such sweet
Soft notes as yet musician's cunning
  Never gave the enraptured air)
There was a rustling that seemed like a bustling
Of merry crowds justling at pitching and hustling,
Small feet were pattering, wooden shoes clattering,
Little hands clapping and little tongues chattering,
And, like fowls in a farmyard when barley is scattering,
Out came the children running.
All the little boys and girls,
With rosy cheeks and flaxen curls,
And sparkling eyes and teeth like pearls,
Tripping and skipping, ran merrily after
The wonderful music with shouting and laughter.

The Mayor was dumb, and the Council stood
As if they were changed into blocks of wood,
Unable to move a step, or cry
To the children merrily skipping by
– Could only follow with the eye

That joyous crowd at the Piper's back.
But how the Mayor was on the rack,
And the wretched Council's bosoms beat,
As the Piper turned from the High Street
To where the Weser rolled its waters
Right in the way of their sons and daughters!
However, he turned from south to west,
And to Koppelberg Hill his steps addressed,
And after him the children pressed;
Great was the joy in every breast.
'He never can cross that mighty top!
He's forced to let the piping drop,
And we shall see our children stop!'
When, lo, as they reached the mountain-side,
A wondrous portal opened wide,
As if a cavern was suddenly hollowed;
And the Piper advanced and the children followed,
And when all were in to the very last,
The door in the mountain-side shut fast.
Did I say, all? No! One was lame,
  And could not dance the whole of the way;
And in after years, if you would blame
  His sadness, he was used to say –
'It's dull in our town since my playmates left!
I can't forget that I'm bereft
Of all the pleasant sights they see,
Which the Piper also promised me.
For he led us, he said, to a joyous land,
Joining the town and just at hand,
Where waters gushed and fruit trees grew
And flowers put forth a fairer hue,
And everything was strange and new;
The sparrows were brighter than peacocks here,

And their dogs outran our fallow deer,
And honey-bees had lost their stings,
And horses were born with eagles' wings:
And just as I became assured
My lame foot would be speedily cured,
The music stopped and I stood still,
And found myself outside the hill,
Left alone against my will,
To go now limping as before,
And never hear of that country more!'

William Shakespeare

WHERE THE BEE SUCKS

Illustrated by Paul Birkbeck

Where the bee sucks, there suck I,
In a cowslip's bell I lie,
There I couch when owls do cry.
On the bat's back I do fly
After summer merrily.
Merrily, merrily shall I live now
Under the blossom that hangs on the bough.

Lewis Carroll

THROUGH THE LOOKING–GLASS

Illustrated by Chris Riddell

When Alice steps through the looking-glass,
she enters a world of chess pieces and nursery-rhyme
characters who behave very oddly.

They were standing under a tree, each with an arm round the other's neck, and Alice knew which was which in a moment, because one of them had 'DUM' embroidered on his collar, and the other 'DEE'. 'I suppose they've each got "TWEEDLE" round at the back of the collar,' she said to herself.

They stood so still that she quite forgot they were alive, and she was just looking round to see if the word 'TWEEDLE' was written at the back of each collar, when she was startled by a voice coming from the one marked 'DUM'.

'If you think we're wax-works,' he said, 'you ought to pay, you know. Wax-works weren't made to be looked at for nothing. Nohow!'

'Contrariwise,' added the one marked 'DEE', 'if you think we're alive, you ought to speak.'

'I'm sure I'm very sorry,' was all Alice could say; for the words of the old song kept ringing through her head like the ticking of a clock, and she could hardly help saying them out loud: –

> *'Tweedledum and Tweedledee*
> *Agreed to have a battle;*
> *For Tweedledum said Tweedledee*
> *Had spoiled his nice new rattle.*
>
> *Just then flew down a monstrous crow,*
> *As black as a tar-barrel;*
> *Which frightened both the heroes so,*
> *They quite forgot their quarrel.'*

'I know what you're thinking about,' said Tweedledum: 'but it isn't so, nohow.'

'Contrariwise,' continued Tweedledee, 'if it was so, it might be; and if it were so, it would be; but as it isn't, it ain't. That's logic.'

'I was thinking,' Alice said very politely, 'which is the best way out of this wood: it's getting so dark. Would you tell me, please?'

But the fat little men only looked at each other and grinned.

They looked so exactly like a couple of great schoolboys, that Alice couldn't help pointing her finger at Tweedledum, and saying 'First Boy!'

'Nohow!' Tweedledum cried out briskly, and shut his mouth up again with a snap.

'Next Boy!' said Alice, passing on to Tweedledee, though she felt quite certain he would only shout out 'Contrariwise!' and so he did.

'You've begun wrong!' cried Tweedledum. 'The first thing in a visit is to say "How d'ye do?" and shake hands!' And here the two brothers gave each other a hug, and then they held out the two hands that were free, to shake hands with her.

Alice did not like shaking hands with either of them first, for fear of hurting the other one's feelings; so, as the best way out of the difficulty, she took hold of both hands at once: the next moment they were dancing round in a ring. This seemed quite natural (she

remembered afterwards), and she was not even surprised to hear music playing: it seemed to come from the tree under which they were dancing and it was done (as well as she could make it out) by the branches rubbing one across the other, like fiddles and fiddle-sticks.

'But it certainly *was* funny,' (Alice said afterwards, when she was telling her sister the history of all this,) 'to find myself singing "*Here we go round the mulberry bush*". I don't know when I began it, but somehow I felt as if I'd been singing it a long long time!'

The other two dancers were fat, and very soon out of breath. 'Four times round is enough for one dance,' Tweedledum panted out, and they left off dancing as suddenly as they had begun: the music stopped at the same moment.

Then they let go of Alice's hands, and stood looking at her for a minute: there was a rather awkward pause, as Alice didn't know how to begin a conversation with people she had just been dancing with. 'It would never do to say "How d'ye do?" *now*,' she said to herself: 'we seem to have got beyond that, somehow!'

'I hope you're not much tired?' she said at last.

'Nohow. And thank you very much for asking,' said Tweedledum.

'So *much* obliged!' added Tweedledee. 'You like poetry?'

'Ye-es, pretty well — some poetry,' Alice said doubtfully. 'Would you tell me which road leads out of the wood?'

'What shall I repeat to her?' said Tweedledee, looking round at Tweedledum with great solemn eyes, and not noticing Alice's question.

'"*The Walrus and the Carpenter*" is the longest,' Tweedledum replied, giving his brother an affectionate hug.

Tweedledee began instantly:

'*The sun was shining —*'

Here Alice ventured to interrupt him. 'If it's *very* long,' she said, as politely as she could, 'would you please tell me first which road —'

Tweedledee smiled gently, and began again:

'The sun was shining on the sea,
 Shining with all his might:
He did his very best to make
 The billows smooth and bright —
And this was odd, because it was
 The middle of the night.

The moon was shining sulkily,
 Because she thought the sun
Had got no business to be there
 After the day was done —
"It's very rude of him," she said,
 "To come and spoil the fun!"

The sea was wet as wet could be,
 The sands were dry as dry.
You could not see a cloud, because
 No cloud was in the sky:
No birds were flying overhead —
 There were no birds to fly.

The Walrus and the Carpenter
 Were walking close at hand;
They wept like anything to see
 Such quantities of sand:
"If this were only cleared away,"
 They said, "it would be grand!"

"If seven maids with seven mops
  Swept it for half a year,
Do you suppose," the Walrus said,
  "That they could get it clear?"
"I doubt it," said the Carpenter,
  And shed a bitter tear.

"O Oysters, come and walk with us!"
  The Walrus did beseech.
"A pleasant walk, a pleasant talk,
  Along the briny beach:
We cannot do with more than four,
  To give a hand to each."

The eldest Oyster looked at him.
  But never a word he said:
The eldest Oyster winked his eye,
  And shook his heavy head —
Meaning to say he did not choose
  To leave the oyster-bed.

But four young Oysters hurried up,
  All eager for the treat:
Their coats were brushed, their faces washed,
  Their shoes were clean and neat —
And this was odd, because, you know,
  They hadn't any feet.

Four other Oysters followed them,
  And yet another four;
And thick and fast they came at last,
  And more, and more, and more —
All hopping through the frothy waves,
  And scrambling to the shore.

The Walrus and the Carpenter
  Walked on a mile or so,
And then they rested on a rock
  Conveniently low:
And all the little Oysters stood
  And waited in a row.

"The time has come," the Walrus said,
  "To talk of many things:
Of shoes — and ships — and sealing-wax —
  Of cabbages — and kings —
And why the sea is boiling hot —
  And whether pigs have wings."

"But wait a bit," the Oysters cried,
  "Before we have our chat;
For some of us are out of breath,
  And all of us are fat!"
"No hurry!" said the Carpenter.
  They thanked him much for that.

"A loaf of bread," the Walrus said,
  "Is what we chiefly need:
Pepper and vinegar besides
  Are very good indeed —
Now if you're ready, Oysters dear,
  We can begin to feed."

"But not on us!" the Oysters cried,
  Turning a little blue.
"After such kindness, that would be
  A dismal thing to do!"
"The night is fine," the Walrus said.
  "Do you admire the view?

"It was so kind of you to come!
  And you are very nice!"
The Carpenter said nothing but
  "Cut us another slice:
I wish you were not quite so deaf —
  I've had to ask you twice!"

"It seems a shame," the Walrus said,
  "To play them such a trick,
After we've brought them out so far,
  And made them trot so quick!"
The Carpenter said nothing but
  "The butter's spread too thick!"

"I weep for you," the Walrus said,
  "I deeply sympathize."
With sobs and tears he sorted out
  Those of the largest size,
Holding his pocket-handkerchief
  Before his streaming eyes.

"O Oysters," said the Carpenter.
  "You've had a pleasant run!
Shall we be trotting home again?"
  But answer came there none —
And this was scarcely odd, because
  They'd eaten every one.'

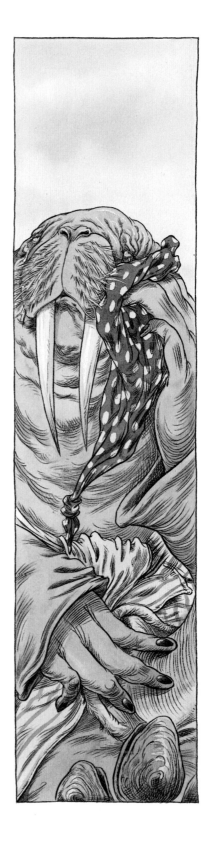

'I like the Walrus best,' said Alice: 'because you see he was a *little* sorry for the poor oysters.'

'He ate more than the Carpenter, though,' said Tweedledee. 'You see he held his handkerchief in front, so that the Carpenter couldn't count how many he took: contrariwise.'

'That was mean!' Alice said indignantly. 'Then I like the Carpenter best – if he didn't eat so many as the Walrus.'

'But he ate as many as he could get,' said Tweedledum.

This was a puzzler. After a pause, Alice began, 'Well! They were *both* very unpleasant characters –' Here she checked herself in some alarm, at hearing something that sounded to her like the puffing of a large steam-engine in the wood near them, though she feared it was more likely to be a wild beast. 'Are there any lions or tigers about here?' she asked timidly.

'It's only the Red King snoring,' said Tweedledee.

'Come and look at him!' the brothers cried, and they took each one of Alice's hands, and led her up to where the King was sleeping.

'Isn't he a *lovely* sight?' said Tweedledum.

Alice couldn't say honestly that he was. He had a tall red night-cap on, with a tassel, and he was lying crumpled up into a sort of untidy heap, and snoring loud – 'fit to snore his head off!' as Tweedledum remarked.

'I'm afraid he'll catch cold with lying on the damp grass,' said Alice, who was a very thoughtful little girl.

'He's dreaming now,' said Tweedledee: 'and what do you think he's dreaming about?'

Alice said, 'Nobody can guess that.'

'Why, about *you*!' Tweedledee exclaimed, clapping his hands triumphantly. 'And if he left off dreaming about you, where do you suppose you'd be?'

'Where I am now, of course,' said Alice.

'Not you!' Tweedledee retorted contemptuously. 'You'd be nowhere. Why, you're only a sort of thing in his dream!'

'If that there King was to wake,' added Tweedledum, 'you'd go out –

bang! – just like a candle!'

'I shouldn't!' Alice exclaimed indignantly. 'Besides, if *I'm* only a sort of thing in his dream, what are *you*, I should like to know?'

'Ditto,' said Tweedledum.

'Ditto, ditto!' cried Tweedledee.

He shouted this so loud that Alice couldn't help saying, 'Hush! You'll be waking him, I'm afraid, if you make so much noise.'

'Well, it's no use *your* talking about waking him,' said Tweedledum, 'when you're only one of the things in his dream. You know very well you're not real.'

'I *am* real!' said Alice, and began to cry.

'You won't make yourself a bit realler by crying,' Tweedledee remarked: 'there's nothing to cry about.'

'If I wasn't real,' Alice said – half-laughing through her tears, it all seemed so ridiculous – 'I shouldn't be able to cry.'

'I hope you don't suppose those are real tears?' Tweedledum interrupted in a tone of great contempt.

'I know they're talking nonsense,' Alice thought to herself: 'and it's foolish to cry about it.' So she brushed away her tears, and went on as cheerfully as she could, 'At any rate I'd better be getting out of the wood, for really it's coming on very dark. Do you think it's going to rain?'

Tweedledum spread a large umbrella over himself and his brother, and looked up into it. 'No, I don't think it is,' he said: 'at least – not under *here*. Nohow.'

'But it may rain *outside*?'

'It may – if it chooses,' said Tweedledee: 'we've no objection. Contrariwise.'

'Selfish things!' thought Alice, and she was just going to say 'Good-night' and leave them, when Tweedledum sprang out from under the umbrella, and seized her by the wrist.

'Do you see *that*?' he said, in a voice choking with passion, and his eyes grew large and yellow all in a moment, as he pointed with a trembling finger at a small white thing lying under the tree.

'It's only a rattle,' Alice said, after a careful examination of the little white thing. 'Not a rattle*snake*, you know,' she added hastily, thinking that he was frightened: 'only an old rattle – quite old and broken.'

'I knew it was!' cried Tweedledum, beginning to stamp about wildly and tear his hair. 'It's spoilt, of course!' Here he looked at Tweedledee, who immediately sat down on the ground, and tried to hide himself under the umbrella.

Alice laid her hand upon his arm, and said in a soothing tone, 'You needn't be so angry about an old rattle.'

'But it isn't old!' Tweedledum cried, in a greater fury than ever. 'It's new, I tell you – I bought it yesterday – my nice NEW RATTLE!' and his voice rose to a perfect scream.

All this time Tweedledee was trying his best to fold up the umbrella, with himself in it: which was such an extraordinary thing to do, that it quite took off Alice's attention from the angry brother. But he couldn't quite succeed, and it ended in his rolling over, bundled up in the umbrella, with only his head out: and there he lay, opening and shutting his mouth and his large eyes – 'looking more like a fish than anything else,' Alice thought.

'Of course you agree to have a battle?' Tweedledum said in a calmer tone.

'I suppose so,' the other sulkily replied, as he crawled out of the umbrella: 'only *she* must help us to dress up, you know.'

So the two brothers went off hand-in-hand into the wood, and returned in a minute with their arms full of things – such as bolsters, blankets, hearth-rugs, table-cloths, dish-covers and coal-scuttles. 'I hope you're a good hand at pinning and tying strings?' Tweedledum remarked. 'Every one of these things has got to go on, somehow or other.'

Alice said afterwards she had never seen such a fuss made about anything in all her life — the way those two bustled about — and the quantity of things they put on — and the trouble they gave her in tying strings and fastening buttons — 'Really they'll be more like bundles of old clothes than anything else, by the time they're ready!' she said to herself, as she arranged a bolster round the neck of Tweedledee, 'to keep his head from being cut off,' as he said.

'You know,' he added very gravely, 'it's one of the most serious things that can possibly happen to one in a battle — to get one's head cut off.'

Alice laughed loud: but she managed to turn it into a cough, for fear of hurting his feelings.

'Do I look very pale?' said Tweedledum, coming up to have his helmet tied on. (He *called* it a helmet, though it certainly looked much more like a saucepan.)

'Well — yes — a *little*,' Alice replied gently.

'I'm very brave generally,' he went on in a low voice: 'only today I happen to have a headache.'

'And *I've* got a toothache!' said Tweedledee, who had overheard the remark. 'I'm far worse than you!'

'Then you'd better not fight to-day,' said Alice thinking it a good opportunity to make peace.

'We *must* have a bit of a fight, but I don't care about going on long,' said Tweedledum. 'What's the time now?'

Tweedledee looked at his watch, and said, 'Half-past four.'

'Let's fight till six, and then have dinner,' said Tweedledum.

'Very well,' the other said, rather sadly: 'and *she* can watch us — only you'd better not come *very* close,' he added: 'I generally hit everything I can see — when I get really excited.'

'And *I* hit everything within reach,' cried Tweedledum, 'whether I can see it or not.'

Alice laughed. 'You must hit the *trees* pretty often, I should think,' she said.

Tweedledum looked round him with a satisfied smile. 'I don't suppose,' he said, 'there'll be a tree left standing, for ever so far round, by the time we've finished!'

'And all about a rattle!' said Alice still hoping to make them a *little* ashamed of fighting for such a trifle.

'I shouldn't have minded it so much,' said Tweedledum, 'if it hadn't been a new one.'

'I wish the monstrous crow would come!' thought Alice.

'There's only one sword, you know,' Tweedledum said to his brother: 'but you can have the umbrella – it's quite as sharp. Only we must begin quick. It's getting as dark as it can.'

'And darker,' said Tweedledee.

It was getting dark so suddenly that Alice thought there must be a thunderstorm coming on. 'What a thick black cloud that is!' she said. 'And how fast it comes! Why, I do believe it's got wings!'

'It's the crow!' Tweedledum cried out in a shrill voice of alarm: and the two brothers took to their heels and were out of sight in a moment.

Alice ran a little way into the wood, and stopped under a large tree. 'It can never get at me *here*,' she thought: 'it's far too large to squeeze itself in among the trees. But I wish it wouldn't flap its wings so – it makes quite a hurricane in the wood – here's somebody's shawl being blown away!'

Percy Bysshe Shelley

OZYMANDIAS

Illustrated by Anthony Browne

I met a traveller from an antique land
Who said: Two vast and trunkless legs of stone
Stand in the desert. Near them, on the sand,
Half sunk, a shattered visage lies, whose frown,
And wrinkled lip, and sneer of cold command,
Tell that its sculptor well those passions read
Which yet survive (stamped on these lifeless things),
The hand that mocked them and the heart that fed;
And on the pedestal these words appear:
'My name is Ozymandias, king of kings;
Look on my works, ye Mighty, and despair!'
Nothing beside remains. Round the decay
Of that colossal wreck, boundless and bare,
The lone and level sands stretch far away.

William Wordsworth

DAFFODILS

Illustrated by Ruth Rivers

I wander'd lonely as a cloud
  That floats on high o'er vales and hills,
When all at once I saw a crowd,
  A host of golden daffodils;
Beside the lake, beneath the trees,
Fluttering and dancing in the breeze.

Continuous as the stars that shine
  And twinkle on the Milky Way,
They stretch'd in never-ending line
  Along the margin of a bay:
Ten thousand saw I at a glance,
Tossing their heads in sprightly dance.

The waves beside them danced, but they
  Out-did the sparkling waves in glee:
A poet could not but be gay,
  In such a jocund company:
I gazed – and gazed – but little thought
What wealth the show to me had brought:

For oft, when on my couch I lie
   In vacant or in pensive mood,
They flash upon that inward eye
   Which is the bliss of solitude;
And then my heart with pleasure fills,
And dances with the daffodils.

Retold by Roger Lancelyn Green

Robin Hood and the Butcher

From
The Adventures of Robin Hood

Illustrated by Paul Young

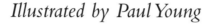

And thou, fine fellowe, who has tasted so
  Of the forester's greenwood game,
Will be in no haste thy time to waste
  In seeking more taste of the same:
Of this can I read thee and riddle thee well,
Thou hast better by far be the devil in hell,
  Than the Sheriff of Nottingham!

Thomas Love Peacock: *Maid Marian*
(1822)

Although there was so much to do in Sherwood where nearly all of the food they ate had to be hunted, trapped, or shot, and they were always in danger of surprise from the Sheriff of Nottingham, Sir Guy of Gisborne, and the rest, Robin Hood occasionally found time hang heavy on his hands.

On one such occasion he and Little John were walking by the high road to Nottingham where it runs through the forest, when they saw a Butcher with his cart of meat come jogging along on his way to market.

'Yonder comes a proud fellow,' said Little John, 'who fancies himself a master with the quarter-staff. He comes through the forest twice every week, and nothing gives him greater pleasure than the chance to thrash someone with his big stick.'

'Twice a week,' said Robin, 'and he has never paid any toll to us! It is long since I fought with the quarter-staff, except in friendly wise with you or Friar Tuck. I'll go and have words with this Butcher – and see if blows come of it!'

'I'll wager a piece of gold he beats you!' said Little John.

'Done!' smiled Robin, and laying aside his weapons, he cut himself a good oak staff and strode down the road until he met the Butcher.

'Now then!' cried the Butcher sharply, as Robin laid a hand on the horse's bridle. 'What do you want, you impudent fellow?'

'You have haunted these ways long enough,' said Robin sternly, 'without paying the due toll that you owe to me! Come, sirrah, pay up at once!'

'And who do you think you are?' cried the Butcher. 'A Forest Guard or what? I serve the good Sheriff of Nottingham – and he'll make your hide smart for this, after I've tanned you myself, and broken your head into the bargain.'

'I am of Robin Hood's company,' was the reply, 'and if you will not pay tribute in gold, get down out of that cart and pay it in blows.'

'Right willingly!' answered the Butcher, and jumping out of his cart he charged at Robin, whirling his staff about his head.

Then there was as good a fight, and as pretty a play of skill with the quarter-staves as ever one might see: but the long and short of it was that though Robin suffered a sore clout over one eye, in the end he brought the Butcher to the ground with a last stunning blow.

'The piece of gold is yours,' said Little John coming up.

'This is a fine fellow,' said Robin as the Butcher sat up and looked about him. 'Give him wine, Little John, I'll warrant his head is ringing even louder than mine!'

'That it is!' groaned the Butcher. 'By the Mass, you are a bonny fighter. I think you must be Robin Hood himself, and no other!'

'That I am indeed!' said Robin.

'Then I think no shame at being beaten,' said the Butcher with a sigh of relief. 'And I'll willingly pay any toll you may ask of me.'

'No, no,' answered Robin, 'you've paid toll enough with that broken head of yours. Come now to our camp and see what good cheer we can make for you.'

When the meal was over, Robin said suddenly to the Butcher:

'Good friend, I have a mind to be a butcher myself. Will you sell me your horse, your cart and the meat now on it for ten pounds – and stay here in the forest with us?'

'Right willingly,' answered the Butcher, and the deal was made.

'You go into danger for no good cause,' said Will Scarlet doubtfully as Robin donned the Butcher's garb.

'Nevertheless I go,' answered Robin. 'I grow weary of this unchanging forest life – and also I would have news of what passes in the world outside. It is said that King Richard is a prisoner somewhere in Europe, and Prince John makes no effort to find and ransom him: I would know more of this. Never fear, not even the Sheriff will know me!'

With that Robin fixed a black patch over one eye, climbed into the cart and went rattling away through the forest and onto the Nottingham road once more. In the afternoon he came to Nottingham, drew up his cart in the market-place, and began to cry:

'Meat to sell! Fresh meat to sell! Fresh meat a penny a pound!'

Then all that saw and heard him at his trade said that he had not been a Butcher for long, since at that price he could not expect to earn

a living. But the thrifty housewives gathered round him eagerly, for never had they bought such cheap meat before.

Among them came the Sheriff's wife, and seeing that the meat was good, fresh and tender – and most unusually cheap – she invited the Butcher to bring his cart up to the Sheriff's house, sell to her what was left, and then sup with her and the Sheriff.

Robin accepted with delight, and as evening fell he stabled his horse and empty cart in the Sheriff's stables and sat down to dine as an honoured guest at the Sheriff's board.

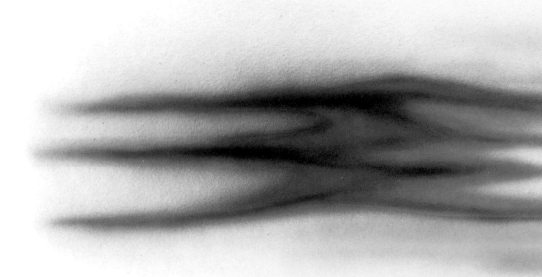

At dinner that night Robin learned many things which he wished to know. He heard that King Richard was in truth a prisoner, but that Prince John was giving out that he was dead so that he himself might become King.

'But a pestilent fellow called Blondel,' added the Sheriff, 'has gone in search of Richard. He is a minstrel, and so can pass unmolested through the most hostile lands: may the plague take him speedily!'

'Will the great Barons and the Lords and Knights accept Prince John as King?' asked Robin.

'There the trouble lies,' said the Sheriff shaking his head sadly. 'Many, like the Earl of Chester, oppose him. But many more will be won over ...'

Later in the evening the Sheriff asked Robin if he had any horned beasts that he could sell to him – meaning live cattle rather than joints of meat.

'Yes, that I have, good master Sheriff,' answered Robin, 'I have two or three hundred of them, and many an acre of good free land, if you please to see it. I can let it to you with as good a right as ever my father made to me.'

'The horned beasts interest me most,' said the Sheriff. 'Good master Butcher, I will come with you on the morrow – and make you a right fair offer for the whole herd, if they please me.'

Robin Hood slept well and comfortably in the Sheriff's house, and ate a fine breakfast in the morning before they set off together, accompanied by only two men, to see the horned beasts.

The Sheriff seemed in high spirits when they started out, jesting and laughing with Robin. But presently as they went deeper and deeper into Sherwood Forest he grew more and more silent.

'Have we much further to go, friend Butcher?' he asked at last. 'God protect us this day from a man they call Robin Hood!'

'The outlaw, you mean?' asked Robin. 'I know him well, and have often shot at the butts with him. I am no bad archer myself, if it comes to that: indeed I dare swear that Robin Hood himself can shoot no better than I.'

'Know you where he lies hid in Sherwood?' asked the Sheriff eagerly.

'Right well,' replied Robin, 'even his most secret place of hiding.'

'I would pay you well if you were to bring me thither,' said the Sheriff.

'That will I do,' answered Robin. 'But hist now: we draw near the place where the horned beasts are to be found. Stay a moment, while I wind my horn so that the herdsmen may drive them hither.'

So saying Robin set his horn to his mouth and blew three blasts. Then he drew a little behind the Sheriff and waited.

Presently there was a crackling in the thicket, and a great troop of red deer came into view, tossing their antlers proudly.

'How like you my horned beasts, Master Sheriff?' asked Robin. 'They be fat and fair to see!'

'Good fellow, I wish I were far from here,' said the Sheriff uncomfortably. 'I like not your company . . .'

'We will have better company anon,' Robin remarked with a smile, and even as he spoke out of the thicket came Little John, followed by Will Scarlet, Much, Reynolde, William of Goldsbrough, and many another of the outlaws of Sherwood.

'What is your will, good master?' said Little John. 'Come, tell us how

54

you fared in Nottingham, and whether you did good trade as a butcher?'

'Fine trade indeed,' answered Robin, pulling off his eye-patch and the rest of his disguise. 'And see, I have brought with me the Sheriff of Nottingham to dine with us this day.'

'He is right welcome,' said Little John. 'And I am sure he will pay well for his dinner.'

'Well indeed,' laughed Robin. 'For he has brought much money with him to buy three hundred head of deer from me. And even now he offered me a great sum to lead him to our secret glade.'

'By the Rood,' said the Sheriff, shaking with terror, 'had I guessed who you were, a thousand pounds would not have brought me into Sherwood!'

'I would that you had a thousand pounds to bring you *out* of Sherwood,' said Robin. 'Now then, bind him and his men, blindfold them, and lead them to dinner. When we reach the glade we can see what they have brought us – and by then I will have earned every penny, ha, ha!'

So the Sheriff and his two trembling followers were blindfolded and led by the secret paths to the hidden glen, and Robin feasted them there full well. But afterwards he bade Little John spread his cloak upon the ground and pour into it all the money the Sheriff had brought with him, and the sum came to nearly five hundred pounds.

'We will keep the three good horses also,' said Robin, 'and let Master Sheriff and his two men walk back to Nottingham – for the good of their health. But let Maid Marian send a present of needlework to the Sheriff's lady, for she entertained me well at dinner and set fair dishes before me.'

Then the Sheriff and his two men were blindfolded once more and taken back to the Nottingham road, and there Robin bade them farewell.

'You shall not defy me for much longer, Robin Hood,' cried the Sheriff, shaking his fist at Robin in farewell. 'I'll come against you with a great force, depend upon it, and hang every man of you from the trees by this road side. And your head shall rot over Nottingham gate.'

'When next you come to visit me in Sherwood,' said Robin quietly, 'you shall not get away on such easy terms. Come when you will, and the more of you the merrier – and I'll send you all packing back to Nottingham in your shirts!'

Then he left them and returned to the secret glade where the Butcher, whose name was Gilbert-of-the-White-Hand, was waiting for him.

'Here are your cart and horses back again, good master Butcher,' said Robin. 'I have had a fine holiday selling meat in your stead – but we must not play too many of such pranks.'

'By the Mass,' swore Gilbert the Butcher, 'I'll sell meat no longer, if you will have me as one of your merry men here in the greenwood. I cannot shoot with any skill – for see how my left hand was burnt white with fire when I once shot a deer to feed my starving family. But you have had some little proof of how I can smite with the quarter-staff.'

'Proof enough, good Gilbert,' cried Robin. 'I am right glad to welcome you as one of us . . . Come, Friar Tuck, propound the oath to him. And then to dinner, and we'll all drink to the health of our new companion, Gilbert-of-the-White-Hand, the jolly Butcher of Nottingham!'

Jonathan Swift

FROM

GULLIVER'S TRAVELS

Illustrated by Paul Birkbeck

Gulliver is shipwrecked and washes up on the island of Lilliput, where he encounters the most extraordinary inhabitants.

When I awaked, it was just daylight. I attempted to rise, but was not able to stir: for as I happened to lie on my back, I found my arms and legs were strongly fastened on each side to the ground; and my hair, which was long and thick, tied down in the same manner. I likewise felt several slender ligatures across my body, from my armpits to my thighs. I could only look upwards, the sun began to grow hot, and the light offended mine eyes. I heard a confused noise about me, but in the posture I lay, could see nothing except the sky. In a little time I felt something alive moving on my left leg, which advancing gently forward over my breast, came almost up to my chin; when bending mine eyes downwards as much as I could, I perceived it to be a human creature not six inches high, with a bow and arrow in his hands, and a quiver at his back. In the mean time, I felt at least forty more of the same kind (as I conjectured) following the first. I was in the utmost astonishment, and roared so loud, that they all ran back in a fright; and some of them, as I was afterwards told,

were hurt with the falls they got by leaping from my sides upon the ground. However, they soon returned, and one of them, who ventured so far as to get a full sight of my face, lifting up his hands and eyes by way of admiration, cried out in a shrill, but distinct voice, *Hekinah degul*: the others repeated the same words several times, but I then knew not what they meant. I lay all this while, as the reader may believe, in great uneasiness: at length, struggling to get loose, I had the fortune to break the strings, and wrench out the pegs that fastened my left arm to the ground; for, by lifting it up to my face, I discovered the methods they had taken to bind me; and, at the same time, with a violent pull, which gave me excessive pain, I a little loosened the strings that tied down my hair on the left side, so that I was just able to turn my head about two inches. But the creatures ran off a second time, before I could seize them; whereupon there was a great shout in a very shrill accent, and after it ceased, I heard one of them cry aloud, *Tolgo phonac*; when in an instant I felt above an hundred arrows discharged on my left hand, which pricked me like so many needles; and besides, they shot another flight into the air, as we do bombs in Europe, whereof many, I suppose, fell on my body (though I felt them not), and some on my face, which I immediately covered with my

left hand. When this shower of arrows was over, I fell a groaning with grief and pain, and then striving again to get loose, they discharged another volley larger than the first, and some of them attempted with spears to stick me in the sides; but, by good luck, I had on me a buff jerkin, which they could not pierce. I thought it the most prudent method to lie still, and my design was to continue so till night, when, my left hand being already loose, I could easily free myself: and as for the inhabitants, I had reason to believe I might be a match for the greatest armies they could bring against me, if they were all of the same size with him that I saw. But Fortune disposed otherwise of me. When the people observed I was quiet, they discharged no more arrows: but, by the noise increasing, I knew their numbers were greater; and about four yards from me, over-against my right ear, I heard a knocking for above an hour, like people at work; when, turning my head that way, as well as the pegs and strings would permit me, I saw a stage erected about a foot and a half from the ground, capable of holding four of the inhabitants, with two or three ladders to mount it: from whence one of them, who seemed to be a person of quality, made me a long speech, whereof I understood not one syllable. But I should have mentioned, that before the principal person began his oration, he cried out three times *Langro dehul san* (these words and the former were afterwards repeated and explained to me): whereupon immediately about fifty of the inhabitants came, and cut the strings that fastened the left side of my head, which gave me the liberty of turning it to the right, and of observing the person and gesture of him who was to speak. He appeared to be of a middle age, and taller than any of the other three who attended him, whereof one was a page who held up his train, and seemed to be somewhat longer than my middle finger; the other two stood one on each side to support him. He acted every part of an orator, and I could observe many periods of threatenings, and others of promises, pity and kindness. I answered in a few words, but in the most submissive manner, lifting up my left hand and both mine eyes to the sun, as calling him for a witness; and being almost famished with hunger, having not eaten a morsel for some hours

before I left the ship, I found the demands of nature so strong upon me, that I could not forbear showing my impatience (perhaps against the strict rules of decency) by putting my finger frequently on my mouth, to signify that I wanted food. The *Hurgo* (for so they call a great lord, as I afterwards learnt) understood me very well. He descended from the stage, and commanded that several ladders should be applied to my sides, on which above an hundred of the inhabitants mounted, and walked towards my mouth, laden with baskets full of meat, which had been provided and sent thither by the King's orders upon the first intelligence he received of me. I observed there was the flesh of several animals, but could not distinguish them by the taste. There were shoulders, legs and loins, shaped like those of mutton, and very well dressed, but smaller than the wings of a lark. I ate them by two or three at a mouthful, and took three loaves at a time, about the bigness of musket bullets. They supplied me as fast as they could, showing a thousand marks of wonder and astonishment at my bulk and appetite. I then made another sign that I wanted drink. They found by my eating that a small quantity would not suffice me; and being a most ingenious people, they slung up with great dexterity one of their largest hogsheads, then rolled it towards my hand, and beat out the top; I drank it off at a draught, which I might well do, for it hardly held half a pint, and tasted like a small wine of Burgundy, but much more delicious. They brought me a second hogshead, which I drank in the same manner, and made signs for more, but they had none to give me. When I had performed these wonders, they shouted for joy, and danced upon my breast, repeating several times as they did at first, *Hekinah degul.* They made me a sign that I should throw down the two hogsheads, but first warned the people below to stand out of the way, crying aloud, *Borach mivola*, and when they saw the vessels in the air,

there was an universal shout of *Hekinah degul*. I confess I was often tempted, while they were passing backwards and forwards on my body, to seize forty or fifty of the first that came in my reach, and dash them against the ground. But the remembrance of what I had felt, which probably might not be the worst they could do, and the promise of honour I made them, for so I interpreted my submissive behaviour, soon drove out those imaginations. Besides, I now considered myself as bound by the laws of hospitality to a people who had treated me with so much expense and magnificence. However, in my thoughts I could not sufficiently wonder at the intrepidity of these diminutive mortals, who durst venture to mount and walk on my body, while one of my hands was at liberty, without trembling at the very sight of so prodigious a creature as I must appear to them. After some time, when they observed that I made no more demands for meat, there appeared before me a person of high rank from his Imperial Majesty. His Excellency having mounted on the small of my right leg, advanced forwards up to my face, with about a dozen of his retinue. And producing his credentials under the Signet Royal, which he applied close to mine eyes, spoke about ten minutes, without any signs of anger,

but with a kind of determinate resolution; often pointing forwards, which, as I afterwards found, was towards the capital city, about half a mile distant, whither it was agreed by his Majesty in council that I must be conveyed. I answered in few words, but to no purpose, and made a sign with my hand that was loose, putting it to the other (but over his Excellency's head, for fear of hurting him or his train) and then to my own head and body, to signify that I desired my liberty. It appeared that he understood me well enough, for he shook his head by way of disapprobation, and held his hand in a posture to show that I must be carried as a prisoner. However, he made other signs to let me understand that I should have meat and drink enough, and very good treatment. Whereupon I once more thought of attempting to break my bonds, but again, when I felt the smart of their arrows upon my face and hands, which were all in blisters, and many of the darts still sticking in them, and observing likewise that the number of my enemies increased, I gave tokens to let them know that they might do with me what they pleased.

Traditional

I SAW A PEACOCK

Illustrated by Emma Chichester Clark

I saw a Peacock with a fiery tail,
I saw a blazing Comet drop down hail,
I saw a Cloud with ivy circled round,
I saw a sturdy Oak creep on the ground,
I saw a Pismire swallow up a whale,
I saw a raging Sea brim full of ale,
I saw a Venice Glass sixteen foot deep,
I saw a Well full of men's tears that weep,
I saw their Eyes all in a flame of fire,
I saw a House as big as the Moon and higher,
I saw the Sun even in the midst of night,
I saw the Man that saw this wondrous sight.

Retold by N. J. Dawood

ALI BABA AND THE FORTY THIEVES

FROM

SINDBAD THE SAILOR AND OTHER TALES FROM THE ARABIAN NIGHTS

Illustrated by Pauline Baynes

Long ago there lived in a city of Persia two brothers whose names were Kassim and Ali Baba.

Though born of the same parents and brought up in the same home, their characters were quite different. Kassim, the elder, was arrogant, shrewd, and greedy, while Ali Baba was unassuming, kind-hearted, and content with his situation. When their father died, they divided all he had between them and started life on an equal footing, but while Kassim married a rich wife and became the owner of a thriving shop in the city's main bazaar, Ali Baba took to wife the daughter of a humble family, and earned a modest living by cutting wood in the forest and selling it in the town.

Ali Baba lived frugally and wisely with his wife, saving as much as his earnings would allow, so that in a few months he was able to buy three donkeys. Every day he would lead his donkeys to the forest and bring them back laden with firewood.

One day, while working at the edge of a far thicket, with his donkeys grazing peacefully near by, he heard the clatter of galloping hoofs in the distance and saw a great cloud of dust approaching. Curious to find out the cause of the commotion, he climbed cautiously into a tall tree that stood on a hillside, giving a clear view of the adjacent plain. From his hiding place he saw a troop of fierce-looking armed horsemen riding towards him. He counted forty of them, and guessed from their appearance and demeanour – their fiery eyes, their black, pointed beards, and the weapons they carried – that they were a band of robbers.

When they came under the tree, the forty thieves dismounted at a signal from the captain and started removing their saddlebags. They carried their loads to a great rock at the bottom of the hill; then the captain went up to the rock and in a loud voice cried, 'Open, Sesame!'

Ali Baba was astonished to notice that, at the mention of this word – the name of a cereal commonly grown in Persia – a hidden door in the rock swung wide open. The entire band of robbers filed in. In a few moments they emerged, carrying their now-empty saddlebags in their hands, and the captain cried, 'Close, Sesame!' The rock at once shut behind them, and no one could have guessed there was any opening in that solid surface.

As soon as the robbers had mounted and ridden off, Ali Baba climbed down from the tree and went up to the mysterious rock. Finding the surface as smooth and solid as before, he marvelled at the magic that had forced it open.

'What priceless treasures must lie within it!' he reflected, and, remembering the captain's words, decided to utter them himself and see what would happen.

'Open, Sesame!' he shouted.

The rock opened, just as it had done before; and Ali Baba walked in. Being a good Muslim, he murmured as he entered, 'In the name of Allah, the Compassionate, the Merciful!' He found himself in a huge cave piled up with rich ornaments, chests brim-full with gold and silver coins, and great bags bursting with precious stones – which must have taken hundreds of years to accumulate. As he scanned the vast treasures, Ali Baba realized that the cave was the secret storehouse of

countless generations of thieves and highwaymen.

Carefully choosing six bags of gold, he loaded them on his donkeys and covered them with brushwood to hide them. Then he cried aloud, 'Close, Sesame!' and in a twinkling the door slid to behind him, leaving not a trace on the rock's outer surface.

When Ali Baba arrived home and his wife saw him unload the bags of gold, she was seized with shame and fear.

'Good husband,' she said, 'do not tell me you have earned all this gold by cutting wood in the forest. Bad luck is sure to enter our humble house if we keep such ill-gotten gains here.'

'Fear nothing, I am no thief,' Ali Baba quickly interrupted. 'Rather rejoice, for it was Allah who guided my footsteps in the forest this morning.' And he told her of his adventure and how he had found the gold in the robbers' hide-out.

When she heard the story, the poor woman was filled with relief and joy. She squatted before the pile of gold that her husband had poured out of the bags and tried to value the incalculable coins.

'Don't try to count them,' said Ali Baba with a laugh. 'It would take you days to do that. Get up now and help me dig a ditch in the kitchen where we can hide them. To leave them here would only rouse the suspicions of our neighbours.'

But his wife wanted to know exactly how rich they were. 'If I cannot count them,' she said, 'I must at least weigh or measure them. I will go and borrow a measure from your brother Kassim's house, and then I can measure the gold while you dig the hole.'

She went over to Kassim's house across the lane and begged his wife to lend her a measure.

'You can have one,' her sister-in-law replied. But she wondered at the same time why Ali Baba should need a measure when he was so poor that he could buy only a day's supply of wheat at a time. So the cunning woman, curious to know what kind of grain he was measuring, devised a trick; she rubbed the bottom of the wooden vessel with some fat.

Ali Baba's wife quickly returned home and, after measuring out the gold, carried the measure back to Kassim's wife, not knowing that a gold piece had stuck to the fat at the bottom.

'What have we here?' cried Kassim's wife as soon as her kinswoman had left her. 'So Ali Baba is now too rich to count his gold and has to measure it!'

Jealousy gripped her soul. She sent a servant to fetch her husband from his shop, and told him the story in a fit of rage. 'We cannot let the matter rest at that,' she screamed. 'You must go now and force that wretched brother of yours to reveal to you the source of his riches!'

Instead of being pleased that his brother was no longer a poor man, Kassim, too, was overwhelmed with envy. His heart burning with spite, he immediately went over to Ali Baba's house.

'How is it that you dare to deceive us so?' he cried. 'You go on pretending to be penniless and humble, when you have so much gold that you cannot even count it. Tell me this moment how you came by it, or I will denounce you as an impostor and a thief!'

He showed his brother the gold piece still smeared with fat, and Ali Baba, seeing at once how his secret had been discovered, confided to Kassim the whole story and begged him to keep quiet about it.

There and then, the greedy Kassim resolved to take possession of the treasure for himself alone. He left his brother and quickly returned home, his head buzzing with a thousand plans.

Early next morning he set out with ten donkeys to find the cave that

Ali Baba had described. When he came to the rock under the tree, he stretched out his arms towards it and shouted, 'Open, Sesame!' And exactly as his brother had told him, the rock opened to let him in. He tied his donkeys to some trees, entered the cave, then closed the rock behind him with the magic words.

Kassim was dumbfounded at the sight of the robbers' treasure, and his very soul was stirred by the prospect of caravan after caravan carrying the riches home. He gathered twenty of the largest sacks of gold and jewels and dragged them to the entrance. Then he tried to remember the magic words. 'Open, Barley!' he cried.

But the rock did not open.

The miserable Kassim, preoccupied with the acquisition of so much gold, had completely forgotten the all-powerful words. Again and again he shouted, 'Open, Wheat! Open, Barley! Open, Beans!' to the door, which obeyed no sound but 'Open, Sesame!'

And as he stood shaking with rage and terror before the impenetrable rock, the forty thieves came riding up to the cave.

When they saw the ten donkeys tethered near the entrance they leaped down from their horses and scattered around in search of the intruder, brandishing their swords and yelling angry curses. Then the captain pointed towards the rock and pronounced the two words that rent it asunder. The robbers were enraged to find a stranger in their treasure house. They swooped upon Kassim with their swords and hacked him into six pieces, then hung the pieces just inside the cave as a lesson and a warning to other would-be intruders.

When night came and Kassim did not return home, his wife grew very anxious. She went over to Ali Baba's house and begged him to go and look for her husband. Fearing that the worst might have happened, Ali Baba took his three donkeys and rode off at sunrise to the robbers' cave.

With a trembling voice he cried, 'Open, Sesame!' and when the rock opened, he walked in. He was stricken with grief at the sight of Kassim's body cut in pieces. With a heavy heart he took down the pieces and put them carefully together into two empty sacks, which he loaded on to one of his donkeys. He loaded the other two beasts with more sacks of gold, then commanded the rocky door to shut and led his donkeys home.

On reaching the courtyard of his house, he knocked at the door, and it was opened by the slave Marjanah, who was the cleverest and most faithful of his servants.

'Marjanah, my girl,' said Ali Baba, 'today you can give us proof of your ingenuity and wisdom. Your master's brother has been killed by robbers and cut into pieces, but no one must know about it. Think of some way by which we can bury him without arousing any suspicions.'

Then he went to his brother's house and broke the bad news to Kassim's wife.

'Do not grieve, dear sister,' he said. 'Allah has given me more riches than I can use. Come and live in our house, and share everything with us. But no one must know our secret.'

They unloaded the pieces of Kassim's body, and discreetly told the neighbours that he had died suddenly in his sleep.

Then Marjanah went to the shop of an old cobbler in another part

of the town where she was quite unknown.

'We want you to do a little sewing,' she said. 'Bring your needles and thread with you. Your work must be secret, and I must blindfold you and lead you to the house.'

At first the old cobbler refused, but when Marjanah slipped a piece of gold into his hand, he allowed himself to be led along the streets and down into the cellar of Ali Baba's house. There she showed him the pieces of Kassim's body, slipped another gold coin into his hand, and bade him sew them together, adding, 'If you work quickly you shall have two more pieces of gold.'

The old man set to work at once and sewed the parts so neatly that no one would see the stitching. She led him back blindfolded to his shop, and returned home to make arrangements for Kassim's funeral. Thus Kassim was buried according to the customary rites, and no one outside the household had the slightest suspicion of the way he had met his death.

When the forty thieves paid their next visit to the cave they were dismayed to find no sign of Kassim's body.

'My men,' the captain said, 'it is clear that someone else knows our secret. We must find out at once who the accomplice of the

man we killed is.'

Calling one of the robbers, he said to him, 'Disguise yourself as a holy dervish. Go into the town and find out the identity of the man whose body we cut to pieces.'

Just before sunrise next morning the robber entered the town, and the first shop he saw open was the old cobbler's. He greeted the old man, praised his wares, and engaged him in a friendly conversation.

'I see, good sir, that you begin work before sunrise,' he began. 'Your eyes must be very good indeed to see so well in the grey light of dawn.'

'Allah be praised, good dervish,' replied the cobbler. 'I can still thread a needle at the first attempt. Why, only yesterday I sewed together the parts of a man's body in a dark cellar without a light.'

'Indeed,' said the robber, 'and who might the man be?'

'That I cannot tell,' the cobbler replied, 'for I was blindfolded and led to the place by an impudent girl, and brought back the same way.'

The robber slipped a gold coin into the cobbler's hand.

'I would like nothing better,' he said, 'than to be taken myself to that house. I will blindfold you, and you can grope your way along the same route you followed yesterday. Take me there and you shall have more gold.'

The cobbler allowed his eyes to be bandaged and, holding on to the robber's sleeve, felt his way slowly to Ali Baba's house; and there he stopped.

'This is most certainly the place,' he cried.

The robber was overjoyed at the discovery. He removed the old man's bandage, slipped a second gold piece into his hand, and sent him back to his shop. Then he took a piece of chalk out of his pocket and with it marked the door of Ali Baba's house. This done, he returned with all possible speed to the forest and told his captain the good news.

When, soon afterward, honest Marjanah went to do the shopping, she noticed the white mark upon the door and thought to herself, 'This is an evil sign, the work of an enemy plotting my master's ruin.'

So she fetched a piece of chalk and made the same mark on the doors of all the houses in the street.

Next morning the thieves came one by one into the town to break into the house their spy had marked for them, and to avenge themselves on everyone who lived in it. But when the robber led them into the street, they were confounded to see that all the doors were marked in the same way, so that it was impossible to tell which was the house they sought. The angry captain sent them back to the forest, with orders to put the foolish spy to death.

'It seems that I shall have to go myself,' said the robber chief.

So next day he rode into the city in disguise

and went straight to the old cobbler, who led him to Ali Baba's house. But the captain did not mark the door this time. He gazed long and carefully at it until its very image was engraved upon his memory, and then he returned to the forest.

He called the thieves together and said to them, 'I know the house for certain now. Tomorrow we shall be avenged. All I require you to do is to bring me thirty-nine earthenware jars, each large enough to contain a full-grown man. One of them must be filled with cooking oil, the rest must be empty.'

The thieves, who always obeyed the captain, rode off at once to the market place and returned with thirty-nine large jars. One of these jars they filled with oil, and in each of the others a robber hid himself, on the captain's orders. The chief armed each with a dagger and club, and covered the mouth of each vessel with a muslin cloth, so that the men inside would be hidden and yet breathe freely. Then he loaded his men's horses with the jars, linked the animals together, and drove them towards the city.

When he came to Ali Baba's house, he found the woodcutter seated on his threshold, enjoying the cool evening air.

'Peace be to you, my master,' said the captain with a low bow. 'I am an oil merchant and have been travelling the road these three days. I am a stranger in this city and do not know where to pass the night. I pray that you will give hospitality, for myself and my horses, in the courtyard of your house.'

'You are most welcome, sir,' said Ali Baba kindly.

He took his guest by the hand and led him into his house. Then he ordered Marjanah to help with the unloading of the jars, to feed the horses, and to prepare a hot meal for the stranger.

Now, the captain had told his men that when he threw a pebble into the jars they were to come out of the jars and join him. So they crouched there, patiently waiting for the signal.

Meanwhile, Marjanah, who was busily cooking the dinner in the

kitchen, found her lamp going out for lack of oil.

'We surely cannot complain of being short of oil,' she said to herself, 'when there are thirty-nine jars full of it in the courtyard. I will go and take a little from one of them.'

She took her lamp and went to fill it, but as she touched the first jar a voice whispered, 'Is it time?'

The quick-witted Marjanah guessed at once what was afoot, and instead of screaming with fright, whispered back in as deep a voice as she could, 'Not yet!'

As she approached the jars in turn, from each came the same question, and to each she gave the same answer, until she came to the last jar, which she found was in fact filled with oil. After taking what she needed, she returned to the kitchen, lit the lamp, and set to work upon a plan to save her master.

From the last jar she quickly filled a great cauldron with oil and set it over the fire to boil. Then she poured the boiling oil into those of the jars in which the thieves were hidden and killed them all.

After dinner the captain of the robbers retired to bed, and at midnight, seeing no light and hearing no sound, he threw his pebble into the yard. But there was no answer, and not one robber appeared.

'The dogs have gone to sleep,' he muttered.

When he ran down to the courtyard and looked into the jars, he found that all his men were dead. Realizing that his plan was discovered and that he himself might be in danger of his life, he leaped over the courtyard wall and fled. On and on he ran until he reached the treasure cave, where he sat brooding over the calamitous end of his followers.

Next morning, Marjanah took Ali Baba into the courtyard and showed him the jars.

He recoiled in horror when he looked into the first and saw a dead man inside, but the girl quickly told him the whole story. Now he rejoiced to hear that all the robbers were dead and was deeply thankful to Marjanah.

'From this moment,' he declared, 'you are no longer a slave, but our own beloved daughter.'

Ali Baba buried the thieves' bodies in a great pit and lived in peace and contentment with his family for many months.

One day, Ali Baba's oldest son, who by now had become a rich merchant with a shop of his own, said to his father, 'I do not know how to repay my neighbour, the merchant Husain, for all the kindness he has shown me since he took the shop next door to mine. I should much like to invite him to our house and give a feast in his honour.'

'Invite him, by all means,' Ali Baba replied. 'He will be most welcome.'

But when the merchant arrived, he said to Ali Baba, 'You do me great honour in inviting me to your house, but alas, I cannot eat with you. I have made a vow never to taste salt or eat any meat flavoured with it.'

'That is no difficult matter,' Ali Baba cried. 'I will give orders that no salt be put into our food tonight.' And he hurried into the kitchen to tell Marjanah that she should use no salt in the cooking.

This odd request aroused the girl's suspicions and she looked closely at the guest when she carried the dishes in. Her horror knew no bounds when she recognized the captain of the robbers and saw that he had a dagger hidden in the folds of his robe.

'So that's why the villain would not eat salt with the man he intends to kill,' she thought.

When the meal was over, Marjanah entered the room, and Ali Baba and his son were astonished to see the dress she had put on; it was that of a dancer. Holding a dagger in one hand, she danced gracefully, to the delight of all the company, particularly that of the disguised robber, who took out his purse to throw a gold coin to her. As he bent forward she flung herself upon him and plunged her dagger into his heart.

'What have you done, you foolish girl!' Ali Baba exclaimed, aghast at the deed.

'You have killed the kind old man!' cried the son.

'I have saved your lives!' Marjanah cried. And she showed them the dagger hidden in the visitor's robe, and then told them who he really was and how she had found him out.

When Ali Baba realized that the girl had saved him yet once more, he took her into his arms and said, 'You shall marry my son and become in all truth my daughter; for you have truly earned this reward.'

And so Marjanah was wedded to Ali Baba's son, amid great rejoicing.

For a long time, Ali Baba kept away from the robbers' cave, but when one year had passed he went there with his son and Marjanah. He found the little path that led up to the rock overgrown with long grass, with not a sign of man or beast, and knew that the cave was now perfectly safe. He flung out his arms towards the rock, crying, 'Open, Sesame!' and once again the door opened, revealing the secret treasure untouched since the death of the robbers.

So Ali Baba became the richest and most influential man of his time, and lived in tranquillity and joy until the end of his life.

Rudyard Kipling

From

THE JUNGLE BOOK

Illustrated by Sally Taylor

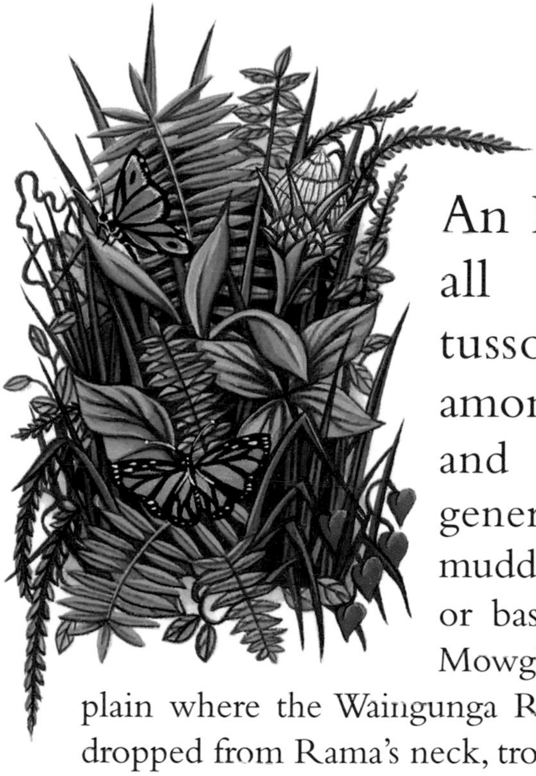

An Indian grazing-ground is all rocks and scrub and tussocks and little ravines, among which the herds scatter and disappear. The buffaloes generally keep to the pools and muddy places, where they lie wallowing or basking in the warm mud for hours. Mowgli drove them on to the edge of the plain where the Waingunga River came out of the Jungle; then he dropped from Rama's neck, trotted off to a bamboo clump, and found Grey Brother. 'Ah!' said Grey Brother. 'I have waited here very many days. What is the meaning of this cattle-herding work?'

'It is an order,' said Mowgli. 'I am a village herd for a while. What news of Shere Khan?'

'He has come back to this country, and has waited here a long time for thee. Now he has gone off again, for the game is scarce. But he means to kill thee.'

'Very good,' said Mowgli. 'So long as he is away do thou or one of the four brothers sit on that rock, so that I can see thee as I come out of the village. When he comes back, wait for me in the ravine by the *dhâk*-tree in the centre of the plain. We need not walk into Shere Khan's mouth.'

Day after day Mowgli would lead the buffaloes out to their wallows, and day after day he would see Grey Brother's back a mile and a half away across the plain (so he knew that Shere Khan had not come back), and day after day he would lie on the grass listening to the noises round him, and dreaming of old days in the Jungle. If Shere Khan had made a false step with his lame paw up in the Jungles by the Waingunga, Mowgli would have heard him in those long, still mornings.

At last a day came when he did not see Grey Brother at the signal-place, and he laughed and headed the buffaloes for the ravine by the *dhâk*-tree, which was all covered with golden-red flowers. There sat Grey Brother, every bristle on his back lifted.

'He has hidden for a month to throw thee off thy guard. He crossed the ranges last night with Tabaqui, hotfoot on thy trail,' said the wolf, panting.

Mowgli frowned. 'I am not afraid of Shere Khan, but Tabaqui is very cunning.'

'Have no fear,' said Grey Brother, licking his lips a little. 'I met Tabaqui in the dawn. Now he is telling all his wisdom to the kites, but he told *me* everything before I broke his back. Shere Khan's plan is to wait for thee at the village gate this evening – for thee and for no one else. He is lying up now in the big dry ravine of the Waingunga.'

'Has he eaten today, or does he hunt empty?' said Mowgli, for the answer meant life or death to him.

'He killed at dawn – a pig – and he has drunk too. Remember, Shere Khan could never fast, even for the sake of revenge.'

'Oh! Fool, fool! What a cub's cub it is! Eaten and drunk too, and he thinks that I shall wait till he has slept! Now, where does he lie up? If there were but ten of us we might pull him down as he lies. These buffaloes will not charge unless they wind him, and I cannot speak their language. Can we get behind his track so that they may smell it?'

'He swam far down the Waingunga to cut that off,' said Grey Brother.

'Tabaqui told him that, I know. He would never have thought of it alone.' Mowgli stood with his finger in his mouth, thinking. 'The big ravine of the Waingunga. That opens out on the plain not half a mile from here. I can take the herd round through the Jungle to the head of the ravine and then sweep down – but he would slink out at the foot. We must block that end. Grey Brother, canst thou cut the herd in two for me?'

'Not I, perhaps – but I have brought a wise helper.' Grey Brother trotted off and dropped into a hole. Then there lifted up a huge grey head that Mowgli knew well, and the hot air was filled with the most desolate cry of all the Jungle – the hunting-howl of a wolf at midday.

'Akela! Akela!' said Mowgli, clapping his hands. 'I might have known that thou wouldst not forget me. We have a big work in hand. Cut the herd in two, Akela. Keep the cows and calves together, and the bulls and the plough-buffaloes by themselves.'

The two wolves ran, ladies'-chain fashion, in and out of the herd, which snorted and threw up its head, and separated into two clumps. In one the cow-buffaloes stood, with their calves in the centre, and glared and pawed, ready, if a wolf would only stay still, to charge down and trample the life out of him. In the other the bulls and the young bulls snorted and stamped; but, though they looked more imposing, they were much less dangerous, for they had no calves to protect. No six men could have divided the herd so neatly.

'What orders?' panted Akela. 'They are trying to join again.'

Mowgli slipped on to Rama's back. 'Drive the bulls away to the left, Akela. Grey Brother, when we are gone, hold the cows together, and drive them into the foot of the ravine.'

'How far?' said Grey Brother, panting and snapping.

'Till the sides are higher than Shere Khan can jump,' shouted Mowgli. 'Keep them there till we come down.' The bulls swept off as Akela bayed, and Grey Brother stopped in front of the cows. They charged down on him and he ran just before them to the foot of the ravine, as Akela drove the bulls far to the left.

'Well done! Another charge and they are fairly started. Careful, now – careful, Akela. A snap too much, and the bulls will charge. *Huyah!* This is wilder work than driving black-buck. Didst thou think these creatures could move so swiftly?' Mowgli called.

'I have – have hunted these too in my time,' gasped Akela in the dust. 'Shall I turn them into the Jungle?'

'Ay, turn! Swiftly turn them! Rama is mad with rage. Oh, if I could only tell him what I need of him today!'

The bulls were turned to the right this time, and crashed into the standing thicket. The other herd-children, watching with the cattle half a mile away, hurried to the village as fast as their legs could carry them, crying that the buffaloes had gone mad and run away.

But Mowgli's plan was simple enough. All he wanted to do was to make a big circle uphill and get at the head of the ravine, and then take the bulls down it and catch Shere Khan between the bulls and the cows; for he knew that after a meal and a full drink Shere Khan would not be in any condition to fight or to clamber up the sides of the ravine. He was soothing the buffaloes now by voice, and Akela had dropped far to the rear, only whimpering once or twice to hurry the rear-guard. It was a long, long circle, for they did not wish to get too near the ravine and give Shere Khan warning. At last Mowgli rounded up the bewildered herd at the head of the ravine on a grassy patch that sloped down to the ravine itself. From that height you could see across the tops of the trees down to the plain below; but what Mowgli looked at was the sides of the ravine, and he saw with a great deal of satisfaction that they ran nearly straight up and down, while the vines and creepers that hung over them would give no foothold to a tiger who wanted to get on.

'Let them breathe, Akela,' he said, holding up his hand. 'They have not winded him yet. Let them breathe. I must tell Shere Khan who comes. We have him in the trap.'

He put his hands to his mouth and shouted down the ravine – it was almost like shouting down a tunnel – and the echoes jumped from rock to rock.

After a long time there came back the drawling, sleepy snarl of a full-fed tiger just wakened.

'Who calls?' said Shere Khan, and a splendid peacock fluttered up out of the ravine screeching.

'I, Mowgli. Cattle thief, it is time to come to the Council Rock! Down – hurry them down, Akela! Down, Rama, down!'

The herd paused for an instant at the edge of the slope, but Akela gave tongue in the full hunting-yell, and they pitched over one after the other, just as steamers shoot rapids, the sand and stones spurting up round them. Once started, there was no chance of stopping, and before they were fairly in the bed of the ravine Rama winded Shere Khan and bellowed.

'Ha! Ha!' said Mowgli, on his back. 'Now thou knowest!' and the torrent of black horns, foaming muzzles, and staring eyes whirled down the ravine like boulders in flood-time; the weaker buffaloes being shouldered out to the sides of the ravine, where they tore through the creepers. They knew what the business was before them – the terrible charge of the buffalo-herd, against which no tiger can hope to stand. Shere Khan heard the thunder of their hoofs, picked himself up, and lumbered down the ravine, looking from side to side for some way of escape; but the walls of the ravine were straight, and he had to keep on, heavy with his dinner and his drink, willing to do anything rather than fight. The herd splashed through the pool he had just left, bellowing till the narrow cut rang. Mowgli heard an answering bellow from the foot of the ravine, saw Shere Khan turn (the tiger knew if the worst came to the worst it was better to meet the bulls than the cows with their calves), and then Rama tripped, stumbled, and went on again over something soft, and, with the bulls at his heels, crashed full into the other herd, while the weaker buffaloes were lifted clean off their feet by the shock of the meeting. That charge carried both herds out into the plain, goring and stamping and snorting. Mowgli watched his time, and slipped off Rama's neck, laying about him right and left with his stick.

'Quick, Akela! Break them up. Scatter them, or they will be fighting one another. Drive them away, Akela. *Hai*, Rama! *Hai! hai! hai!* my children. Softly now, softly! It is all over.'

Akela and Grey Brother ran to and fro nipping the buffaloes' legs, and though the herd wheeled once to charge up the ravine again, Mowgli managed to turn Rama, and the others followed him to the wallows.

Shere Khan needed no more trampling. He was dead, and the kites were coming for him already.

Robert Louis Stevenson

WINDY NIGHTS

Illustrated by Ian Beck

Whenever the moon and stars are set,
  Whenever the wind is high,
All night long in the dark and wet,
  A man goes riding by.
Late in the night when the fires are out,
Why does he gallop and gallop about?

Whenever the trees are crying aloud,
  And ships are tossed at sea,
By, on the highway, low and loud,
  By at the gallop goes he.
By at the gallop he goes, and then
By he comes back at the gallop again.

Rudyard Kipling

IF

Illustrated by Sue Williams

If you can keep your head when all about you
  Are losing theirs and blaming it on you,
If you can trust yourself when all men doubt you,
  But make allowance for their doubting too;
If you can wait and not be tired by waiting,
  Or being lied about, don't deal in lies,
Or being hated don't give way to hating,
  And yet don't look too good, nor talk too wise:

If you can dream – and not make dreams your master;
  If you can think – and not make thoughts your aim,
If you can meet with Triumph and Disaster
  And treat these two impostors just the same;
If you can bear to hear the truth you've spoken
  Twisted by knaves to make a trap for fools,
Or watch the things you gave your life to, broken,
  And stoop and build 'em up with worn-out tools:

If you can make one heap of all your winnings
   And risk it on one turn of pitch-and-toss,
And lose, and start again at your beginnings
   And never breathe a word about your loss;
If you can force your heart and nerve and sinew
   To serve your turn long after they are gone,
And so hold on when there is nothing in you
   Except the Will which says to them: 'Hold on!'

If you can talk with crowds and keep your virtue,
   Or walk with Kings – nor lose the common touch,
If neither foes nor loving friends can hurt you,
   If all men count with you, but none too much;
If you can fill the unforgiving minute
   With sixty seconds' worth of distance run,
Yours is the Earth and everything that's in it,
   And – which is more – you'll be a Man, my son!

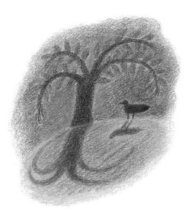

John Masefield

SEA FEVER

Illustrated by Geoff Hunt

I must go down to the seas again, to the lonely sea
  and the sky,
And all I ask is a tall ship and a star to steer her by,
And the wheel's kick and the wind's song and the
  white sail's shaking,
And a grey mist on the sea's face, and a grey dawn
  breaking.

I must go down to the seas again, for the call of the
  running tide
Is a wild call and a clear call that may not be denied;
And all I ask is a windy day with the white clouds
  flying,
And the flung spray and the blown spume, and the
  seagulls crying.

I must go down to the seas again, to the vagrant gypsy
  life,
To the gull's way and the whale's way where the wind's
  like a whetted knife;
And all I ask is a merry yarn from a laughing fellow-rover,
And quiet sleep and a sweet dream when the long trick's
  over.

Jack London

From

THE CALL OF THE WILD

Illustrated by John Butler

Buck is a dog born to luxury, but betrayed and sold to be a sledge dog in the harsh and frozen Yukon.

Buck's first day on the Dyea beach was like a nightmare. Every hour was filled with shock and surprise. He had been suddenly jerked from the heart of civilization and flung into the heart of things primordial. No lazy, sunkissed life was this, with nothing to do but loaf and be bored. Here was neither peace, nor rest, nor a moment's safety. All was confusion and action, and every moment life and limb were in peril. There was imperative need to be constantly alert; for these dogs and men were not town dogs and men. They were savages, all of them; who knew no law but the law of club and fang.

He had never seen dogs fight as these wolfish creatures fought, and his first experience taught him an unforgettable lesson. It is true, it was a vicarious experience, else he would not have lived to profit by it. Curly was the victim. They were camped near the log store, where she, in her friendly way, made advances to a husky dog the size of a full-grown wolf, though not half so large as she. There was no warning,

94

only a leap in like a flash, a metallic clip of teeth, a leap out equally swift, and Curly's face was ripped open from eye to jaw.

It was the wolf manner of fighting, to strike and leap away; but there was more to it than this. Thirty or forty huskies ran to the spot and surrounded the combatants in an intent and silent circle. Buck did not comprehend that silent intentness, nor the eager way with which they were licking their chops. Curly rushed her antagonist, who struck again and leaped aside. He met her next rush with his chest, in a peculiar fashion that tumbled her off her feet. She never regained them. This was what the onlooking huskies had waited for. They closed in upon her, snarling and yelping, and she was buried, screaming with agony, beneath the bristling mass of bodies.

So sudden was it, and so unexpected, that Buck was taken aback. He saw Spitz run out his scarlet tongue in a way he had of laughing; and he saw François swinging an axe, spring into the mess of dogs. Three men with clubs were helping him to scatter them. It did not take long. Two minutes from the time Curly went down, the last of her assailants were clubbed off. But she lay there limp and lifeless in the bloody, trampled snow, almost literally torn to pieces, the swart half-breed standing over her and cursing horribly. The scene often came back to Buck to trouble him in his sleep. So that was the way. No fair play. Once down, that was the end of you. Well, he would see to it that he never went down. Spitz ran out his tongue and laughed again and from that moment Buck hated him with a bitter and deathless hatred.

Before he had recovered from the shock caused by the tragic passing of Curly, he received another shock. François fastened upon him an arrangement of straps and buckles. It was a harness, such as he had seen the grooms put on the horses at home. And as he had seen horses work, so he was set to work, hauling François on a sled to the forest that fringed the valley, and returning with a load of firewood. Though his dignity was sorely hurt by thus being made a draught animal, he was too wise to rebel. He buckled down with a will and did his best, though it was all new and strange. François was stern, demanding instant obedience; and by virtue of his whip receiving instant obedience; while Dave, who was an experienced wheeler, nipped Buck's hindquarters whenever he was in error. Spitz was the leader, likewise experienced, and while he could not always get at Buck, he growled sharp reproof now and again, or cunningly threw his weight in the traces to jerk Buck into the way he should go. Buck learned easily, and under the combined tuition of his two mates and François made remarkable progress. Ere they returned to camp he knew enough to stop at 'ho', to go ahead at 'mush', to swing wide on the bends; and to keep clear of the wheeler when the loaded sled shot downhill at their heels.

'T'ree vair' good dogs,' François told Perrault. 'Dat Buck, heem pool lak hell, I tich heem queek as anyt'ing.'

By afternoon, Perrault, who was in a hurry to be on the trail with his dispatches, returned with two more dogs. 'Billee' and 'Joe' he called them, two brothers, and true huskies both. Sons of the one mother though they were, they were as different as day and night. Billee's one fault was his excessive good nature, while Joe was the very opposite, sour and introspective, with a perpetual snarl and a malignant eye. Buck received them in comradely fashion. Dave ignored them; while Spitz proceeded to thrash first one and then the other. Billee wagged his tail appeasingly, turned to run when he saw that appeasement was of no avail, and cried (still appeasingly) when Spitz's sharp teeth scored his flank. But no matter how Spitz circled, Joe whirled around on his heels to face him, mane bristling, ears laid back, lips writhing and snarling, jaws clipping together as fast as he could snap, and eyes diabolically gleaming – the incarnation of belligerent fear. So terrible was his appearance that Spitz was forced to forego disciplining him; but to cover his own discomfiture he turned upon the inoffensive and wailing Billee and drove him to the confines of the camp.

By evening Perrault secured another dog, an old husky, long and

lean and gaunt, with a battle-scarred face and a single eye which flashed a warning of prowess that commanded respect. He was called Sol-leks, which means the Angry One. Like Dave, he asked nothing, gave nothing, expected nothing; and when he marched slowly and deliberately into their midst, even Spitz left him alone. He had one peculiarity which Buck was unlucky enough to discover. He did not like to be approached on his blind side. Of this offence Buck was unwittingly guilty, and the first knowledge he had of his indiscretion was when Sol-leks whirled upon him and slashed his shoulder to the bone for three inches up and down. Forever after Buck avoided his blind side, and to the last of their comradeship had no more trouble. His only apparent ambition, like Dave's, was to be left alone; though, as Buck was afterward to learn, each of them possessed one other and even more vital ambition.

That night Buck faced the great problem of sleeping. The tent, illumined by a candle, glowed warmly in the midst of the white plain; and when he, as a matter of course, entered it, both Perrault and François bombarded him with curses and cooking utensils till he recovered from his consternation and fled ignominiously into the outer cold. A chill wind was blowing that nipped him sharply and bit with especial venom into his wounded shoulder. He lay down on the snow and attempted to sleep, but the frost soon drove him shivering to his feet. Miserable and disconsolate, he wandered about among the many tents, only to find that one place was as cold as another. Here and there savage dogs rushed upon him, but he bristled his neck-hair and snarled (for he was learning fast), and they let him go his way unmolested.

Finally an idea came to him. He would return and see how his own team-mates were making out. To his astonishment, they had disappeared. Again he wandered about through the great camp, looking for them, and again he returned. Were they in the tent? No, that could not be, else he would not have been driven out. Then where could they possibly be? With dropping tail and shivering body, very forlorn indeed, he aimlessly circled the tent. Suddenly the snow gave way beneath his fore legs and he sank down. Something wriggled under his feet. He sprang back, bristling and snarling, fearful of the unseen and unknown. But a friendly little yelp reassured him, and he went back to investigate. A whiff of warm air ascended to his nostrils, and there, curled up under the snow in a snug ball, lay Billee. He whined placatingly, squirmed and wriggled to show his good will and intention, and even ventured, as a bribe for peace, to lick Buck's face with his warm wet tongue.

Another lesson. So that was the way they did it, eh? Buck confidently selected a spot, and with much fuss and wasted effort proceeded to dig a hole for himself. In a trice the heat from his body filled the confined space and he was asleep.

Lewis Carroll

JABBERWOCKY

Illustrated by Chris Riddell

'Twas brillig, and the slithy toves
   Did gyre and gimble in the wabe;
All mimsy were the borogroves,
   And the mome raths outgrabe.

'Beware the Jabberwock, my son!
   The jaws that bite, the claws that catch!
Beware the Jubjub bird, and shun
   The frumious Bandersnatch!'

He took his vorpal sword in hand:
   Long time the manxome foe he sought –
So rested he by the Tumtum tree,
   And stood awhile in thought.

And, as in uffish thought he stood,
   The Jabberwock, with eyes of flame,
Came whiffling through the tulgy wood,
   And burbled as it came!

One, two! One, two! And through and through
   The vorpal blade went snicker-snack!
He left it dead, and with its head
   He went galumphing back.

'And hast thou slain the Jabberwock?
    Come to my arms, my beamish boy!
O frabjous day! Callooh! Callay!'
    He chortled in his joy.

'Twas brillig, and the slithy toves
    Did gyre and gimble in the wabe:
All mimsy were the borogroves,
    And the mome raths outgrabe.

Robert Louis Stevenson

FROM A RAILWAY CARRIAGE

Illustrated by Ian Beck

Faster than fairies, faster than witches,
Bridges and houses, hedges and ditches;
And charging along like troops in a battle,
All through the meadows the horses and cattle:
All of the sights of the hill and the plain
Fly as thick as driving rain;
And ever again, in the wink of an eye,
Painted stations whistle by.

Here is a child who clambers and scrambles,
All by himself and gathering brambles;
Here is a tramp who stands and gazes;
And there is the green for stringing the daisies!
Here is a cart run away in the road
Lumping along with man and load;
And here is a mill, and there is a river:
Each a glimpse and gone for ever!

P. L. Travers

FROM

MARY POPPINS

Illustrated by Emma Chichester Clark

Mary Poppins is no ordinary nanny,
as Jane and Michael soon discover.

'Are you quite sure he will be at home?' said Jane, as they got off the Bus, she and Michael and Mary Poppins.

'Would my Uncle ask me to bring you to tea if he intended to go out, I'd like to know?' said Mary Poppins, who was evidently very offended by the question. She was wearing her blue coat with the silver buttons and the blue hat to match, and on the days when she wore these it was the easiest thing in the world to offend her.

All three of them were on the way to pay a visit to Mary Poppins' uncle, Mr Wigg, and Jane and Michael had looked forward to the trip for so long that they were more than half afraid that Mr Wigg might not be in, after all.

'Why is he called Mr Wigg — does he wear one?' asked Michael, hurrying along beside Mary Poppins.

'He is called Mr Wigg because Mr Wigg is his name. And he doesn't wear one. He is bald,' said Mary Poppins. 'And if I have any more questions we will just go Back Home.' And she sniffed her usual sniff of displeasure.

Jane and Michael looked at each other and frowned. And the frown meant: 'Don't let's ask her anything else or we'll never get there.'

Mary Poppins put her hat straight at the Tobacconist's Shop at the corner. It had one of those curious windows where there seem to be three of you instead of one, so that if you look long enough at them you begin to feel you are not yourself but a whole crowd of somebody else. Mary Poppins sighed with pleasure, however, when she saw three of herself, each wearing a blue coat with silver buttons and a blue hat to match. She thought it was such a lovely sight that she wished there had been a dozen of her or even thirty. The more Mary Poppins the better.

'Come along,' she said sternly, as though they had kept *her* waiting. Then they turned the corner and pulled the bell of Number Three, Robertson Road. Jane and Michael could hear it faintly echoing from a long way away and they knew that in one minute or two at the most, they would be having tea with Mary Poppins' uncle, Mr Wigg, for the first time ever.

'If he's in, of course,' Jane said to Michael in a whisper.

At that moment the door flew open and a thin, watery-looking lady appeared.

'Is he in?' said Michael quickly.

'I'll thank you,' said Mary Poppins, giving him a terrible glance, 'to let *me* do the talking.'

'How do you do, Mrs Wigg,' said Jane politely.

'Mrs Wigg!' said the thin lady, in a voice even thinner than herself. 'How dare you call me Mrs Wigg? No, thank you! I'm plain Miss Persimmon and proud of it. Mrs Wigg indeed!' She seemed to be quite upset, and they thought Mr Wigg must be a very odd person if Miss Persimmon was so glad not to be Mrs Wigg.

'Straight up and first door on the landing,' said Miss Persimmon, and she went hurrying away down the passage saying: 'Mrs Wigg indeed!' to herself in a high, thin, outraged voice.

Jane and Michael followed Mary Poppins upstairs. Mary Poppins knocked at the door.

'Come in! Come in! And welcome!' called a loud, cheery voice from inside. Jane's heart was pitter-pattering with excitement.

'He *is* in!' she signalled to Michael with a look.

Mary Poppins opened the door and pushed them in front of her.

A large cheerful room lay before them. At one end of it a fire was burning brightly and in the centre stood an enormous table laid for tea – four cups and saucers, piles of bread and butter, crumpets, coconut cakes and a large plum cake with pink icing.

'Well, this is indeed a Pleasure,' a huge voice greeted them, and Jane and Michael looked round for its owner. He was nowhere to be seen. The room appeared to be quite empty. Then they heard Mary Poppins saying crossly:

'Oh, Uncle Albert – not *again*? It's not your birthday, is it?'

And as she spoke she looked up at the ceiling. Jane and Michael looked up too and to their surprise saw a round, fat, bald man who was hanging in the air without holding on to anything. Indeed, he appeared to be *sitting* on the air, for his legs were crossed and he had just put down the newspaper which he had been reading when they came in.

'My dear,' said Mr Wigg, smiling down at the children, and looking apologetically at Mary Poppins, 'I'm very sorry, but I'm afraid it *is* my birthday.'

'Tch, tch, tch!' said Mary Poppins.

'I only remembered last night and there was no time then to send you a postcard asking you to come another day. Very distressing, isn't it?' he said, looking down at Jane and Michael.

'I can see you're rather surprised,' said Mr Wigg. And, indeed, their mouths were so wide open with astonishment that Mr Wigg, if he had been a little smaller, might almost have fallen into one of them.

'I'd better explain, I think,' Mr Wigg went on calmly. 'You see, it's this way. I'm a cheerful sort of man and very disposed to laughter. You wouldn't believe, either of you, the number of things that strike me as being funny. I can laugh at pretty nearly everything, I can.'

And with that Mr Wigg began to bob up and down, shaking with laughter at the thought of his own cheerfulness.

'Uncle Albert!' said Mary Poppins, and Mr Wigg stopped laughing with a jerk.

'Oh, beg pardon, my dear. Where was I? Oh, yes. Well, the funny thing about me is – all right, Mary, I won't laugh if I can help it! – that whenever my birthday falls on a Friday, well, it's all up with me. Absolutely U.P.,' said Mr Wigg.

'But why –?' began Jane.

'But how –?' began Michael.

'Well, you see, if I laugh on that particular day I become so filled with Laughing Gas that I simply can't keep on the ground. Even if I smile it happens. The first funny thought, and I'm up like a balloon. And until I can think of something serious I can't get down again.' Mr Wigg began to chuckle at that, but he caught sight of Mary Poppins' face and stopped the chuckle, and continued:

'It's awkward, of course, but not unpleasant. Never happens to either of you, I suppose?'

Jane and Michael shook their heads.

'No, I thought not. It seems to be my own special habit. Once, after I'd been to the Circus the night before, I laughed so much that – would you believe it? – I was up here for a whole twelve hours, and couldn't get down till the last stroke of midnight. Then, of course, I come down with a flop because it was Saturday and not my birthday any more. It's rather odd, isn't it? Not to say funny?

'And now here it is Friday again and my birthday, and you two and Mary P. to visit me. Oh, Lordy, Lordy, don't make me laugh, I beg of you –' But although Jane and Michael had done nothing very amusing, except to stare at him in astonishment, Mr Wigg began to laugh again loudly, and as he laughed he went bouncing and bobbing about in the air, with the newspaper rattling in his hand and his spectacles half on and half off his nose.

He looked so comic, floundering in the air like a great human bubble, clutching at the ceiling sometimes and sometimes at the gas-bracket as he passed it, that Jane and Michael, though they were trying hard to be polite, just couldn't help doing what they did. They laughed. *And* they laughed. They shut their mouths tight to prevent the laughter escaping, but that didn't do any good. And presently they were rolling over and over on the floor, squealing and shrieking with laughter.

'Really!' said Mary Poppins. 'Really, *such* behaviour!'

'I can't help it, I can't help it!' shrieked Michael, as he rolled into the fender. 'It's so terribly funny. Oh, Jane, *isn't* it funny?'

Jane did not reply, for a curious thing was happening to her. As she laughed she felt herself growing lighter and lighter, just as though she were being pumped full of air. It was a curious and delicious feeling and it made her want to laugh all the more. And then suddenly, with a bouncing bound, she felt herself jumping through the air. Michael, to his astonishment, saw her go soaring up through the room. With a little bump her head touched the ceiling and then she went bouncing along it till she reached Mr Wigg.

'*Well!*' said Mr Wigg, looking very surprised indeed. 'Don't tell me it's *your* birthday, too?' Jane shook her head.

'It's not? Then this Laughing Gas must be catching! Hi – whoa there, look out for the mantelpiece!' This was to Michael, who had suddenly risen from the floor and was swooping through the air, roaring with laughter, and just grazing the china ornaments on the mantelpiece as he passed. He landed with a bounce right on Mr Wigg's knee.

'How do you do,' said Mr Wigg, heartily shaking Michael by the hand. 'I call this really friendly of you – bless my soul, I do! To come up to me since I couldn't come down to you – eh?' And then he and Michael looked at each other and flung back their heads and simply howled with laughter.

'I say,' said Mr Wigg to Jane, as he wiped his eyes. 'You'll be thinking I have the worst manners in the world. You're standing and

you ought to be sitting – a nice young lady like you. I'm afraid I can't offer you a chair up here, but I think you'll find the air quite comfortable to sit on. I do.'

Jane tried it and found she could sit down quite comfortably on the air. She took off her hat and laid it down beside her and it hung there in space without any support at all.

'That's right,' said Mr Wigg. Then he turned and looked down at Mary Poppins.

'Well, Mary, we're fixed. And now I can enquire about *you*, my dear. I must say, I am very glad to welcome you and my two young friends here to-day – why, Mary, you're frowning. I'm afraid you don't approve of – er – all this.'

He waved his hand at Jane and Michael, and said hurriedly:

'I apologize, Mary, my dear. But you know how it is with me. Still, I must say I never thought my two young friends here would catch it, really I didn't, Mary! I suppose I should have asked them for another day or tried to think of something sad or something –'

'Well, I must say,' said Mary Poppins primly, 'that I have never in my life seen such a sight. And at your age, Uncle –'

'Mary Poppins, Mary Poppins, do come up!' interrupted Michael. 'Think of something funny and you'll find it's quite easy.'

'Ah, now do, Mary!' said Mr Wigg persuasively.

'We're lonely up here without you!' said Jane, and held out her arms towards Mary Poppins. '*Do* think of something funny!'

'Ah, *she* doesn't need to,' said Mr Wigg sighing. 'She can come up if she wants to, even without laughing – and she knows it.' And he looked mysteriously and secretly at Mary Poppins as she stood down there on the hearth-rug.

'Well,' said Mary Poppins, 'it's all very silly and undignified, but, since you're all up there and don't seem able to get down, I suppose I'd better come up, too.'

With that, to the surprise of Jane and Michael, she put her hands down at her sides and without a laugh, without even the faintest glimmer of a smile, she shot up through the air and sat down beside Jane.

'How many times, I should like to know,' she said snappily, 'have I told you to take off your coat when you come into a hot room?' And she unbuttoned Jane's coat and laid it neatly on the air beside the hat.

'That's right, Mary, that's right,' said Mr Wigg contentedly, as he leant down and put his spectacles on the mantelpiece. 'Now we're all comfortable –'

'There's comfort *and* comfort,' sniffed Mary Poppins.

'And we can have tea,' Mr Wigg went on, apparently not noticing her remark. And then a startled look came over his face.

'My goodness!' he said. 'How dreadful! I've just realized – the table's down there and we're up here. What *are* we going to do? We're here and it's there. It's an awful tragedy – awful! But oh, it's terribly comic!' And he hid his face in his handkerchief and laughed loudly into it. Jane and Michael, though they did not want to miss the crumpets and the cakes, couldn't help laughing too, because Mr Wigg's mirth was so infectious.

Mr Wigg dried his eyes.

'There's only one thing for it,' he said. 'We must think of something serious. Something sad, very sad. And then we shall be able to get down. Now – one, two, three! Something *very* sad, mind you!'

They thought and thought, with their chins on their hands.

Michael thought of school, and that one day he would have to go there. But even that seemed funny today and he had to laugh.

Jane thought: 'I shall be grown up in another fourteen years!' But that didn't sound sad at all but quite nice and rather funny. She could not help smiling at the thought of herself grown up, with long skirts and a hand-bag.

'There was my poor old Aunt Emily,' thought Mr Wigg out loud. 'She was run over by an omnibus. Sad. Very sad. Unbearably sad. Poor Aunt Emily. But they saved her umbrella. That was funny, wasn't it?' And before he knew where he was, he was heaving and trembling and bursting with laughter at the thought of Aunt Emily's umbrella.

'It's no good,' he said, blowing his nose. 'I give it up. And my young friends here seem to be no better at sadness than I am. Mary, can't *you* do something? We want our tea.'

To this day Jane and Michael cannot be sure of what happened then. All they know for certain is that, as soon as Mr Wigg had appealed to Mary Poppins, the table below began to wriggle on its legs.

Presently it was swaying dangerously, and then with a rattle of china and with cakes lurching off their plates on to the cloth, the table came soaring through the room, gave one graceful turn, and landed beside them so that Mr Wigg was at its head.

'Good girl!' said Mr Wigg, smiling proudly upon her. 'I knew you'd fix something. Now, will you take the foot of the table and pour out, Mary? And the guests on either side of me. That's the idea,' he said, as Michael ran bobbing through the air and sat down on Mr Wigg's right. Jane was at his left hand. There they were, all together, up in the air and the table between them. Not a single piece of bread-and-butter or a lump of sugar had been left behind.

Mr Wigg smiled contentedly.

'It is usual, I think, to begin with bread-and-butter,' he said to Jane and Michael, 'but as it's my birthday we will begin the wrong way – which I always think is the *right* way – with the Cake!'

And he cut a large slice for everybody.

'More tea?' he said to Jane. But before she had time to reply there

113

was a quick, sharp knock at the door.

'Come in!' called Mr Wigg.

The door opened, and there stood Miss Persimmon with a jug of hot water on a tray.

'I thought, Mr Wigg,' she began, looking searchingly round the room, 'you'd be wanting some more hot – Well, I never! I simply *never*!' she said, as she caught sight of them all seated on the air round the table. 'Such goings on I never did see! In all my born days I never saw such. I'm sure, Mr Wigg, I always knew *you* were a bit odd. But I've closed my eyes to it – being as how you paid your rent regular. But such behaviour as this having tea in the air with your guests – Mr Wigg, sir, I'm astonished at you! It's that undignified, and for a gentleman of your age – I never did.'

'But perhaps you will, Miss Persimmon!' said Michael.

'Will what?' said Miss Persimmon haughtily.

'Catch the Laughing Gas, as we did,' said Michael.

Miss Persimmon flung back her head scornfully.

'I hope, young man,' she retorted, 'I have more respect for myself than to go bouncing about in the air like a rubber ball on the end of a bat. I'll stay on my own feet, thank you, or my name's not Amy Persimmon, and – oh dear, oh *dear*, my goodness, oh *DEAR* – what *is* the matter? I can't walk, I'm going, I – oh, help, *HELP*!'

For Miss Persimmon, quite against her will, was off the ground and was stumbling through the air, rolling from side to side like a very thin barrel, balancing the tray in her hand. She was almost weeping with distress as she arrived at the table and put down her jug of hot water.

'Thank you,' said Mary Poppins in a calm, very polite voice.

Then Miss Persimmon turned and went wafting down again, murmuring as she went: 'So undignified – and me a well-behaved, steady-going woman. I must see a doctor –'

When she touched the floor she ran hurriedly out of the room, wringing her hands, and not giving a single glance backwards.

'So undignified!' they heard her moaning as she shut the door behind her.

'Her name can't be Amy Persimmon, because she *didn't* stay on her own feet!' whispered Jane to Michael.

But Mr Wigg was looking at Mary Poppins – a curious look, half-amused, half-accusing.

'Mary, Mary, you shouldn't — bless my soul, you shouldn't, Mary. The poor old body will never get over it. But, oh, my goodness, didn't she look funny waddling through the air — my Gracious Goodness, but didn't she?'

And he and Jane and Michael were off again, rolling about the air, clutching their sides and gasping with laughter at the thought of how funny Miss Persimmon had looked.

'Oh dear!' said Michael. 'Don't make me laugh any more. I can't stand it. I shall break!' 'Oh, oh, oh!' cried Jane, as she gasped for breath, with her hand over her heart. 'Oh, my Gracious, Glorious, Galumphing Goodness!' roared Mr Wigg, dabbing his eyes with his coat-tail because he couldn't find his handkerchief.

'IT IS TIME TO GO HOME.' Mary Poppins' voice sounded above the roars of laughter like a trumpet.

And suddenly, with a rush, Jane and Michael and Mr Wigg came down. They landed on the floor with a huge bump, all together. The thought that they would have to go home was the first sad thought of the afternoon, and the moment it was in their minds the Laughing Gas went out of them.

Jane and Michael sighed as they watched Mary Poppins come slowly down the air, carrying Jane's coat and hat.

Mr Wigg sighed, too. A great, long, heavy sigh.

'Well, isn't that a pity?' he said soberly. 'It's very sad that you've got to go home. I never enjoyed an afternoon so much — did you?'

'Never,' said Michael sadly, feeling how dull it was to be down on the earth again with no Laughing Gas inside him.

'Never, never,' said Jane, as she stood on tip-toe and kissed Mr Wigg's withered-apple cheek. 'Never, never, never, never . . .!'

Frances Hodgson Burnett

FROM

A LITTLE PRINCESS

Illustrated by George Smith

When her father is made bankrupt, Sara, once a
privileged student at Miss Minchin's school, is forced
to work as a servant and live alone in the attic.

Sara mounted her table and stood looking out. It was a wonderful moment. There were floods of molten gold covering the west, as if a glorious tide was sweeping over the world. A deep, rich yellow light filled the air; the birds flying across the tops of the houses showed quite black against it.

'It's a Splendid one,' said Sara softly to herself. 'It makes me feel almost afraid — as if something strange was just going to happen. The Splendid ones always make me feel like that.'

She suddenly turned her head because she heard a sound a few yards away from her. It was an odd sound, like a queer little squeaky chattering. It came from the window of the next attic. Someone had come to look at the sunset as she had. There was a head and part of a body emerging from the skylight, but it was not the head or body of a little girl or a housemaid; it was the picturesque white-swathed form and dark-faced, gleaming-eyed, white-turbaned head of a native Indian – 'a lascar', Sara said to herself quickly – and the sound she had heard came from a small monkey he held in his arms as if he were fond of it, and which was snuggling and chattering against his breast.

As Sara looked toward him he looked toward her. The first thing she thought was that his dark face looked sorrowful and homesick. She felt absolutely sure he had come up to look at the sun, because he had seen it so seldom in England that he longed for a sight of it. She looked at him interestedly for a second, and then smiled across the slates. She had learned to know how comforting a smile, even from a stranger, may be.

Hers was evidently a pleasure to him. His whole expression altered, and he showed such gleaming white teeth as he smiled back that it was as if a light had been illuminated in his dusky face. The friendly look in Sara's eyes was always very effective when people felt tired or dull.

It was perhaps in making his salute to her that he loosened his hold on the monkey. He was an impish monkey and always ready for adventure, and it is probable that the sight of a little girl excited him. He suddenly broke loose, jumped on to the slates, ran across them chattering, and actually leaped on to Sara's shoulder, and from there down into her attic room. It made her laugh and delighted her; but she knew he must be restored to his master – if the lascar was his master – and she wondered how this was to be done. Would he let her catch him, or would he be naughty and refuse to be caught, and perhaps get away and run off over the roofs and be lost? That would not do at all. Perhaps he belonged to the Indian gentleman, and the poor man was fond of him.

She turned to the lascar, feeling glad that she remembered still some of the Hindustani she had learned when she lived with her father. She could make the man understand. She spoke to him in the language he knew.

'Will he let me catch him?' she asked.

She thought she had never seen more surprise and delight than the dark face expressed when she spoke in the familiar tongue. The truth was that the poor fellow felt as if his gods had intervened, and the kind little voice came from heaven itself. At once Sara saw that he had been

accustomed to European children. He poured forth a flood of respectful thanks. He was the servant of Missee Sahib. The monkey was a good monkey and would not bite; but, unfortunately, he was difficult to catch. He would flee from one spot to another, like the lightning. He was disobedient, though not evil. Ram Dass knew him as if he were his child, and Ram Dass he would sometimes obey, but not always. If Missee Sahib would permit Ram Dass, he himself could cross the roof to her room, enter the window, and regain the unworthy little animal. But he was evidently afraid Sara might think he was taking a great liberty and perhaps would not let him come.

But Sara gave him leave at once.

'Can you get across?' she inquired.

'In a moment,' he answered her.

'Then come,' she said, 'he is flying from side to side of the room as if he was frightened.'

Ram Dass slipped through his attic window and crossed to hers as steadily and lightly as if he had walked on roofs all his life. He slipped through the skylight and dropped upon his feet without a sound. Then he turned to Sara and salaamed again. The monkey saw him and uttered a little scream. Ram Dass hastily took the precaution of shutting the skylight, and then went in chase of him. It was not a very long chase. The monkey prolonged it a few minutes evidently for the mere fun of it, but presently he sprang chattering on to Ram Dass's shoulder and sat there chattering and clinging to his neck with a weird little skinny arm.

Ram Dass thanked Sara profoundly. She had seen that his quick native eyes had taken in at a glance all the bare shabbiness of the room, but he spoke to her as if he were speaking to the little daughter of a rajah, and pretended that he observed nothing. He did not presume to remain more than a few moments after he had caught the monkey, and those moments were given to further deep and grateful obeisance to her in return for her indulgence. This little evil one, he said, stroking the monkey, was, in truth, not so evil as he seemed, and his master, who was ill, was sometimes amused by him. He would have been made sad if his favourite had run away and been lost. Then he salaamed once more, and got through the skylight and across the slates again with as much agility as the monkey himself had displayed.

When he had gone Sara stood in the middle of her attic and thought of many things his face and his manner had brought back to her. The sight of his native costume and the profound reverence of his manner stirred all her past memories. It seemed a strange thing to remember that she – the drudge whom the cook had said insulting things to an hour ago – had only a few years ago been surrounded by people who all treated her as Ram Dass had treated her; who salaamed when she went by, whose foreheads almost touched the ground when she spoke to them, who were her servants and her slaves. It was like a sort of dream. It was all over, and it could never come back. It certainly seemed that there was no way in which any change could take place. She knew what Miss Minchin intended that her future should be. So long as she was too young to be used as a regular teacher, she would be used as an errand girl and servant, and yet expected to remember what she had learned and in some mysterious way to learn more. The greater number of her evenings she was supposed to spend at study, and knew she would have been severely admonished if she had not advanced as was expected of her. The truth, indeed, was that Miss Minchin knew that she was too anxious to learn to require teachers. Give her books, and she would devour them and end by knowing them by heart. She might be trusted to be equal to teaching a good deal in the course of a few years. This was what would happen; when she was older she would be expected to drudge in the schoolroom as she drudged now in various parts of the house; they would be obliged to give her more respectable clothes, but they would be sure to be plain and ugly, and to make her look somehow like a servant. That was all there seemed to be to look forward to, and Sara stood quite still for several minutes and thought it over.

Then a thought came back to her which made the colour rise in her cheek and a spark light itself in her eyes. She straightened her thin little body and lifted her head.

'Whatever comes,' she said, 'cannot alter one thing. If I am a princess in rags and tatters, I can be a princess inside. It would be easy to be a princess if I were dressed in cloth of gold, but it is a great deal more of a triumph to be one all the time when no one knows it. There was Marie Antoinette when she was in prison and her throne was gone and she had only a black gown on, and her hair was white, and they insulted her and called her Widow Capet. She was a great deal more like a queen then than when she was so gay and everything was so grand. I like her best then. Those howling mobs of people did not frighten her. She was stronger than they were, even when they cut her head off.'

This was not a new thought, but quite an old one, by this time. It had consoled her through many a bitter day, and she had gone about the house with an expression in her face which Miss Minchin could not understand and which was a source of great annoyance to her, as it seemed as if the child were mentally living a life which held her above the rest of the world. It was as if she scarcely heard the rude and acid things said to her; or, if she heard them, did not care for them at all. Sometimes, when she was in the midst of some harsh, domineering speech, Miss Minchin would find the still, unchildish eyes fixed upon her with something like a proud smile in them. At such times she did not know that Sara was saying to herself:

'You don't know that you are saying these things to a princess, and that if I chose I could wave my hand and order you to execution. I only spare you because I *am* a princess, and you are a poor, stupid, unkind, vulgar old thing, and don't know any better.'

This used to interest and amuse her more than anything else; and queer and fanciful as it was, she found comfort in it and it was a good thing for her. While the thought held possession of her, she could not be made rude and malicious by the rudeness and malice of those about her.

'A princess must be polite,' she said to herself.

And so when the servants, taking their tone from their mistress, were insolent and ordered her about, she would hold her head erect and reply to them with a quaint civility which often made them stare at her.

'She's got more airs and graces than if she come from Buckingham Palace, that young one,' said the cook, chuckling a little sometimes. 'I lose my temper with her often enough, but I will say she never forgets her manners. "If you please, cook"; "Will you be so kind, cook?"; "I beg your pardon, cook"; "May I trouble you, cook?" She drops 'em about the kitchen as if they was nothing.'

The morning after the interview with Ram Dass and his monkey, Sara was in the schoolroom with her small pupils. Having finished giving them their lessons, she was putting the French exercise books together and thinking, as she did it, of the various things royal personages in disguise were called upon to do: Alfred the Great, for instance, burning the cakes and getting his ears boxed by the wife of the neatherd. How frightened she must have been when she found out what she had done. If Miss Minchin should find out that she – Sara, whose toes were almost sticking out of her boots – was a princess – a real one! The look in her eyes was exactly the look which Miss Minchin most disliked. She would not have it; she was quite near her, and was so enraged that she actually flew at her and boxed her ears – exactly as the neatherd's wife had boxed King Alfred's. It made Sara start. She wakened from her dream at the shock, and, catching her breath, stood still a second. Then, not knowing she was going to do it, she broke into a little laugh.

'What are you laughing at, you bold, impudent child?' Miss Minchin exclaimed.

It took Sara a few seconds to control herself sufficiently to remember that she was a princess. Her cheeks were red and smarting from the blows she had received.

'I was thinking,' she answered.

'Beg my pardon immediately,' said Miss Minchin.

Sara hesitated a second before she replied.

'I will beg your pardon for laughing, if it was rude,' she said then, 'but I won't beg your pardon for thinking.'

'What were you thinking?' demanded Miss Minchin. 'How dare you think? What were you thinking?'

Jessie tittered, and she and Lavinia nudged each other in unison. All the girls looked up from their books to listen. Really, it always interested them a little when Miss Minchin attacked Sara. Sara always said something queer, and never seemed the least bit frightened. She was not in the least frightened now, though her boxed ears were scarlet and her eyes were as bright as stars.

'I was thinking,' she answered grandly and politely, 'that you did not know what you were doing.'

'That I did not know what I was doing?' Miss Minchin fairly gasped.

'Yes,' said Sara. 'And I was thinking what would happen if I were a princess and you boxed my ears – what I should do to you. And I was

124

thinking that if I were one, you would never dare to do it, whatever I said or did. And I was thinking how surprised and frightened you would be if you suddenly found out –'

She had the imagined future so clearly before her eyes that she spoke in a manner which had an effect even upon Miss Minchin. It almost seemed for the moment to her narrow, unimaginative mind that there must be some real power hidden behind this candid daring.

'What?' she exclaimed. 'Found out what?'

'That I really was a princess,' said Sara, 'and could do anything – anything I liked.'

Every pair of eyes in the room widened to its full limit. Lavinia leaned forward on her seat to look.

'Go to your room,' cried Miss Minchin breathlessly, 'this instant! Leave the schoolroom! Attend to your lessons, young ladies!'

Sara made a little bow.

'Excuse me for laughing if it was impolite,' she said, and walked out of the room, leaving Miss Minchin struggling with her rage, and the girls whispering over their books.

'Did you see her? Did you see how queer she looked?' Jessie broke out. 'I shouldn't be at all surprised if she did turn out to be something. Suppose she should!'

James Hogg

A Boy's Song

Illustrated by Tim Clarey

Where the pools are bright and deep,
Where the grey trout lies asleep,
Up the river and over the lea –
That's the way for Billy and me.

Where the blackbird sings the latest,
Where the hawthorn blooms the sweetest,
Where the nestlings chirp and flee,
That's the way for Billy and me.

Where the mowers mow the cleanest,
Where the hay lies thick and greenest;
There to trace the homeward bee,
That's the way for Billy and me.

Where the hazel bank is steepest,
Where the shadow falls the deepest,
Where the clustering nuts fall free,
That's the way for Billy and me.

Why the boys should drive away
Little sweet maidens from their play,
Or love to banter and fight so well,
That's the thing I never could tell.

But this I know, I love to play,
Through the meadow, among the hay;
Up the water and over the lea,
That's the way for Billy and me.

Walter de la Mare

TARTARY

Illustrated by Pauline Baynes

If I were Lord of Tartary,
  Myself and me alone,
My bed should be of ivory,
  Of beaten gold my throne;
And in my court should peacocks flaunt,
And in my forests tigers haunt,
And in my pools great fishes slant
  Their fins athwart the sun.

If I were Lord of Tartary,
  Trumpeters every day
To every meal would summon me,
  And in my courtyard bray;
And in the evening lamps would shine,
Yellow as honey, red as wine,
While harp, and flute, and mandoline,
  Made music sweet and gay.

If I were Lord of Tartary,
  I'd wear a robe of beads,
White, and gold, and green they'd be –
  And clustered thick as seeds;
And ere should wane the morning-star,
I'd don my robe and scimitar,
And zebras seven should draw my car
  Through Tartary's dark glades.

Lord of the fruits of Tartary,
  Her rivers silver-pale!
Lord of the hills of Tartary,
  Glen, thicket, wood, and dale!
Her flashing stars, her scented breeze,
Her trembling lakes, like foamless seas,
Her bird-delighting citron-trees
  In every purple vale!

Robert Louis Stevenson

TREASURE ISLAND

Illustrated by Richard Jones

Jim Hawkins, cabin-boy on the Hispaniola, *overhears*
Long John Silver plotting a mutiny.

We had some heavy weather, which only proved the qualities of the *Hispaniola*. Every man on board seemed well content, and they must have been hard to please if they had been otherwise; for it is my belief there was never a ship's company so spoiled since Noah put to sea. Double grog was going on the least excuse; there was duff on odd days, as, for instance, if the squire heard it was any man's birthday; and always a barrel of apples standing broached in the waist, for anyone to help himself that had a fancy.

'Never knew good come of it yet,' the captain said to Dr Livesey. 'Spoil foc's'le hands, make devils. That's my belief.'

But good did come of the apple barrel, as you shall hear; for if it had not been for that, we should have had no note of warning, and might all have perished by the hand of treachery.

This was how it came about.

We had run up the trades to get the wind of the island we were after

– I am not allowed to be more plain – and now we were running down for it with a bright look-out day and night. It was about the last day of our outward voyage, by the largest computation; some time that night, or, at latest, before noon of the morrow, we should sight the Treasure Island. We were heading SSW., and had a steady breeze abeam and a quiet sea. The *Hispaniola* rolled steadily, dipping her bowsprit now and then with a whiff of spray. All was drawing alow and aloft; everyone was in the bravest spirits, because we were now so near an end of the first part of our adventure.

Now, just after sundown, when all my work was over and I was on my way to my berth, it occurred to me that I should like an apple. I ran on deck. The watch was all forward looking out for the island. The

man at the helm was watching the luff of the sail, and whistling away gently to himself; and that was the only sound excepting the swish of the sea against the bows and around the sides of the ship.

In I got bodily into the apple barrel, and found there was scarce an apple left; but, sitting down there in the dark, what with the sound of the waters and the rocking movement of the ship, I had either fallen asleep, or was on the point of doing so, when a heavy man sat down with rather a clash close by. The barrel shook as he leaned his shoulders against it, and I was just about to jump up when the man began to speak. It was Silver's voice, and, before

I had heard a dozen words, I would not have shown myself for all the world, but lay there, trembling and listening, in the extreme of fear and curiosity; for from these dozen words I understood that the lives of all the honest men aboard depended upon me alone.

'No, not I,' said Silver. 'Flint was cap'n; I was quartermaster, along of my timber leg. The same broadside I lost my leg, old Pew lost his deadlights. It was a master surgeon, him that ampytated me – out of college and all – Latin by the bucket, and what not; but he was hanged like a dog, and sun-dried like the rest, at Corso Castle. That was Roberts' men, that was, and comed of changing names of their ships – *Royal Fortune* and so on. Now, what a ship was christened, so let her stay, I says. So it was with the *Cassandra*, as brought us all safe home from Malabar, after England took the Viceroy of the Indies; so it was with the old *Walrus*, Flint's old ship, as I've seen a'muck with the red blood and fit to sink with gold.'

'Ah!' cried another voice, that of the youngest hand on board, and evidently full of admiration, 'he was the flower of the flock, was Flint!'

'Davis was a man, too, by all accounts,' said Silver. 'I never sailed along of him; first with England, then with Flint, that's my story; and now here on my own account, in a manner of speaking. I laid by nine hundred safe, from England, and two thousand after Flint. That ain't bad for a man before the mast – all safe in bank. 'Tain't earning now, it's saving does it, you may lay to that. Where's all England's men now? I dunno. Where's Flint's? Why, most on 'em aboard here, and glad to get the duff – been begging before that, some on 'em. Old Pew, as had lost his sight, and might have thought shame, spends twelve hundred pounds in a year, like a lord in Parliament. Where is he now? Well, he's dead now and under hatches; but for two year before that, shiver my timbers! the man was starving. He begged, and he stole, and he cut throats, and starved at that, by the powers!'

'Well, it ain't much use, after all,' said the young seaman.

''Tain't much use for fools, you may lay to it – that, nor nothing,' cried Silver. 'But now, you look here: you're young, you are, but you're as smart as paint. I see that when I set my eyes on you, and I'll talk to you like a man.'

You may imagine how I felt when I heard this abominable old rogue addressing another in the very same words of flattery as he had used to myself. I think, if I had been able, that I would have killed him through the barrel. Meantime, he ran on, little supposing he was overheard.

'Here it is about gentlemen of fortune. They lives rough, and they risk swinging, but they eat and drink like fighting-cocks, and when a cruise is done, why it's hundreds of pounds instead of hundreds of farthings in their pockets. Now, the most goes for rum and a good fling, and to sea again in their shirts. But that's not the course I lay. I puts it all away, some here, some there, and none too much anywheres, by reason of suspicion. I'm fifty, mark you; once back from this cruise, I set up gentleman in earnest. Time enough, too, says you. Ah, but I've lived easy in the meantime; never denied myself o' nothing heart desires, and slep' soft and ate dainty all my days, but when at sea. And how did I begin? Before the mast, like you!'

'Well,' said the other, 'but all the other money's gone now, ain't it? You daren't show face in Bristol after this.'

'Why, where might you suppose it was?' asked Silver, derisively.

'At Bristol, in banks and places,' answered his companion.

'It were,' said the cook; 'it were when we weighed anchor. But my old missis has it all by now. And the "Spy-glass" is sold, lease and goodwill and rigging; and the old girl's off to meet me. I would tell you where, for I trust you; but it 'ud make jealousy among the mates.'

'And can you trust your missis?' asked the other.

'Gentlemen of fortune,' returned the cook, 'usually trust little among themselves, and right they are, you may lay to it. But I have a way with me, I have. When a mate brings a slip on his cable – one as knows me, I mean – it won't be in the same world with old John. There was some that was feared of Pew, and some that was feared of Flint; but Flint his own self was feared of me. Feared he was, and proud. They was the roughest crew afloat, was Flint's; the devil himself would have been

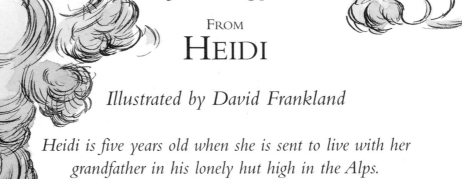

Johanna Spyri

FROM

HEIDI

Illustrated by David Frankland

Heidi is five years old when she is sent to live with her grandfather in his lonely hut high in the Alps.

As soon as Detie had disappeared, the old man sat down again on the bench. He stared at the ground in silence, blowing great clouds of smoke from his pipe, while Heidi explored her new surroundings with delight. She went up to the goat stall which was built on to the side of the hut, but found it empty. Then she went round to the back and stood for a while listening to the noise the wind made whistling through the branches of the old fir trees. Presently it died down, and she came back to the front of the hut, where she found her grandfather still sitting in the same position. As she stood watching him, hands behind her back, he looked up and said, 'What do you want to do now?'

'I want to see what is inside the hut,' she answered.

'Come on, then,' he said, and he got up and led the way indoors. 'Bring the bundle of clothes in with you,' he added.

'I shan't want them any more,' she declared.

The old man turned and looked sharply at her, and saw her black

140

eyes shining with anticipation.

'She's no fool,' he muttered to himself, and added aloud, 'Why's that?'

'I want to be able to run about like the goats do.'

'Well, so you can,' said her grandfather, 'but bring the things inside all the same. They can go in the cupboard.'

Heidi picked up the bundle and followed the old man into a biggish room which was the whole extent of his living quarters. She saw a table and a chair, and his bed over in one corner. Opposite that was a stove, over which a big pot was hanging. There was a door in one wall which the old man opened, and she saw it was a large cupboard with his clothes hanging in it. There were shelves in it too. One held his shirts, socks, and handkerchiefs, another plates, cups, and glasses, while on the top one were a round loaf, some smoked meat, and some cheese. Here, in fact, were all the old man's possessions. Heidi went inside the open cupboard and pushed her bundle right away to the back so that it would not easily be seen again.

'Where shall I sleep, Grandfather?' she asked next.

'Where you like,' he replied.

This answer pleased Heidi, and as she was looking round the room for a good place she noticed a ladder propped against the wall near her grandfather's bed. She climbed up it at once and found herself in a hay loft. A pile of fresh, sweet-smelling hay lay there, and there was a round hole in the wall of the loft, through which she could see right down the valley.

'I shall sleep up here,' she called down. 'It's a splendid place. Just come and see, Grandfather.'

'I know it well,' he called back.

'I'm going to make my bed now,' she went on, 'but you'll have to come up and bring me a sheet to lie on.'

'All right,' said her grandfather, and he went to the cupboard and searched among his belongings until he found a piece of coarse cloth, which he carried up to her. He found she had already made herself a sort of mattress and pillow of the hay, and had placed them so that she would be able to look through the hole in the wall when she was in bed.

'That's right,' said the old man, 'but it needs to be thicker than that,' and he spread a lot more hay over hers so that she would not feel the hard floor through it. The thick cloth which he had brought for a sheet was so heavy that she could hardly lift it by herself, but its thickness made it a good protection against the prickly hay stalks. Together they spread it out, and Heidi tucked the ends under her 'mattress' to make it all neat and comfortable. Then she looked at her bed thoughtfully for a moment, and said, 'We've forgotten something, Grandfather.'

'What's that?' he asked.

'A blanket to cover it, so that I can creep under it when I go to bed.'

'That's what you think, is it? Suppose I haven't got one?'

'Oh, well then, it doesn't matter,' said Heidi, 'I can easily cover myself with hay,' and she was just going to fetch some more when her grandfather stopped her. 'Wait a bit,' he said, and he went down the ladder, and took from his own bed a great sack made of heavy linen which he brought up to the loft.

'There, isn't that better than hay?' he asked, as they put it over the bed. Heidi was delighted with the result.

'That's a wonderful blanket, and my whole bed's lovely. I wish it was bedtime now so that I could get in it.'

'I think we might have something to eat first, don't you?' said her grandfather. Heidi had forgotten everything else in her excitement over the bed, but at the mention of food, she realized how hungry she was, as she had eaten nothing all day except a piece of bread and a cup of weak coffee before setting out on her long journey. So she replied eagerly, 'Oh, yes.'

'Well then, if we are agreed, let us go and see about a meal,' and he followed Heidi down the ladder. He went to the stove, lifted the big pot off the chain and put a smaller one in its place, then sat himself down on a three-legged stool and blew up the fire with the bellows till it was red and glowing. As the pot began to sing, he put a large piece of cheese on a toasting fork and moved it to and fro in front of the fire until it became golden yellow all over. At first Heidi just stood and watched with great interest, then she thought of something else and ran to the cupboard. When her grandfather brought the steaming pot and the toasted cheese to the table, he found it was laid with two plates, two knives, and the round loaf. Heidi had noticed these things in the cupboard and knew they would be needed for the meal.

'I'm glad to see you can think things out for yourself,' he said, 'but there is something missing.'

Heidi looked at the steaming pot and went back to the cupboard. She could see one mug there and two glasses, so she took the mug and one of the glasses and put them on the table.

'That's right. You know how to be helpful,' said her grandfather. 'Now where are you going to sit?' He himself was in the only chair so Heidi fetched the three-legged stool and sat down on that.

'You've got a seat all right, but rather a low one, and even with my chair you would not be high enough to reach the table.' So saying, the old man got up and pushed his chair in front of Heidi's stool and put the mug filled with milk on it, and a plate on which was a slice of bread covered with the golden toasted cheese. 'Now you have a table to yourself and can start to eat,' he said. Then he perched himself on a corner of the big table and began his own meal.

Heidi took up the mug and drained it thirstily. After that she drew a deep breath – for she had been too busy drinking to breathe – and set the empty mug down.

'Is the milk good?' asked her grandfather.

'The best I've ever drunk,' replied Heidi.

'You must have some more then,' and he refilled her mug.

She ate her bread and cheese, which tasted delicious, and every now and then she took a drink. She looked as happy and contented as anyone could be.

After the meal her grandfather went to the goat-stall and Heidi watched him sweep the floor with a broom and then put down fresh straw for the animals to sleep on. When that job was done he went into the shed, which was built on to the side of the hut, and sawed off several round sticks of wood. Then he bored holes to fit them in a strong flat piece of board, and when he had fitted them all together, the result was a high chair. Heidi watched him, silent in her amazement.

'Do you know what this is?' he asked, when he had finished.

'It's a chair specially for me,' she said wonderingly. 'And how quickly you made it!'

'She's got eyes in her head and knows how to use them,' thought the old man. Next he busied himself with some small repairs in the hut, driving in a nail here and there, tightening a screw in the door and so on. Heidi followed at his heels, watching him with the closest attention, for everything was new and interesting to her.

Thus the afternoon passed. A strong wind sprang up again, whistling and rustling through the fir trees. The sound pleased Heidi so much that she began dancing and jumping about, and her grandfather stood watching her from the door of the shed. Suddenly there was a shrill whistle and Peter appeared in the midst of his herd of goats. Heidi gave a cry of delight and rushed to greet her friends of the morning. As the goats reached the hut they all stood still, except for two graceful animals, one brown and one white, which detached themselves from the others and went up to the old man. Then they began to lick his hands for he was holding a little salt in them, as he did every evening to welcome them home.

Peter went away with the rest of the herd, and Heidi ran to the two goats and began to pat them gently. 'Are these ours, Grandfather?' she asked. 'Both of them? Do they go into the stall? Will they always be here with us?' Her questions followed so closely on each other that her grandfather could hardly get an answer in edgeways. When the goats had finished the salt, the old man said, 'Now go and fetch your mug and the bread.' She obeyed and was back in a flash. Then he filled her mug with milk from the white goat and gave it to her with a slice of bread. 'Eat that and then go to bed,' he said. 'If you want a nightdress or anything like that, you'll find it in the bundle your aunt brought. Now I must see to the goats. Sleep well.'

'Good night, Grandfather,' she called, as he walked off with the animals. Then she ran after them to ask what the goats' names were.

'The white one is called Daisy and the brown Dusky,' replied her grandfather.

'Good night, Daisy, good night, Dusky,' called Heidi after the goats, who had disappeared into their stall. She ate her supper on the bench outside the hut. The wind was so strong, it almost blew her away, so she finished her bread and milk quickly and went indoors and up to bed. There she was soon sleeping as soundly as if she was tucked up in the finest bed in the world.

Her grandfather went to bed also before it was dark, for he always got up with the sun, and that came over the mountain tops very early in the summer. During the night the wind blew so hard that it shook the whole hut and made its beams creak. It shrieked down the chimney and brought one or two of the old fir trees' branches crashing down. So after a while the old man got up, thinking, 'The child may be frightened.'

He climbed up the ladder and went over to her bed. Just then the moon, which had been covered by scudding clouds, shone straight through the hole in the wall on to Heidi's face. She was fast asleep under her heavy coverlet, one rosy cheek resting on her chubby little arm, and with such a happy expression on her face that she must surely have been dreaming of pleasant things. He stood looking down at her till clouds covered the moon again, darkening the room. Then he went back to bed.

William Blake

THE TYGER

Illustrated by Sally Taylor

Tyger! Tyger! burning bright
In the forests of the night,
What immortal hand or eye
Could frame thy fearful symmetry?

In what distant deeps or skies
Burnt the fire of thine eyes?
On what wings dare he aspire?
What the hand dare seize the fire?

And what shoulder, and what art,
Could twist the sinews of thy heart?
And when thy heart began to beat,
What dread hand? and what dread feet?

What the hammer? what the chain?
In what furnace was thy brain?
What the anvil? what dread grasp
Dare its deadly terrors clasp?

When the stars threw down their spears,
And watered heaven with their tears,
Did he smile his work to see?
Did he who made the Lamb make thee?

Tyger! Tyger! burning bright
In the forests of the night,
What immortal hand or eye,
Dare frame thy fearful symmetry?

Felicia D. Hemans

CASABIANCA

Illustrated by Gino D'Achille

The boy stood on the burning deck,
  Whence all but he had fled;
The flame that lit the battle's wreck
  Shone round him o'er the dead.

Yet beautiful and bright he stood,
  As born to rule the storm;
A creature of heroic blood,
  A proud though childlike form.

The flames rolled on; he would not go
  Without his father's word;
That father, faint in death below,
  His voice no longer heard.

He called aloud, 'Say, Father, say,
  If yet my task be done!'
He knew not that the chieftain lay
  Unconscious of his son.

'Speak, Father!' once again he cried,
  'If I may yet be gone!'
And but the booming shots replied,
  And fast the flames rolled on.

Upon his brow he felt their breath,
  And in his waving hair,
And looked from that lone post of death
  In still yet brave despair;

And shouted but once more aloud,
  'My Father! must I stay?'
While o'er him fast, through sail and shroud,
  The wreathing fires made way.

They wrapped the ship in splendour wild,
  They caught the flag on high,
And streamed above the gallant child,
  Like banners in the sky.

There came a burst of thunder sound;
  The boy – Oh! where was he?
Ask of the winds, that far around
  With fragments strewed the sea –

With mast and helm and pennon fair,
  That well had borne their part –
But the noblest thing that perished there
  Was that young, faithful heart.

Sir Arthur Conan Doyle

from THE PRIORY SCHOOL

FROM

THE GREAT ADVENTURES OF SHERLOCK HOLMES

Illustrated by Adrian Chesterman

Sherlock Holmes, private detective, and his assistant, Dr Watson, embark on a thrilling investigation into the disappearance of the son of a duke.

That evening found us in the cold, bracing atmosphere of the Peak country, in which Dr Huxtable's famous school is situated. It was already dark when we reached it. A card was lying on the hall table, and the butler whispered something to his master, who turned to us with agitation in every heavy feature.

'The duke is here,' said he. 'The duke and Mr Wilder are in the study. Come, gentlemen, and I will introduce you.'

I was, of course, familiar with the pictures of the famous statesman, but the man himself was very different from his representation. He was a tall and stately person, scrupulously dressed, with a drawn, thin face, and a nose which was grotesquely curved and long. His complexion was of a dead pallor, which was more startling by contrast with a long, dwindling beard of vivid red, which flowed down over his white waistcoat, with his watch-chain gleaming through its fringe. Such was the stately presence who looked stonily at us from the centre of Dr

152

Huxtable's hearthrug. Beside him stood a very young man, whom I understood to be Wilder, the private secretary. He was small, nervous, alert, with intelligent, light blue eyes and mobile features. It was he who at once, in an incisive and positive tone, opened the conversation.

'I called this morning, Dr Huxtable, too late to prevent you from starting for London. I learned that your object was to invite Mr Sherlock Holmes to undertake the conduct of this case. His Grace is surprised, Dr Huxtable, that you should have taken such a step without consulting him.'

'When I learned the police had failed –'

'His Grace is by no means convinced that the police have failed.'

'But surely, Mr Wilder –'

'You are well aware, Dr Huxtable, that his Grace is particularly anxious to avoid all public scandal. He prefers to take as few people as possible into his confidence.'

'The matter can be easily remedied,' said the brow-beaten doctor. 'Mr Sherlock Holmes can return to London by the morning train.'

'Hardly that, Doctor, hardly that,' said Holmes, in his blandest voice. 'This northern air is invigorating and pleasant, so I propose to spend a few days upon your moors, and to occupy my mind as best I may. Whether I have the shelter of your roof or of the village inn is, of course, for you to decide.'

I could see that the unfortunate doctor was in the last stage of indecision, from which he was rescued by the deep, sonorous voice of the red-bearded duke, which boomed out like a dinner-gong.

'I agree with Mr Wilder, Dr Huxtable, that you would have done wisely to consult me. But since Mr Holmes has already been taken into your confidence, it would indeed be absurd that we should not avail ourselves of his services. Far from going to the inn, Mr Holmes, I should be pleased if you would come and stay with me at Holdernesse Hall?'

'I thank your Grace. For the purposes of my investigation I think that it would be wiser for me to remain at the scene of the mystery.'

'Just as you like, Mr Holmes. Any information which Mr Wilder or I can give you is, of course, at your disposal.'

'It will probably be necessary for me to see you at the Hall,' said Holmes. 'I would only ask you now, sir, whether you have formed any explanation in your own mind as to the mysterious disappearance of your son?'

'No, sir, I have not.'

'Excuse me if I allude to that which is painful to you, but I have no alternative. Do you think that the duchess had anything to do with the matter?'

The great minister showed perceptible hesitation.

'I do not think so,' he said at last.

'The other most obvious explanation is that the child has been kidnapped for the purpose of levying ransom. You have not had any demand of the sort?'

'No, sir.'

'One more question, your Grace. I understand that you wrote to your son upon the day when this incident occurred.'

'No! I wrote upon the day before.'

'Exactly. But he received it on that day?'

'Yes.'

'Was there anything in your letter which might have unbalanced him or induced him to take such a step?'

'No, sir, certainly not.'

'Did you post that letter yourself?'

The nobleman's reply was interrupted by his secretary, who broke in with some heat.

'His Grace is not in the habit of posting letters himself,' said he. 'The letter was laid with others upon the study table, and I

154

myself put them in the post-bag.'

'You are sure this one was among them?'

'Yes; I observed it.'

'How many letters did your Grace write that day?'

'Twenty or thirty. I have a large correspondence. But surely this is somewhat irrelevant?'

'Not entirely,' said Holmes.

'For my own part,' the duke continued, 'I have advised the police to turn their attention to the South of France. I have already said that I do not believe that the duchess would encourage so monstrous an action, but the lad had the most wrong-headed opinions, and it is possible that he may have fled to her, aided and abetted by this German. I think, Dr Huxtable, that we will now return to the Hall.'

I could see that there were other questions which Holmes would have wished to put; but the nobleman's abrupt manner showed that the interview was at end. It was evident that to his intensely aristocratic nature this discussion of his intimate family affairs with a stranger was most abhorrent, and that he feared lest every fresh question would throw a fiercer light into the discreetly shadowed corners of his ducal history.

When the nobleman and his secretary had left, my friend flung himself at once with characteristic eagerness into the investigation.

The boy's chamber was carefully examined, and yielded nothing save the absolute conviction that it was only through the window that he could have escaped. The German master's room and effects gave no further clue. In his case a trailer of ivy had given way under his weight, and we saw by the light of a lantern the mark on the lawn where his heels had come down. That one dent in the short green grass was the only material witness left of this inexplicable nocturnal flight.

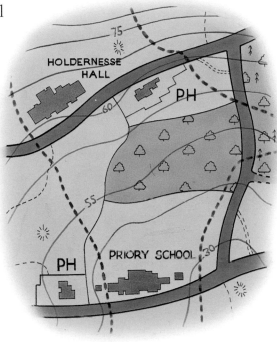

Sherlock Holmes left the house alone, and only returned after eleven. He had obtained a large ordnance map of the neighbourhood, and this he brought into my room, where he laid it out on the bed, and, having balanced the lamp in the middle of it, he began to smoke over it, and occasionally to point out objects of interest with the reeking amber of his pipe.

'This case grows upon me, Watson,' said he. 'There are decidedly some points of interest in connection with it. In this early stage I want you to realize these geographical features, which may have a good deal to do with our investigation.

'Look at this map. This dark square is the Priory School. I'll put a pin in it. Now, this line is the main road. You see that it runs east and west past the school, and you see also there is no side-road for a mile either way. If these two folk passed away by road it was *this* road.'

'Exactly.'

'By a singular and happy chance we are able to some extent to check what passed along this road during the night in question. At this point, where my pipe is now resting, a country constable was on duty from twelve to six. It is, as you perceive, the first crossroad on the east side. This man declares that he was not absent from his post for an instant, and he is positive that neither boy nor man could have gone that way unseen. I have spoken with this policeman tonight, and he appears to me to be a perfectly reliable person. That blocks this end. We have now to deal with the other. There is an inn here, the Red Bull, the landlady of which was ill. She had sent to Mackleton for a doctor, but he did not arrive until morning, being absent at another case. The people at the inn were alert all night, awaiting his coming, and one or other of them seems to have continually had an eye upon the road. They declare that no one passed. If their evidence is good, then we are fortunate enough to be able to block the west, and also to be able to say that the fugitives did *not* use the road at all.'

'But the bicycle?' I objected.

'Quite so. We will come to the bicycle presently. To continue our reasoning: if these people did not go by the road, they must have traversed the country to the north of the house or to the south of the house. That is certain. Let us weigh the one against the other. On the south of the house is, as you perceive, a large district of arable land, cut up into small fields, with stone walls between them. There, I admit that a bicycle is impossible. We can dismiss the idea. We turn to the country on the north. Here there lies a grove of trees, marked as the "Ragged Shaw", and on the farther side stretches a great rolling moor, Lower Gill Moor, extending for ten miles, and sloping gradually upwards. Here, at one side of this wilderness, is Holdernesse Hall, ten miles by road, but only six across the moor. It is a peculiarly desolate plain. A few moor farmers have small holdings, where they rear sheep and cattle. Except these, the plover and the curlew are the only inhabitants until you come to the Chesterfield high-road. There is a church there, you see, a few cottages, and an inn. Beyond that the hills become precipitous. Surely it is here to the north that our quest must lie.'

'But the bicycle?' I persisted.

'Well, well!' said Holmes impatiently. 'A good cyclist does not need a high road. The moor is intersected with paths, and the moon was at the full. Halloa! What is this?'

There was an agitated knock at the door, and an instant afterwards Dr Huxtable was in the room. In his hand he held a blue cricket-cap, with a white chevron on the peak.

'At last we have a clue!' he cried. 'Thank Heaven, at last we are on the dear boy's track! It is his cap.'

'Where was it found?'

'In the van of the gipsies who camped on the moor. They left on Tuesday. Today the police traced them down and examined their caravan. This was found.'

'How do they account for it?'

'They shuffled and lied – said that they found it on the moor on Tuesday morning. They know where he is, the rascals! Thank goodness, they are all safe under lock and key. Either the fear of the law or the duke's purse will certainly get out of them all that they know.'

'So far, so good,' said Holmes, when the doctor had at last left the room. 'It at least bears out the theory that it is on the side of the Lower Gill Moor that we must hope for results. The police have really done nothing locally, save the arrest of these gipsies. Look here, Watson! There is a watercourse across the moor. You see it marked here in the

map. In some parts it widens into a morass. This is particularly so in the region between Holdernesse Hall and the school. It is vain to look elsewhere for tracks in this dry weather; but at *that* point there is certainly a chance of some record being left. I will call you early tomorrow morning, and you and I will try if we can to throw some light upon the mystery.'

The day was just breaking when I woke to find the long, thin form of Holmes by my bedside. He was fully dressed, and had apparently already been out.

'I have done the lawn and the bicycle shed,' said he. 'I have also had a ramble through the Ragged Shaw. Now, Watson, there is cocoa ready in the next room. I must beg you to hurry, for we have a great day before us.'

His eyes shone, and his cheek was flushed with the exhilaration of the master workman who sees his work lies ready before him. A very different Holmes, this active, alert man, from the introspective and pallid dreamer of Baker Street. I felt, as I looked upon that supple figure, alive with nervous energy, that it was indeed a strenuous day that awaited us.

And yet it opened in the blackest disappointment. With high hopes we struck across the peaty, russet moor, intersected with a thousand sheep-paths, until we came to the broad light-green belt which marked the morass between us and Holdernesse. Certainly, if the lad had gone homewards, he must have passed this, and he would not pass it without leaving his trace. But no sign of him or the German could be seen. With a darkening face my friend strode along the margin, eagerly observant of every muddy stain upon the mossy surface. Sheep-marks there were in profusion, and at one place, some miles down, cows had left their tracks. Nothing more.

'Check number one,' said Holmes, looking gloomily over the rolling expanse of the moor. 'There is another morass down yonder, and a narrow neck between. Halloa! halloa! halloa! What have we here?'

We had come on a small black ribbon of pathway. In the middle of it, clearly marked on the sodden soil, was the track of a bicycle.

161

'Hurrah!' I cried. 'We have it.'

But Holmes was shaking his head, and his face was puzzled and expectant rather than joyous.

'A bicycle certainly, but not *the* bicycle,' said he. 'I am familiar with forty-two different impressions left by tyres. This, as you perceive, is a Dunlop, with a patch upon the outer cover. Heidegger's tyres were Palmers', leaving longitudinal stripes. Aveling, the mathematical master, was sure upon the point. Therefore it is not Heidegger's track.'

'The boy's, then?'

'Possibly, if we could prove a bicycle to have been in his possession. But this we have utterly failed to do. This track, as you perceive, was made by a rider who was going from the direction of the school.'

'Or towards it?'

'No, no, my dear Watson. The more deeply sunk impression is, of course, the hind wheel, upon which the weight rests. You perceive several places where it has passed across and obliterated the more shallow mark of the front one. It was undoubtedly heading away from the school. It may or may not be connected with our inquiry, but we will follow it backwards before we go any farther.'

We did so, and at the end of a few hundred yards lost the tracks as we emerged from the boggy portion of the moor. Following the path backwards, we picked out another spot, where a spring trickled across it. Here, once again, was the mark of the bicycle, though nearly obliterated by the hoofs of cows. After that there was no sign, but the path ran right on into Ragged Shaw, the wood which backed on to the school. From this wood the cycle must have emerged. Holmes sat down on a boulder and rested his chin in his hands. I had smoked two cigarettes before he moved.

'Well, well,' said he at last. 'It is, of course, possible that a cunning man might change the tyre of his bicycle in order to leave unfamiliar tracks. A criminal who was capable of such a thought is a man whom I should be proud to do business with. We will leave this question undecided and hark back to our morass again, for we have left a good deal unexplored.'

We continued our systematic survey of the edge of the sodden portion of the moor, and soon our perseverance was gloriously rewarded.

Right across the lower part of the bog lay a miry path. Holmes gave a cry of delight as he approached it. An impression like a fine bundle of telegraph wires ran down the centre of it. It was the Palmer tyre.

'Here is Herr Heidegger, sure enough!' cried Holmes exultantly. 'My reasoning seems to have been pretty sound, Watson.'

'I congratulate you.'

'But we have a long way still to go. Kindly walk clear of the path. Now let us follow the trail. I fear that it will not lead very far.'

We found, however, as we advanced, that this portion of the moor was intersected with soft patches, and, though we frequently lost sight of the track, we always succeeded in picking it up once more.

'Do you observe,' said Holmes, 'that the rider is now undoubtedly forcing the pace? There can be no doubt of it. Look at this impression, where you get both tyres clear. The one is as deep as the other. That can only mean that the rider is throwing his weight on to the handle-bar as a man does when he is sprinting. By Jove! he has had a fall.'

There was a broad irregular smudge covering some yards of the track. Then there were a few footmarks, and the tyre reappeared once more.

'A side-slip,' I suggested.

Holmes held up a crumpled branch of flowering gorse. To my horror I perceived that the yellow blossoms were all dabbled with crimson. On the path, too, and among the heather were dark stains of clotted blood.

'Bad!' said Holmes. 'Bad! Stand clear, Watson! Not an unnecessary footstep! What do I read here? He fell wounded, he stood up, he remounted, he proceeded. But there is no other track. Cattle on this side-path. He was surely not gored by a bull? Impossible! But I see no traces of anyone else. We must push on, Watson. Surely, with stains as well as the track to guide us, he cannot escape us now.'

Our search was not a very long one. The tracks of the tyre began to curve fantastically upon the wet and shining path. Suddenly, as I looked ahead, the gleam of metal caught my eye from amid the thick gorse bushes. Out of them we dragged a bicycle, Palmer-tyred, one pedal bent, and the whole front of it horribly smeared and slobbered with blood. On the other side of the bushes a shoe was projecting. We ran round, and there lay the unfortunate rider. He was a tall man, full bearded, with spectacles, one glass of which had been knocked out. The cause of his death was a frightful blow upon the head, which had crushed in part of his skull. That he could have gone on after receiving such an injury said much for the vitality and courage of the man. He wore shoes, but no socks, and his open coat disclosed a night-shirt beneath it. It was undoubtedly the German master.

Holmes turned the body over reverently, and examined it with great attention. He then sat in deep thought for a time, and I could see by his ruffled brow that this grim discovery had not, in his opinion, advanced us much in our inquiry.

'It is a little difficult to know what to do, Watson,' said he, at last. 'My own inclinations are to push this inquiry on, for we have already lost so much time that we cannot afford to waste another hour. On the other hand, we are bound to inform the police of this discovery, and to see that this poor fellow's body is looked after.'

'I could take a note back.'

'But I need your company and assistance. Wait a bit! There is a fellow cutting peat up yonder. Bring him over here, and he will guide the police.'

I brought the peasant across, and Holmes dispatched the frightened man with a note to Dr Huxtable.

'Now, Watson,' said he, 'we have picked up two clues this morning.

One is the bicycle with the Palmer tyre, and we see what that has led to. The other is the bicycle with the patched Dunlop. Before we start to investigate that, let us try to realize what we *do* know, so as to make the most of it, and to separate the essential from the accidental.

'First of all, I wish to impress upon you that the boy certainly left of his own free will. He got down from his window and he went off, either alone or with someone. That is sure.'

I assented.

'Well, now, let us turn to this unfortunate German master. The boy was fully dressed when he fled. Therefore he foresaw what he would do. But the German went without his socks. He certainly acted on very short notice.'

'Undoubtedly.'

'Why did he go? Because, from his bedroom window, he saw the flight of the boy. Because he wished to overtake him and bring him back. He seized his bicycle, pursued the lad, and in pursuing him met his death.'

166

'So it would seem.'

'Now I come to the critical part of my argument. The natural action of a man in pursuing a little boy would be to run after him. He would know that he could overtake him. But the German does not do so. He turns to his bicycle. I am told that he was an excellent cyclist. He would not do this if he did not see that the boy had some swift means of escape.'

'The other bicycle.'

'Let us continue our reconstruction. He meets his death five miles from the school – not by a bullet, mark you, which even a lad might conceivably discharge, but by a savage blow dealt by a vigorous arm. The lad, then, *had* a companion in his flight. And the flight was a swift one, since it took five miles before an expert cyclist could overtake them. Yet we survey the ground round the scene of the tragedy. What do we find? A few cattle tracks, nothing more. I took a wide sweep round, and there is no path within fifty yards. Another cyclist could have had nothing to do with the actual murder. Nor were there any human footmarks.'

'Holmes,' I cried, 'this is impossible.'

'Admirable!' he said. 'A most illuminating remark. It *is* impossible as I state it, and therefore I must in some respect have stated it wrong. Yet you saw for yourself. Can you suggest any fallacy?'

'He could not have fractured his skull in a fall?'

'In a morass, Watson?'

'I am at my wits' end.'

'Tut, tut; we have solved some worse problems. At least we have plenty of material, if we can only use it. Come, then, and, having exhausted the Palmer, let us see what the Dunlop with the patched cover has to offer us.'

Lewis Carroll

YOU ARE OLD, FATHER WILLIAM

Illustrated by Chris Riddell

'You are old, Father William,' the young man said,
  'And your hair has become very white;
And yet you incessantly stand on your head –
  Do you think, at·your age, it is right?'

'In my youth,' Father William replied to his son,
  'I feared it might injure the brain;
But, now that I'm perfectly sure I have none,
  Why, I do it again and again.'

'You are old,' said the youth, 'as I mentioned before,
  And have grown most uncommonly fat;
Yet you turned a back-somersault in at the door –
  Pray, what is the reason for that?'

'In my youth,' said the sage, as he shook his grey locks,
  'I kept all my limbs very supple
By the use of this ointment – one shilling the box –
  Allow me to sell you a couple?'

'You are old,' said the youth, 'and your jaws are too weak
  For anything tougher than suet;
Yet you finished the goose, with the bones and the beak –
  Pray, how did you manage to do it?'

'In my youth,' said his father, 'I took to the law,
  And argued each case with my wife;
And the muscular strength, which it gave to my jaw,
  Has lasted the rest of my life.'

'You are old,' said the youth, 'one would hardly suppose
  That your eye was as steady as ever;
Yet you balanced an eel on the end of your nose –
  What made you so awfully clever?'

'I have answered three questions, and that is enough,'
  Said his father. 'Don't give yourself airs!
Do you think I can listen all day to such stuff?
  Be off, or I'll kick you downstairs!'

Edgar Allan Poe

ANNABEL LEE

Illustrated by Rosemary Woods

It was many and many a year ago,
  In a kingdom by the sea,
That a maiden there lived whom you may know
  By the name of Annabel Lee;
And this maiden she lived with no other thought
  Than to love and be loved by me.

She was a child and *I* was a child,
  In this kingdom by the sea,
But we loved with a love that was more than love –
  I and my Annabel Lee –
With a love that the wingèd seraphs of Heaven
  Coveted her and me.

And this was the reason that, long ago,
  In this kingdom by the sea,
A wind blew out of a cloud, by night
  Chilling my Annabel Lee;
So that her highborn kinsmen came
  And bore her away from me,
To shut her up in a sepulchre
  In this kingdom by the sea.

The angels, not half so happy in Heaven,
　Went envying her and me: –
Yes! – that was the reason (as all men know,
　In this kingdom by the sea)
That the wind came out of the cloud, chilling
　And killing my Annabel Lee.

But our love it was stronger by far than the love
　Of those who were older than we –
　Of many far wiser than we –
And neither the angels in Heaven above
　Nor the demons down under the sea,
Can ever dissever my soul from the soul
　Of the beautiful Annabel Lee: –

For the moon never beams, without bringing me dreams
　Of the beautiful Annabel Lee;
And the stars never rise but I see the bright eyes
　Of the beautiful Annabel Lee:
And so, all the night-tide, I lie down by the side
Of my darling, my darling, my life and my bride,
　In the sepulchre there by the sea –
　In her tomb by the side of the sea.

Kenneth Grahame

FROM
THE WIND IN THE WILLOWS

Illustrated by E. H. Shepard

When Mole goes boating with the Water Rat instead of spring-cleaning, he discovers a world he never knew about.

Leaving the main stream, they now passed into what seemed at first sight like a little landlocked lake. Green turf sloped down to either edge, brown snaky tree-roots gleamed below the surface of the quiet water, while ahead of them the silvery shoulder and foamy tumble of a weir, arm-in-arm with a restless dripping mill-wheel, that held up in its turn a grey-gabled mill-house, filled the air with a soothing murmur of sound, dull and smothery, yet with little clear voices speaking up cheerfully out of it at intervals. It was so very beautiful that the Mole could only hold up both fore-paws and gasp, 'O my! O my! O my!'

The Rat brought the boat alongside the bank, made her fast, helped the still awkward Mole safely ashore, and swung out the luncheon-basket. The Mole begged as a favour to be allowed to unpack it all by himself; and the Rat was very pleased to indulge him, and to sprawl at full length on the grass and rest, while his excited friend shook out the table-cloth and spread it, took out all the mysterious packets one by one and arranged their contents in due order, still gasping, 'O my! O my!' at each fresh revelation. When all was ready, the Rat said, 'Now, pitch in, old fellow!' and the Mole was indeed very glad to obey, for he had started his spring-cleaning at a very early hour that morning, as people *will* do, and had not paused for bite or sup; and he had been through a very great deal since that distant time which now seemed so many days ago.

'What are you looking at?' said the Rat presently, when the edge of their hunger was somewhat dulled, and the Mole's eyes were able to wander off the table-cloth a little.

'I am looking,' said the Mole, 'at a streak of bubbles that I see travelling along the surface of the water. That is a thing that strikes me as funny.'

'Bubbles? Oho!' said the Rat, and chirruped cheerily in an inviting sort of way.

A broad glistening muzzle showed itself above the edge of the bank, and the Otter hauled himself out and shook the water from his coat.

'Greedy beggars!' he observed, making for the provender. 'Why didn't you invite me, Ratty?'

'This was an impromptu affair,' explained the Rat. 'By the way – my friend, Mr Mole.'

'Proud, I'm sure,' said the Otter, and the two animals were friends forthwith.

'Such a rumpus everywhere!' continued the Otter. 'All the world seems out on the river today. I came up this backwater to try and get a moment's peace, and then stumble upon you fellows! At least – I beg pardon – I don't exactly mean that, you know.'

There was a rustle behind them, proceeding from a hedge wherein last year's leaves still clung thick, and a stripy head, with high shoulders behind it, peered forth on them.

'Come on, old Badger!' shouted the Rat.

The Badger trotted forward a pace or two; then grunted, 'H'm! Company,' and turned his back and disappeared from view.

'That's *just* the sort of fellow he is!' observed the disappointed Rat.

'Simply hates Society! Now we shan't see any more of him today. Well, tell us *who's* out on the river?'

'Toad's out, for one,' replied the Otter. 'In his brand-new wager-boat; new togs, new everything!'

The two animals looked at each other and laughed.

'Once, it was nothing but sailing,' said the Rat. 'Then he tired of that and took to punting. Nothing would please him but to punt all day and every day, and a nice mess he made of it. Last year it was house-boating, and we all had to go and stay with him in his house-boat, and pretend we liked it. He was going to spend the rest of his life in a house-boat. It's all the same, whatever he takes up; he gets tired of it, and starts on something fresh.'

'Such a good fellow, too,' remarked the Otter reflectively. 'But no stability – especially in a boat!'

From where they sat they could get a glimpse of the main stream across the island that separated them; and just then a wager-boat flashed into view, the rower – a short, stout figure – splashing badly and rolling a good deal, but working his hardest. The Rat stood up and hailed him, but Toad – for it was he – shook his head and settled sternly to his work.

'He'll be out of the boat in a minute if he rolls like that,' said the Rat, sitting down again.

'Of course he will,' chuckled the Otter. 'Did I ever tell you that good story about Toad and the lock-keeper? It happened this way. Toad...'

An errant May-fly swerved unsteadily athwart the current in the intoxicated fashion affected by young bloods of May-flies seeing life. A swirl of water and a 'cloop!' and the May-fly was visible no more.

Neither was the Otter.

The Mole looked down. The voice was still in his ears, but the turf whereon he had sprawled was clearly vacant. Not an Otter to be seen, as far as the distant horizon.

But again there was a streak of bubbles on the surface of the river.

The Rat hummed a tune, and the Mole recollected that animal-etiquette forbade any sort of comment on the sudden disappearance of one's friends at any moment, for any reason or no reason whatever.

'Well, well,' said the Rat. 'I suppose we ought to be moving. I wonder which of us had better pack the luncheon-basket?' He did not speak as if he was frightfully eager for the treat.

'O, please let me,' said the Mole. So, of course, the Rat let him.

Packing the basket was not quite such pleasant work as unpacking the basket. It never is. But the Mole was bent on enjoying everything, and although just when he had got the basket packed and strapped up tightly he saw a plate staring up at him from the grass, and when the job had been done again the Rat pointed out a fork which anybody ought to have seen, and last of all, behold! the mustard-pot, which he had been sitting on without knowing it – still, somehow, the thing got finished at last, without much loss of temper.

The afternoon sun was getting low as the Rat sculled gently homewards in a dreamy mood, murmuring poetry-things over to himself,

and not paying much attention to Mole. But the Mole was very full of lunch, and self-satisfaction, and pride, and already quite at home in a boat (so he thought) and was getting a bit restless besides: and presently he said, 'Ratty! Please, *I* want to row, now!'

The Rat shook his head with a smile. 'Not yet, my young friend,' he said – 'wait till you've had a few lessons. It's not so easy as it looks.'

The Mole was quiet for a minute or two. But he began to feel more and more jealous of Rat, sculling so strongly and so easily along, and his pride began to whisper that he could do it every bit as well. He jumped up and seized the sculls, so suddenly, that the Rat, who was gazing out over the water and saying more poetry-things to himself, was taken by surprise and fell backwards off his seat with his legs in the air for the second time, while the triumphant Mole took his place and grabbed the sculls with entire confidence.

'Stop it, you *silly* ass!' cried the Rat, from the bottom of the boat. 'You can't do it! You'll have us over!'

The Mole flung his sculls back with a flourish, and made a great dig at the water. He missed the surface altogether, his legs flew up above his head, and he found himself lying on the top of the prostrate Rat. Greatly alarmed, he made a grab at the side of the boat, and the next moment – Sploosh!

Over went the boat, and he found himself struggling in the river.

O my, how cold the water was, and O, how *very* wet it felt. How it sang in his ears as he went down, down, down! How bright and welcome the sun looked as he rose to the surface coughing and spluttering! How black was his despair when he felt himself sinking again! Then a firm paw gripped him by the back of his neck. It was the Rat, and he was evidently laughing – the Mole could *feel* him laughing, right down his arm and through his paw, and so into his – the Mole's – neck.

The Rat got hold of a scull and shoved it under the Mole's arm; then he did the same by the other side of him and, swimming behind, propelled the helpless animal to shore, hauled him out, and set him down on the bank, a squashy, pulpy lump of misery.

When the Rat had rubbed him down a bit, and wrung some of the wet out of him, he said, 'Now then, old fellow! Trot up and down the towing-path as hard as you can, till you're warm and dry again, while I dive for the luncheon-basket.'

So the dismal Mole, wet without and ashamed within, trotted about till he was fairly dry, while the Rat plunged into the water again, recovered the boat, righted her and made her fast, fetched his floating property to shore by degrees, and finally dived successfully for the luncheon-basket and struggled to land with it.

When all was ready for a start once more, the Mole, limp and dejected, took his seat in the stern of the boat; and as they set off, he said in a low voice, broken with emotion, 'Ratty, my generous friend! I am very sorry indeed for my foolish and ungrateful conduct. My heart quite fails me when I think how I might have lost that beautiful luncheon-basket. Indeed, I have been a complete ass, and I know it.

Will you overlook it this once and forgive me, and let things go on as before?'

'That's all right, bless you!' responded the Rat cheerily. 'What's a little wet to a Water Rat? I'm more in the water than out of it most days. Don't you think any more about it; and, look here! I really think you had better come and stop with me for a little time. It's very plain and rough, you know – not like Toad's house at all – but you haven't seen that yet; still, I can make you comfortable. And I'll teach you to row, and to swim, and you'll soon be as handy on the water as any of us.'

The Mole was so touched by his kind manner of speaking that he could find no voice to answer him; and he had to brush away a tear or two with the back of his paw. But the Rat kindly looked in another direction, and presently the Mole's spirits revived again, and he was even able to give some straight back-talk to a couple of moorhens who were sniggering to each other about his bedraggled appearance.

When they got home, the Rat made a bright fire in the parlour, and planted the Mole in an armchair in front of it, having fetched down a dressing-gown and slippers for him, and told him river stories till supper-time. Very thrilling stories they were, too, to an earth-dwelling animal like Mole. Stories about weirs, and sudden floods, and leaping pike, and steamers that flung hard bottles – at least bottles were certainly flung, and *from* steamers, so presumably *by* them; and about herons, and how particular they were whom they spoke to; and about adventures down drains, and night-fishings with Otter, or excursions far afield with Badger. Supper was a most cheerful meal; but very shortly afterwards a terribly sleepy Mole had to be escorted upstairs by his considerate host, to the best bedroom, where he soon laid his head on his pillow in great peace and contentment, knowing that his new-found friend the River was lapping the sill of his window.

This day was only the first of many similar ones for the emancipated Mole, each of them longer and fuller of interest as the ripening summer moved onward. He learnt to swim and to row, and entered into the joy of running water; and with his ear to the reed-stems he caught, at intervals, something of what the wind went whispering so constantly among them.

Carlo Collodi

From

PINOCCHIO

Illustrated by Mauro Evangelista

*Pinocchio, the puppet who wants to be a real boy, meets his
'friends' — the fox and the cat — and goes with them to sow his
money in the Field of Miracles.*

As you may imagine, the
fairy let the puppet scream
and cry a good half hour
because of his long nose which
he could not get through the
door. She did this to teach him a
good lesson, and to correct him of the
very bad habit of lying, which is one of
the worst habits a boy can have. But when
she saw his face disfigured from crying, and his eyes sticking out of
his head, she pitied him. So she clapped her hands, at which signal a
thousand big woodpeckers flew in at the window and, perching on
Pinocchio's nose, pecked away at it with so much zeal that in a few
minutes the big, ridiculous thing was reduced to its usual size.

'How good you are, dear fairy,' said the puppet, wiping his eyes. 'I
love you so much!'

'I love you too,' answered the fairy, 'and if you want to stay with me,
you shall be my little brother, and I will be your darling sister.'

'I'd like to stay with you, but what about my daddy?'

'I have thought of everything, and your father already knows everything. He will be here tonight.'

'Really?' exclaimed Pinocchio, jumping for joy. 'Then, dearest fairy, if you don't mind, I shall go out to meet him. I can't wait any longer to see and kiss that poor old man, who has suffered so much for me!'

'Go, by all means, but don't get lost. Take the road through the wood, and you will surely meet him.'

Pinocchio left; and as soon as he reached the wood he began to run like a deer. At a certain place, in front of the big oak tree, he stopped, because he thought he heard people moving in the bushes. And indeed, there appeared all at once on the road – can you guess who? – the fox and the cat, his two travelling companions, with whom he had supped at the Red Crab Inn.

'Here is our dear Pinocchio,' exclaimed the fox, embracing and kissing him. 'How do you come to be here?'

'How do you come to be here?' repeated the cat.

'It's a very long story,' said the puppet. 'I'll tell it when I have time, though you should know this much – that the other night, when you left me alone in the inn, I encountered assassins on the road.'

'Assassins? Oh, my poor friend Pinocchio! And what did they want?'

'They wanted to rob me of my gold.'

'Infamous people!' said the fox.

'Most infamous people!' added the cat.

'But I ran away,' continued the puppet, 'and they chased me until they caught me, and hung me to a branch of that oak tree.' And Pinocchio pointed to the big oak.

'Did you ever hear anything more horrible!' said the fox. 'What a world we are condemned to live in! Where can honest people like us find shelter?'

While talking, Pinocchio noticed that the cat was lame of her right foreleg, since the paw with all its claws was missing. So he said to her, 'What has become of your paw?'

The cat wanted to say something, but got confused – so the fox answered quickly, 'My friend is too modest. That is why she doesn't answer, but I shall answer for her. About an hour ago we met an old

wolf on the road, who was almost fainting from hunger. He asked alms of us, but we hadn't even a fish bone to give him; so what do you think my friend did – my friend, who has the heart of a Caesar? She bit off her own paw, and gave it to the poor beast, so that he could eat something.' As he told this, the fox wiped a tear.

Pinocchio was so deeply touched that he went to the cat, and whispered in her ear, 'If all cats were like you, mice would be fortunate creatures!'

'And what are you doing here?' asked the fox.

'I'm waiting for my father; he might come any moment.'

'And your gold pieces?'

'They are all in my pocket, except the one I spent at the inn of the Red Crab.'

'And to think that, by tomorrow, instead of four gold pieces they might be a thousand, or two thousand! Why not follow my advice, and bury them in the Field of Miracles?'

'Impossible, today. I'll go another time.'

'Another time will be too late,' said the fox.

'Why?'

'Because a rich man has bought the field, and after tomorrow nobody will be allowed to bury his money there.'

'How far away is the Field of Miracles?'

'Hardly two miles. Will you come with us? You will be there in half an hour, and bury your four gold pieces at once, and after a few minutes you shall have two thousand, and return in the evening with your pockets full. Will you come?'

Pinocchio remembered the good fairy, old Geppetto, and the

warnings of the talking cricket; yet in the end he did as all boys do who have no sense, and no heart – that is, he shook his head and said to the fox and the cat, 'Let's go! I'll come with you.'

And off they went.

They had walked about half a day when they came to a place called Fools' Trap. As soon as they entered the city, Pinocchio saw that the streets were full of dogs who had lost their hair, and whose mouths were wide open from hunger. There were shorn sheep, trembling with cold; roosters without their crests and combs, who were begging for a grain of maize; butterflies who could not fly, because they had sold their beautiful wings; peacocks without tails, who were ashamed to be seen; and pheasants who were crawling along, mourning for their beautiful gold and silver feathers, lost for ever.

In the midst of these beggars and shame-faced beasts, from time to time elegant carriages passed by, with a fox, or a thievish magpie, or some bird of prey inside.

'But where is the Field of Miracles?' asked Pinocchio.

'Just a few yards from here.'

They crossed the city and, going beyond the walls, they came to a lonely field that looked just like any other field.

'Here we are,' said the fox. 'Now, get to work and dig a small hole with your hands and put your gold pieces in.'

Pinocchio obeyed. He dug a hole, put into it the four gold pieces he still had, and covered them up with some earth.

'Now, then,' said the fox, 'go to the dam close by, bring a bucket of water, and water the ground where you have sown your fortune.'

Pinocchio went to the dam and, as he did not have a

bucket, he took one of his old shoes, filled it with water, and watered the earth which covered his money.

'What else must I do?'

'Nothing else,' answered the fox. 'Now we can go away. You must come back in about twenty minutes, and you will see a little tree already growing through the earth, with its branches covered with money.'

The poor puppet was beside himself with joy, and he thanked the fox and the cat a thousand times, and promised them a lovely present.

'We don't want presents,' answered those two scoundrels. 'It's quite enough for us to have shown you how to get rich without hard work. That makes us as happy as can be.'

With these words they said good-bye to Pinocchio and, wishing him a splendid harvest, they went about their business.

Charles Dickens

FROM
OLIVER TWIST

Illustrated by Simon Dewey and Mark Longworth

*When Oliver runs away from the workhouse orphanage
he falls into the company of a gang of pickpockets, including
Fagin, Bill Sykes and the Artful Dodger.*

It was late next morning when Oliver awoke from a sound, long sleep. There was no other person in the room but the old Jew, who was boiling some coffee in a saucepan for breakfast, and whistling softly to himself as he stirred it round and round, with an iron spoon. He would stop every now and then to listen when there was the least noise below; and when he had satisfied himself, he would go on, whistling and stirring again, as before.

Oliver had scarcely washed himself, and made everything tidy, by emptying the basin out of the window, agreeably to the Jew's directions, when the Dodger returned: accompanied by a very sprightly young friend, whom Oliver had seen smoking on the previous night, and who was now formally introduced to him as Charley Bates. The four sat down, to breakfast, on the coffee and some hot rolls and ham which the Dodger had brought home in the crown of his hat.

'Well,' said the Jew, glancing slyly at Oliver, and addressing himself to the Dodger, 'I hope you've been at work this morning, my dears?'

'Hard,' replied the Dodger.

'As nails,' added Charley Bates.

'Good boys, good boys!' said the Jew. 'What have *you* got, Dodger?'

'A couple of pocket-books,' replied that young gentleman.

'Lined?' inquired the Jew, with eagerness.

'Pretty well,' replied the Dodger, producing two pocket-books; one green, and the other red.

'Not so heavy as they might be,' said the Jew, after looking at the insides carefully; 'but very neat and nicely made. Ingenious workman, ain't he, Oliver?'

'Very, indeed, sir,' said Oliver. At which Mr Charles Bates laughed uproariously; very much to the amazement of Oliver, who saw nothing to laugh at, in anything that had passed.

'And what have you got, my dear?' said Fagin to Charley Bates.

'Wipes,' replied Master Bates; at the same time producing four pocket-handkerchiefs.

'Well,' said the Jew, inspecting them closely; 'they're very good ones, very. You haven't marked them well, though, Charley; so the marks shall be picked out with a needle, and we'll teach Oliver how to do it. Shall us, Oliver, eh? Ha! ha! ha!'

'If you please, sir,' said Oliver.

'You'd like to be able to make pocket-handkerchiefs as easy as Charley Bates, wouldn't you, my dear?' said the Jew.

'Very much, indeed, if you'll teach me, sir,' replied Oliver.

Master Bates saw something so exquisitely ludicrous in this reply that he burst into another laugh; which laugh, meeting the coffee he was drinking, and carrying it down some wrong channel, very nearly terminated in his premature suffocation.

The Dodger said nothing, but he smoothed Oliver's hair over his eyes, and said he'd know better, by-and-by; upon which the old gentleman, observing Oliver's colour mounting, changed the subject by asking whether there had been much of a crowd at the execution that morning? This made him wonder more and more; for it was plain from the replies of the two boys that they had both been there; and Oliver naturally wondered how they could possibly have found time to be so very industrious.

When the breakfast was cleared away, the merry old gentleman and the two boys played at a very curious and uncommon game, which was performed in this way. The merry old gentleman, placing a snuff-box in one pocket of his trousers, a note-case in the other, and a watch in his waistcoat pocket, with a guard-chain round his neck, and sticking a mock diamond pin in his shirt: buttoned his coat tight round him, and putting his spectacle-case and handkerchief in his pockets, trotted up and down the room with a stick, in imitation of the manner in which old gentlemen walk about the streets any hour in the day. Sometimes he stopped at the fireplace, and sometimes at the door, making believe that he was staring with all his might into shop-windows. At such times he would look constantly round him, for fear of thieves, and would keep slapping all his pockets in turn, to see that he hadn't lost anything, in such a very funny and natural manner, that Oliver laughed till the tears ran down his face. All this time, the two boys followed him closely about, getting out of his sight, so nimbly, every time he turned round, that it was impossible to follow their motions. At last, the Dodger trod upon his toes, or ran upon his boot accidentally, while Charley Bates stumbled up against him behind; and in that one moment they took from him, with the most extraordinary rapidity, snuff-box, note-case, watch-guard, chain, shirt-pin, pocket-handkerchief, – even the spectacle-case. If the old gentleman felt a hand in any one of his pockets, he cried out where it was; and then the game began all over again.

When this game had been played a great many times, a couple of young ladies called to see the young gentlemen; one of whom was named Bet, and the other Nancy. They wore a good deal of hair, not very neatly turned up behind, and were rather untidy about the shoes and stockings. They were not exactly pretty, perhaps; but they had a great deal of colour in their faces, and looked quite stout and hearty. Being remarkably free and agreeable in their manners, Oliver thought them very nice girls indeed. As there is no doubt they were.

These visitors stopped a long time. Spirits were produced, in consequence of one of the young ladies complaining of a coldness in her inside; and the conversation took a very convivial and improving turn. At length, Charley Bates expressed his opinion that it was time to pad the hoof. This, it occurred to Oliver, must be French for going out; for, directly afterwards, the Dodger, and Charley, and the two young ladies, went away together, having been kindly furnished by the amiable old Jew with money to spend.

'There, my dear,' said Fagin. 'That's a pleasant life, isn't it? They have gone out for the day.'

'Have they done work, sir?' inquired Oliver.

'Yes,' said the Jew; 'that is, unless they should unexpectedly come across any, when they are out; and they won't neglect it, if they do, my dear, depend upon it. Make 'em your models, my dear. Make 'em your models,' tapping the fire-shovel on the hearth to add force to his words; 'do everything they bid you, and take their advice in all matters – especially the Dodger's, my dear. He'll be a great man himself, and will make you one too, if you take pattern by him. – Is my handkerchief hanging out of my pocket, my dear?' said the Jew, stopping short.

'Yes, sir,' said Oliver.

'See if you can take it out, without my feeling it: as you saw them do, when we were at play this morning.'

Oliver held up the bottom of the pocket with one hand, as he had seen the Dodger hold it, and drew the handkerchief lightly out of it with the other.

'Is it gone?' cried the Jew.

'Here it is, sir,' said Oliver, showing it in his hand.

'You're a clever boy, my dear,' said the playful old gentleman, patting Oliver on the head approvingly. 'I never saw a sharper lad. Here's a shilling for you. If you go on, in this way, you'll be the greatest man of the time. And now come here, and I'll show you how to take the marks out of the handkerchiefs.'

Oliver wondered what picking the old gentleman's pocket in play, had to do with his chances of being a great man. But, thinking that the Jew, being so much his senior, must know best, he followed him quietly to the table, and was soon deeply involved in his new study.

For many days, Oliver remained in the Jew's room, picking the marks out of the pocket-handkerchiefs, (of which a great number were brought home,) and sometimes taking part in the game already described: which the two boys and the Jew played, regularly, every morning. At length, he began to languish for fresh air, and took many occasions of earnestly entreating the old gentleman to allow him to go out to work, with his two companions.

At length, one morning, Oliver obtained the permission he had so eagerly sought. There had been no handkerchiefs to work upon, for two or three days, and the dinners had been rather meagre. Perhaps these were reasons for the old gentleman's giving his assent; but, whether they were or no, he told Oliver he might go, and placed him under the joint guardianship of Charley Bates, and his friend the Dodger.

The three boys sallied out; the Dodger with his coat-sleeves tucked up, and his hat cocked, as usual; Master Bates sauntering along with his hands in his pockets; and Oliver between them, wondering where they were going, and what branch of manufacture he would be instructed in, first.

The pace at which they went, was such a very lazy, ill-looking saunter, that Oliver soon began to think his companions were going to deceive the old gentleman, by not going to work at all. The Dodger had a vicious propensity, too, of pulling the caps from the heads of small boys and tossing them down areas, while Charley Bates exhibited some very loose notions concerning the rights of property, by pilfering divers apples and onions from the stalls at the kennel sides, and thrusting them into pockets which were so surprisingly capacious, that they seemed to undermine his whole suit of clothes in every direction. These things looked so bad, that Oliver was on the point of declaring his intention of seeking his way back, in the best way he could, when his thoughts were suddenly directed into another channel, by a very mysterious change of behaviour on the part of the Dodger.

They were just emerging from a narrow court not far from the open square in Clerkenwell, when the Dodger made a sudden stop; and, laying his finger on his lip, drew his companions back again, with the greatest caution and circumspection.

'What's the matter?' demanded Oliver.

'Hush!' replied the Dodger. 'Do you see that old cove at the bookstall?'

'The old gentleman over the way?' said Oliver. 'Yes, I see him.'

'He'll do,' said the Dodger.

'A prime plant,' observed Master Charley Bates.

Oliver looked from one to the other, with the greatest surprise; but he was not permitted to make any inquiries; for the two boys walked stealthily across the road, and slunk close behind the old gentleman towards whom his attention had been directed. Oliver walked a few paces after them; and, not knowing whether to advance or retire, stood looking on in silent amazement.

The old gentleman was a very respectable-looking personage, with a powdered head and gold spectacles. He was dressed in a bottle-green coat with a black velvet collar; wore white trousers; and carried a smart bamboo cane under his arm. He had taken up a book from the stall, and there he stood, reading away, as hard as if he were in his elbow-chair, in his own study. It is very possible that he fancied himself there, indeed; for it was plain, from his abstraction, that he saw not the bookstall, nor the street, nor the boys, nor, in short, anything but the book itself.

What was Oliver's horror and alarm as he stood a few paces off, looking on with his eyelids as wide open as they would possibly go, to see the Dodger plunge his hand into the old gentleman's pocket, and draw from thence a handkerchief! To see him hand the same to Charley Bates; and finally to behold them, both, running away round the corner at full speed.

In an instant the whole mystery of the handkerchiefs, and the watches, and the jewels, and the Jew, rushed upon the boy's mind. He stood, for a moment, with the blood so tingling through all his veins from terror, that he felt as if he were in a burning fire; then, confused and frightened, he took to his heels; and, not knowing what he did, made off as fast as he could lay his feet to the ground.

This was all done in a minute's space, and the very instant that Oliver began to run, the old gentleman, putting his hand to his pocket, and missing his handkerchief, turned sharp round. Seeing the boy scudding away at such a rapid pace, he very naturally concluded him to be the depredator; and, shouting 'Stop thief!' with all his might, made off after him, book in hand.

But the old gentleman was not the only person who raised the hue-and-cry. The Dodger and Master Bates, unwilling to attract public attention by running down the open street, had merely retired into the very first doorway round the corner. They no sooner heard the cry, and saw Oliver running, than, guessing exactly how the matter stood, they issued forth with great promptitude; and, shouting 'Stop thief!' too, joined in the pursuit like good citizens.

'Stop thief! Stop thief!' There is a magic in the sound. The cry is taken up by a hundred voices, and the crowd accumulate at every turning. Away they fly, splashing through the mud, and rattling along the pavements; up go the windows, out run the people, onward bear the mob.

'Stop thief! Stop thief!' There is a passion *for hunting something* deeply implanted in the human breast. One wretched breathless child, panting with exhaustion; terror in his looks; agony in his eyes; large drops of perspiration streaming down his face, strains every nerve to make head upon his pursuers; and as they follow on his track, and gain upon him every instant, they hail his decreasing strength with still louder shouts, and whoop and scream with joy. 'Stop thief!' Ay, stop him for God's sake, were it only in mercy!

Stopped at last! A clever blow. He is down upon the pavement; and

the crowd eagerly gather round him: each new-comer jostling and struggling with the others to catch a glimpse. 'Stand aside!' – 'Give him a little air!' – 'Nonsense! he don't deserve it.' – 'Where's the gentleman?' – 'Here he is, coming down the street.' – 'Make room there for the gentleman!' – 'Is this the boy, sir!' – 'Yes.'

Oliver lay, covered with mud and dust, and bleeding from the mouth, looking wildly round upon the heap of faces that surrounded him, when the old gentleman was officiously dragged and pushed into the circle by the foremost of the pursuers.

'Yes,' said the gentleman, 'I am afraid it is the boy.'

'Afraid!' murmured the crowd. 'That's a good 'un!'

'Poor fellow!' said the gentleman, 'he has hurt himself.'

A police officer (who is generally the last person to arrive in such cases) at that moment made his way through the crowd, and seized Oliver by the collar.

'Come, get up,' said the man, roughly.

'It wasn't me indeed, sir. Indeed, indeed, it was two other boys,' said Oliver, clasping his hands passionately, and looking round. 'They are here somewhere.'

'Oh no, they ain't,' said the officer. He meant this to be ironical, but it was true besides; for the Dodger and Charley Bates had filed off down the first convenient court they came to. 'Come, get up!'

'Don't hurt him,' said the old gentleman, compassionately.

'Oh no, I won't hurt him,' replied the officer, tearing his jacket half off his back, in proof thereof. 'Come, I know you; it won't do. Will you stand upon your legs, you young devil?'

Oliver, who could hardly stand, made a shift to raise himself on his feet, and was at once lugged along the streets by the jacket-collar, at a rapid pace. The gentleman walked on with them by the officer's side; and as many of the crowd as could achieve the feat, got a little a-head, and stared back at Oliver from time to time.

Eric Knight

From

LASSIE COME-HOME

Illustrated by Kaye Hodges

*Although hundreds of miles from home, Lassie is determined to do
her duty and meet young Joe from school.*

The van with its grilled door drew into a courtyard. The iron gates set in the great wall clanged behind it. The van backed up so that it was tight against a raised entrance.

Inside, Lassie lay quietly in a corner. There were other dogs in the van. During the ride through the city, they had lifted their voices in clamour. But Lassie had lain still, like a captive queen among lesser prisoners. She had lain there, only her eyes alert, shutting out the exterior world just as she had done when she lay ill beneath the gorse clump.

She did not drop this air of dignity even when the grilled backdrop of the van was opened. The other dogs of mixed breeds yelped anew and darted about. The two men seized them and urged them along towards a large, concrete chamber. But Lassie did not move. Then she was the only one left in the van.

Perhaps it was her calm and regal air that misled the man. Or perhaps, too, he remembered the facility with which the young woman had placed the dog in the truck.

He entered the van with a small leash. Lassie lay quietly, and as she had been too proud to struggle and yelp for freedom as the other dogs had done, now she calmly suffered the hands to slip the thong over her head. As the lead was about to tighten she rose obediently, and as she had been taught to do from youth, began to follow the man. Down they came over the tailboard of the van and into the echoing corridor, Lassie going without either pulling ahead on the leash or dragging behind on it.

This, too, may have lulled the man, for, just as they reached the place where his assistant was holding open the barred door, he leaned down to unslip the leash.

In that flash, Lassie was free.

She leaped away like the passing of a beam of light. The man jumped to bar her path, but his human coordination was snail-like compared to that of the animal. Lassie turned herself in flight even as he started to move and drove herself between his legs and the wall.

Down the corridor she went, and then she pulled to a halt. Her way was blocked. There was nothing before her but the looming interior of the van which she had just left, backed so truly against the entrance that there was not an inch of space on any side.

She turned and dashed back — straight into the faces of the men who charged after her. Dodging their arms and legs, she catapulted past them again. At the left was a stairway. She raced for it. At the top a corridor stretched crosswise. One direction went south. She raced down it.

Now, behind her, the building began to echo with cries. There were people in the corridor. Hands grabbed at her as she raced along. Twisting like a football 'back', she went the length of the corridor. And then she halted. The corridor ended at a blank wall. There was a window, but it was closed.

Lassie wheeled. Now, back down the long hall men were gathered. They were advancing. Lassie looked about her. There were many doors at each side of the way, but they were all closed. There was no escape.

Her captors seemed to be confident of that, for now the two men

with peaked caps appeared, and the voice of the dog catcher rose.

'Stay where ye are, everyone, please. We've got her now. Just stay where ye are so's she can't get back down the corridor. She won't bite anybody. She's not a bad dog.'

Slowly the man advanced. Behind him was his assistant with the net. They came nearer and nearer.

Proudly Lassie stood at bay. With head high, she waited.

And then escape came. For right beside Lassie, one of the forbidding doors opened, and a voice sounded. It was an important voice – an official voice.

'What's going on out here? Do you realize there's a Court of Law sitting . . .'

That was as far as he got. For at that moment a tawny figure streaked by him, almost upsetting him as it cannoned off his legs. His face twisted itself into an expression of horror and outraged dignity. He gave one glance of utter contempt at the two men with the net. Then he shut the door.

Now, inside the room the air echoed with sound, for Lassie was racing about, looking for some means of escape. But in that large room there seemed to be none. All the doors were closed. At last, in a corner, Lassie stood at bay. People moved away from her, leaving her isolated. The banging and scraping of chairs and the cries slowly sank, and the only noise left was that of a thumping gavel. Then a sombre voice spoke.

'Do I understand that this is the surprise witness that the defence has promised?'

Immediately the room rocked with laughter. Young men in sombre costumes smiled broadly. The imperious figure wearing the enormous white wig allowed himself to smile, too, for he was famed far and wide for his piercing wit. And, moreover, this case had been long and tedious. His remark would be repeated and reprinted in newspapers the length and breadth of the land:

'Another report comes today of the sparkling humour of that renowned legal wit, Justice McQuarrie, sitting at . . .'

The great man nodded affably so that his wig almost came on to his forehead.

At that moment, Lassie barked, once, shortly.

The great man beamed.

'I presume that is an answer in the affirmative. And I may add that this is the most intelligent witness I have had before me in twenty years, for it is the first one that can answer yes or no without equivocation.'

Again the great room rocked with laughter. The young men in gowns nodded like mandarins and turned to one another. Old McQuarrie was in excellent form today!

Now, as though deciding that he alone should decree how long laughter should last, the judge thumped with the gavel. His brow furrowed. His eyes were stern.

'Usher,' he roared. 'Usher!'

A uniformed man hastened before the tribunal and stood at attention.

'Usher. What is that?'

'It is a dog, My Lord.'

'A dog!'

The judge turned his glance on the animal, still at bay in the corner.

'You confirm my own suspicions, Usher. It is a dog,' the judge said affably. Then his voice broke into a roar. 'Well, what do I want done with it?'

'I think I know what is in your mind, Your Lordship.'

'What is in my mind, Usher?'

'You wish it removed, Your Lordship.'

'I do! Remove it! Remove it!'

The Usher looked about him in hurt amazement. In all his years as an official, such a problem had never before arisen. Perhaps it had never arisen in all the history of law. Perhaps there was no official and recognized procedure set down by any book or statute for the proper engineering of such a matter. Every other possible thing had been thought of, but – dogs? Not that the Usher could remember.

Dogs – from court, removal of. Perhaps it was listed somewhere. But the Usher couldn't remember it. And if there were no official course of action to be followed, how should one . . .

The Usher's face suddenly brightened. He had solved it. The stairway of authority. He turned towards the man who had opened the door and allowed Lassie to enter.

'McLosh! Remove this dog. Where did it come from?'

The red-faced guardian of the door looked reproachfully at his superior.

'Na doot she's wiggled awa' fra' Fairgusson and Donnell. They twa's oot there the noo wi' a lashin' o' ropes.'

The Usher turned and translated in more official language to the judge.

'The dog's escaped from the pound authorities, Your Lordship. Two of them are outside now. And since the apprehension and detention of stray dogs properly come within the duties of the pound . . .'

'I won't make an official ruling on that, but

unofficially, Usher – unofficially . . .'

Again the delighted young men in robes smiled at each other.

'. . . Unofficially I should say it is in their province. Admit them and order them to remove this animal.'

'Very good, Your Lordship.'

Escaping hurriedly, the Usher went to the door.

'Get it oot o' here, quick. Before he loses his temper,' he whispered huskily.

Bearing the net, the two men entered the court. The legal array stood in eager interest. It was certainly a relief from the droning on this dull day.

The two men crept towards the corner, slowly – warily.

'We'll soon ha' her out o' here, Your Lordship,' one said in a conciliating tone.

But as he spoke, Lassie wheeled away. She knew that net. It was a hateful enemy. She must escape it.

Again the room became bedlam. The younger men took every advantage of the situation, and like schoolboys they lifted their voices in hunting cries.

'Yoicks! Gone away!'

'Look! Hallo, Watson. There by the desk!'

'Tallyho! Hiii! Ow, my shin.'

Cheerily they whooped, and in high glee did their best in every way to impede the men with the net – managing to upset them at every opportunity as they pretended to help corner the dog.

But at last the fun had run its course. Lassie was penned by the wall. The ring of men crept nearer. Above her was an open window. She leaped to the ledge – and then stood there in hesitation, for below her was the courtyard where the van still stood. There was a sheer drop of twenty feet to the concrete below.

The men came forward confidently. They knew that it was too far to leap. They spread out the net.

On the ledge Lassie trembled. Off to the left was the roof of the van. It was only ten feet below, but it was too far away. She crouched, her paws dancing as if to get better footing. Her muscles trembled.

For a dog is not like a cat. Like men, a dog has learned to fear heights. And yet it was the only way.

Crouching, gathering her muscles, Lassie stood. Then she leaped. Out she drove, as far as she could, towards the top of the van. Even as she went through the air, she knew she was falling short. Her sense of time and balance told her she could not land safely.

Reaching out with her forelegs, she just touched. For a brief second she hung there, as her hind legs scrambled on the side. Then she dropped to the ground heavily. And she lay, stunned.

Above, in the courtroom, the windows were lined with faces. The dog catcher gave a sharp cry.

'Now we've got her.'

William Blake

From

AUGURIES OF INNOCENCE

Illustrated by Siân Bailey

To see a World in a Grain of Sand
And a Heaven in a Wild Flower,
Hold Infinity in the palm of your hand
And Eternity in an hour.

Rudyard Kipling

A SMUGGLERS' SONG

Illustrated by David Frankland

If you wake at midnight and hear a horse's feet,
Don't go drawing back the blind, or looking in the street,
Them that asks no questions isn't told a lie.
Watch the wall, my darling, while the Gentlemen go by!
        Five and twenty ponies,
        Trotting through the dark –
        Brandy for the Parson,
        'Baccy for the Clerk;
        Laces for a lady; letters for a spy,
And watch the wall, my darling, while the Gentlemen go by!

Running round the woodlump if you chance to find
Little barrels, roped and tarred, all full of brandy-wine,
Don't you shout to come and look, nor take 'em for your play;
Put the brushwood back again, – and they'll be gone next day!

If you see the stableyard setting open wide;
If you see a tired horse lying down inside;
If your mother mends a coat cut about and tore;
If the lining's wet and warm – don't you ask no more!

If you meet King George's men, dressed in blue and red,
You be careful what you say, and mindful what is said.
If they call you 'pretty maid', and chuck you 'neath the chin,
Don't you tell where no one is, nor yet where no one's been!

Knocks and footsteps round the house – whistles after dark –
You've no call for running out till the housedogs bark.
Trusty's here and Pincher's here, and see how dumb they lie –
They don't fret to follow when the Gentlemen go by!

If you do as you've been told, likely there's a chance,
You'll be give a dainty doll, all the way from France,
With a cap of Valenciennes, and a velvet hood –
A present from the Gentlemen, along o' being good!
       Five and twenty ponies,
       Trotting through the dark –
       Brandy for the Parson,
       'Baccy for the Clerk.
Them that asks no questions isn't told a lie –
Watch the wall, my darling, while the Gentlemen go by!

Mary Howitt

THE SPIDER AND THE FLY

Illustrated by Fritz Wegner

'Will you walk into my parlour?' said the Spider to the Fly,
''Tis the prettiest little parlour that ever you did spy;
The way into my parlour is up a winding stair,
And I have many curious things to show when you are there.'
'Oh no, no,' said the little Fly, 'to ask me is in vain,
For who goes up your winding stair can ne'er come down again.'

sweet creature!

'I'm sure you must be weary, dear, with soaring up so high;
Will you rest upon my little bed?' said the Spider to the Fly.
'There are pretty curtains drawn around, the sheets are fine and thin;
And if you like to rest awhile, I'll snugly tuck you in!'
'Oh no, no,' said the little Fly, 'for I've often heard it said,
They never, never wake again, who sleep upon your bed!'

Said the cunning Spider to the Fly, 'Dear friend, what can I do,
To prove the warm affection I've always felt for you?
I have within my pantry good store of all that's nice;
I'm sure you're very welcome – will you please to take a slice?'
'Oh no, no,' said the little Fly, 'kind sir, that cannot be,
I've heard what's in your pantry, and I do not wish to see.'

'Sweet creature,' said the Spider, 'you're witty and you're wise;
How handsome are your gauzy wings, how brilliant are your eyes!
I have a little looking-glass upon my parlour shelf,
If you'll step in a moment, dear, you shall behold yourself.'
'I thank you, gentle sir,' she said, 'for what you're pleased to say,
And bidding you good morning now, I'll call another day.'

The Spider turned him round about, and went into his den,
For well he knew the silly Fly would soon come back again;
So he wove a subtle web, in a little corner sly,
And set his table ready, to dine upon the Fly.
Then he came out to his door again, and merrily did sing:
'Come hither, hither, pretty Fly, with the pearl and silver wing;
Your robes are green and purple – there's a crest upon your head;
Your eyes are like the diamond bright, but mine are dull as lead.'

Alas, alas! how very soon this silly little Fly,
Hearing his wily, flattering words, came slowly flitting by;
With buzzing wings she hung aloft, then near and nearer drew,
Thinking only of her brilliant eyes, and green and purple hue;
Thinking only of her crested head – poor foolish thing! At last,
Up jumped the cunning Spider, and fiercely held her fast.
He dragged her up his winding stair, into his dismal den,
Within his little parlour – but she ne'er came out again!

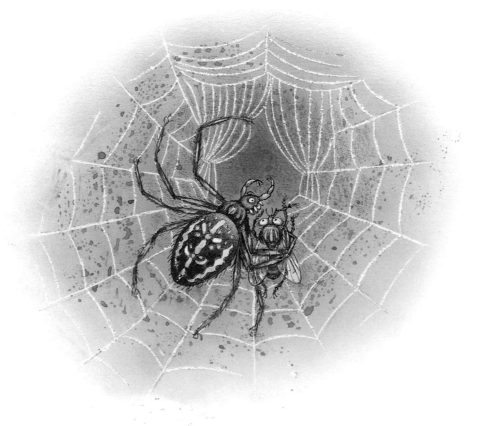

Lady Lindsay

DAY AND NIGHT

Illustrated by Alison Jay

Said Day to Night,
'I bring God's light.
  What gift have you?'
  Night said, 'The dew.'

'I give bright hours,'
Quoth Day, 'and flowers.'
  Said Night, 'More blest,
  I bring sweet rest.'

it made me deaf with the noise and pretty near blind with the smoke, and I judged I was gone. If they'd a had some bullets in, I reckon they'd a got the corpse they was after. Well, I see I warn't hurt, thanks to goodness. The boat floated on and went out of sight around the shoulder of the island. I could hear the booming, now and then, further and further off, and by-and-by after an hour, I didn't hear it no more. The island was three mile long. I judged they had got to the foot, and was giving it up. But they didn't yet awhile. They turned around the foot of the island and started up the channel on the Missouri side, under steam, and booming once in a while as they went. I crossed over to that side and watched them. When they got abreast the head of the island they quit shooting and dropped over to the Missouri shore and went home to the town.

I knowed I was all right now. Nobody else would come a-hunting after me. I got my traps out of the canoe and made me a nice camp in the thick woods. I made a kind of a tent out of my blankets to put my things under so the rain couldn't get at them. I catched a cat-fish and haggled him open with my saw, and towards sundown I started my camp-fire and had supper. Then I set out a line to catch some fish for breakfast.

When it was dark I set by my camp-fire smoking, and feeling pretty satisfied; but by-and-by it got sort of lonesome, and so I went and set on the bank and listened to the currents washing along, and counted the stars and drift-logs and rafts that come down, and then went to bed; there ain't no better way to put in time when you are lonesome; you can't stay so, you soon get over it.

And so for three days and nights. No difference – just the same thing. But the next day I went exploring around down through the island. I was boss of it; it all belonged to me, so to say, and I wanted to know all about it; but mainly I wanted to put in the time. I found plenty strawberries, ripe and prime; and green summer-grapes, and green razberries; and the green blackberries was just beginning to show. They would all come handy by-and-by, I judged.

Well, I went fooling along in the deep woods till I judged I warn't

far from the foot of the island. I had my gun along, but I hadn't shot nothing; it was for protection; thought I would kill some game nigh home. About this time I mighty near stepped on a good-sized snake, and it went sliding off through the grass and flowers, and I after it, trying to get a shot at it. I clipped along, and all of a sudden I bounded right on to the ashes of a camp-fire that was still smoking.

My heart jumped up amongst my lungs. I never waited for to look further, but uncocked my gun and went sneaking back on my tip-toes as fast as ever I could. Every now and then I stopped a second, amongst the thick leaves, and listened; but my breath come so hard I couldn't hear nothing else. I slunk along another piece further, then listened again; and so on, and so on; if I see a stump, I took it for a man; if I trod on a stick and broke it, it made me feel like a person had cut one of my breaths in two and I only got half, and the short half, too.

When I got to camp I warn't feeling very brash, there warn't much sand in my craw; but I says, this ain't no time to be fooling around. So I got all my traps into my canoe again so as to have them out of sight, and I put out the fire and scattered the ashes around to look like an old last year's camp, and then clumb a tree.

I reckon I was up in the tree two hours; but I didn't see nothing, I didn't hear nothing – I only thought I heard and seen as much as a thousand things. Well, I couldn't stay up there for ever; so at last I got down, but I kept in the thick woods and on the look-out all the time. All I could get to eat was berries and what was left over from breakfast.

By the time it was night I was pretty hungry. So when it was good and dark, I slid out from shore before moonrise and paddled over to the Illinois bank – about a quarter of a mile. I went out in the woods and cooked a supper, and I had about made up my mind I would stay there all night, when I hear a *plunkety-plunk, plunkety-plunk*, and says to myself, horses coming; and next I hear people's voices. I got everything into the canoe as quick as I could, and then went creeping through the woods to see what I could find out. I hadn't got far when I hear a man say:

'We better camp here, if we can find a good place; the horses is about beat out. Let's look around.'

I didn't wait, but shoved out and paddled away easy. I tied up in the old place, and reckoned I would sleep in the canoe.

I didn't sleep much. I couldn't, somehow, for thinking. And every time I waked up I thought somebody had me by the neck. So the sleep didn't do me no good. By-and-by I says to myself, I can't live this way; I'm agoing to find out who it is that's here on the island with me; I'll find it out or bust. Well, I felt better, right off.

So I took my paddle and slid out from shore just a step or two, and then let the canoe drop along down amongst the shadows. The moon was shining, and outside of the shadows it made it most as light as day. I poked along well on to an hour, everything still as rocks and sound asleep. Well, by this time I was most down to the foot of the island. A little ripply, cool breeze begun to blow, and that was as good as saying the night was about done. I give her a turn with the paddle and brung her nose to shore; then I got my gun and slipped out and into the edge of the woods. I set down there on a log and looked out through the leaves. I see the moon go off watch and the darkness begin to blanket the river. But in a little while I see a pale streak over the tree-tops, and knowed the day was coming. So I took my gun and slipped off towards where I had run across that camp-fire, stopping every minute or two to listen. But I hadn't no luck, somehow; I couldn't seem to find the place. But by-and-by, sure enough, I catched a glimpse of fire, away through the trees. I went for it, cautious and slow. By-and-by I was close enough to have a look, and there laid a man on the ground. It most give me the fan-tods. He had a blanket around his head, and his head was nearly in the fire. I set there behind a clump of bushes, in about six foot of him, and kept my eyes on him steady. It was getting grey daylight, now. Pretty soon he gapped, and stretched himself, and hove off the blanket, and it was Miss Watson's Jim! I bet I was glad to see him. I says:

'Hello, Jim!' and skipped out.

He bounced up and stared at me wild. Then he drops down on his knees, and puts his hands together and says:

'Doan' hurt me – don't! I hain't ever done no harm to a ghos'. I awluz liked dead people, en done all I could for 'em. You go en git in de river agin, whah you b'longs, en doan' do nuffin' to Ole Jim, 'at 'uz awluz yo' fren'.'

Well, I warn't long making him understand I warn't dead. I was ever so glad to see Jim. I warn't lonesome, now. I told him I warn't afraid of *him* telling the people where I was. I talked along, but he only set there and looked at me; never said nothing. Then I says:

'It's good daylight. Le's get breakfast. Make up your camp-fire good.'

'What's de use er makin' up de camp-fire to cook strawbries en sich truck? But you got a gun, hain't you? Den we kin git sumfin' better den strawbries.'

'Strawberries and such truck,' I says. 'Is that what you live on?'

'I couldn' git nuffin' else,' he says.

'Why, how long you been on the island, Jim?'

'I come heah de night arter you's killed.'

'What, all that time?'

'Yes-indeedy.'

'And ain't you had nothing but that kind of rubbage to eat?'

'No, sah – nuffn' else.'

'Well, you must be most starved, ain't you?'

'I reck'n I could eat a hoss. I think I could. How long you ben on de islan'?'

'Since the night I got killed.'

'No! W'y, what has you lived on? But you got a gun? Oh, yes, you got a gun. Dat's good. Now you kill sumfn' en I'll make up de fire.'

So we went over to where the canoe was, and while he built a fire in a grassy open place amongst the trees, I fetched meal and bacon and coffee, and coffee-pot and frying-pan, and sugar and tin cups, and the

nigger was set back considerable, because he reckoned it was all done with witchcraft. I catched a good big cat-fish, too, and Jim cleaned him with his knife, and fried him.

When breakfast was ready, we lolled on the grass and eat it smoking hot; Jim laid it in with all his might, for he was most about starved. Then when we had got pretty well stuffed, we laid off and lazied.

By-and-by Jim says:

'But looky here, Huck, who wuz it dat 'uz killed in dat shanty, ef it warn't you?'

Then I told him the whole thing, and he said it was smart. He said Tom Sawyer couldn't get up no better plan than what I had. Then I says:

'How do you come to be here, Jim, and how'd you get here?'

He looked pretty uneasy, and didn't say nothing for a minute. Then he says:

'Maybe I better not tell.'

'Why, Jim?'

'Well, dey's reasons. But you wouldn't tell on me ef I 'uz to tell you, would you, Huck?'

'Blamed if I would, Jim.'

'Well, I b'lieve you, Huck. I — I run *off.*'

'Jim!'

'But mind, you said you wouldn't tell — you know you said you wouldn't tell, Huck.'

'Well, I did. I said I wouldn't, and I'll stick to it. Honest *injun* I will. People would call me a low-down Ablitionist and despise me for keeping mum — but that don't make no difference. I ain't agoing to tell, and I ain't agoing back there anyways. So now, le's know all about it.'

Alfred, Lord Tennyson

THE EAGLE

Illustrated by Sue Williams

He clasps the crag with crooked hands;
Close to the sun in lonely lands,
Ringed with the azure world, he stands.

The wrinkled sea beneath him crawls;
He watches from his mountain walls,
And like a thunderbolt he falls.

Samuel Taylor Coleridge

FROM

THE RIME OF THE
ANCIENT MARINER

Illustrated by Geoff Hunt

The ancient Mariner tells of his fateful deed.

'And now there came both mist and snow,
And it grew wondrous cold:
And ice, mast-high, came floating by,
As green as emerald.

And through the drifts the snowy clifts
Did send a dismal sheen:
Nor shapes of men nor beasts we ken –
The ice was all between.

The ice was here, the ice was there,
The ice was all around:
It cracked and growled, and roared and howled,
Like noises in a swound!

At length did cross an Albatross,
Through the fog it came;
As if it had been a Christian soul,
We hailed it in God's name.

It ate the food it ne'er had eat,
And round and round it flew.
The ice did split with a thunder-fit;
The helmsman steered us through!

And a good south wind sprung up behind;
The Albatross did follow,
And every day, for food or play,
Came to the mariner's hollo!

In mist or cloud, on mast or shroud,
It perched for vespers nine;
Whiles all the night, through fog-smoke white,
Glimmered the white Moon-shine.'

'God save thee, ancient Mariner!
From the fiends, that plague thee thus! –
Why look'st thou so?' – 'With my cross-bow
I shot the ALBATROSS.'

William Shakespeare

WITCHES' CHANT

FROM
MACBETH

Illustrated by Paul Birkbeck

Round about the cauldron go:
In the poisoned entrails throw.
Toad, that under cold stone
Days and nights has thirty-one
Sweated venom sleeping got,
Boil thou first in the charmèd pot.
  Double, double toil and trouble;
  Fire burn and cauldron bubble.

Fillet of a fenny snake,
In the cauldron boil and bake;
Eye of newt and toe of frog,
Wool of bat and tongue of dog,
Adder's fork and blindworm's sting,
Lizard's leg and owlet's wing.
For a charm of powerful trouble,
Like a hell-broth boil and bubble.
  Double, double toil and trouble;
  Fire burn and cauldron bubble.

224

Scale of dragon, tooth of wolf,
Witch's mummy, maw and gulf
Of the ravenous salt-sea shark,
Root of hemlock digged in the dark,
Make the gruel thick and slab:
Add thereto a tiger's chaudron,
For the ingredients of our cauldron.
　Double, double toil and trouble,
　Fire burn and cauldron bubble.

George MacDonald

FROM

THE PRINCESS AND THE GOBLIN

Illustrated by Mark Robertson

*Curdie, a friend of Princess Irene, learns two important things
about the fiendish goblins who live below the mountain.*

For some time Curdie worked away briskly, throwing all the ore he had disengaged on one side behind him, to be ready for carrying out in the morning. He heard a good deal of goblin-tapping, but it all sounded far away in the hill, and he paid it little heed. Towards midnight he began to feel rather hungry; so he dropped his pickaxe, got out a lump of bread which in the morning he had laid in a damp hole in the rock, sat down on a heap of ore, and ate his supper. Then he leaned back for five minutes' rest before beginning his work again, and laid his head against the rock. He had not kept the position for one minute before he heard something which made him sharpen his ears. It sounded like a voice inside the rock. After a while he heard it again. It was a goblin voice – there could be no doubt about that – and this time he could make out the words.

'Hadn't we better be moving?' it said.

A rougher and deeper voice replied:

'There's no hurry. That wretched little mole won't be through tonight, if he work ever so hard. He's not by any means at the thinnest place.'

'But you still think the lode does come through into our house?' said the first voice.

'Yes, but a good bit farther on than he has got to yet. If he had struck a stroke more to the side just here,' said the goblin, tapping the very stone, as it seemed to Curdie, against which his head lay, 'he would have been through; but he's a couple of yards past it now, and if he follow the lode it will be a week before it leads him in. You see it back there – a long way. Still, perhaps, in case of accident it would be as well to be getting out of this. Helfer, you'll take the great chest. That's your business, you know.'

'Yes, dad,' said a third voice. 'But you must help me to get it on my back. It's awfully heavy, you know.'

'Well, it isn't just a bag of smoke, I admit. But you're as strong as a mountain, Helfer.'

'You say so, dad. I think myself I'm all right. But I could carry ten times as much if it wasn't for my feet.'

'That *is* your weak point, I confess, my boy.'

'Ain't it yours too, father?'

'Well, to be honest, it is a goblin weakness. Why *they* come so soft, I declare I haven't an idea.'

'Specially when your head's so hard, you know, father.'

'Yes, my boy. The goblin's glory is his head. To think how the fellows up above there have to put on helmets and things when they go fighting! Ha! ha!'

'But why don't we wear shoes like them, father? I should like it – especially when I've got a chest like that on my head.'

'Well, you see, it's not the fashion. The king never wears shoes.'

'The queen does.'

'Yes; but that's for distinction. The first queen, you see – I mean the king's first wife – wore shoes, of course, because she came from upstairs; and so, when she died, the next queen would not be inferior to her as she called it, and would wear shoes too. It was all pride. She is the hardest in forbidding them to the rest of the women.'

'I'm sure I wouldn't wear them – no, not for – that I wouldn't!' said the first voice, which was evidently that of the mother of the family. 'I can't think why either of them should.'

'Didn't I tell you the first was from upstairs?' said the other. 'That was the only silly thing I ever knew His Majesty guilty of. Why should he marry an outlandish woman like that – one of our natural enemies too?'

'I suppose he fell in love with her.'

'Pooh! pooh! He's just as happy now with one of his own people.'

'Did she die *very* soon? They didn't tease her to death, did they?'

'Oh, dear, no! The king worshipped her very footmarks.'

'What made her die, then? Didn't the air agree with her?'

'She died when the young prince was born.'

'How silly of her! *We* never do that. It must have been because she wore shoes.'

'I don't know that.'

'Why do they wear shoes up there?'

'Ah, now that's a sensible question, and I will answer it. But in order to do so, I must first tell you a secret. I once saw the queen's feet.'

'Without her shoes?'

'Yes – without her shoes.'

'No! Did you? How was it?'

'Never you mind how it was. *She* didn't know I saw them. And what do you think! – they had *toes*!'

'Toes! What's that?'

'You may well ask! I should never have known if I had not seen the queen's feet. Just imagine! the ends of her feet were split up into five or six thin pieces!'

'Oh, horrid! How *could* the king have fallen in love with her?'

'You forget that she wore shoes. That is just why she wore them. That is why all the men, and women too, upstairs wear shoes. They can't bear the sight of their own feet without them.'

'Ah! now I understand. If ever you wish for shoes again, Helfer, I'll hit your feet – I will.'

'No, no, mother; pray don't.'

'Then don't you.'

'But with such a big box on my head –'

A horrid scream followed, which Curdie interpreted as in reply to a blow from his mother upon the feet of her eldest goblin.

'Well, I never knew so much before!' remarked a fourth voice.

'Your knowledge is not universal quite yet,' said the father. 'You were only fifty last month. Mind you see to the bed and bedding. As soon as we've finished our supper, we'll be up and going. Ha! ha! ha!'

'What are you laughing at, husband?'

'I'm laughing to think what a mess the miners will find themselves in – somewhere before this day ten years.'

'Why, what do you mean?'

'Oh, nothing.'

'Oh, yes, you do mean something. You always do mean something.'

'It's more than you do, then, wife.'

'That may be; but it's not more than I find out, you know.'

'Ha! ha! You're a sharp one. What a mother you've got, Helfer!'

'Yes, father.'

'Well, I suppose I must tell you. They're all at the palace consulting about it tonight; and as soon as we've got away from this thin place I'm going

230

there to hear what night they fix upon. I should like to see that young ruffian there on the other side, struggling in the agonies of –'

He dropped his voice so low that Curdie could hear only a growl. The growl went on in the low bass for a good while, as inarticulate as if the goblin's tongue had been a sausage; and it was not until his wife spoke again that it rose to its former pitch.

'But what shall we do when you are at the palace?' she asked.

'I will see you safe in the new house I've been digging for you for the last two months. Podge, you mind the table and chairs. I commit them to your care. The table has seven legs – each chair three. I shall require them all at your hands.'

After this arose a confused conversation about the various household goods and their transport; and Curdie heard nothing more that was of any importance.

He now knew at least one of the reasons for the constant sound of the goblin hammers and pickaxes at night. They were making new houses for themselves, to which they might retreat when the miners should threaten to break into their dwellings. But he had learned two things of far greater importance. The first was, that some grievous calamity was preparing, and almost ready to fall upon the heads of the miners; the second was – the one weak point of a goblin's body; he had not known that their feet were so tender as he had now reason to suspect. He had heard it said that they had no toes: he had never had opportunity of inspecting them closely enough, in the dusk in which they always appeared, to satisfy himself whether it was a correct report. Indeed, he had not been able even to satisfy himself as to whether they had no fingers, although that also was commonly said to be the fact. One of the miners, indeed, who had had more schooling than the rest, was wont to argue that such must have been the primordial condition of humanity, and that education and handicraft had developed both toes and fingers – with which proposition Curdie had once heard his father sarcastically agree, alleging in support of it the probability that babies' gloves were a traditional remnant of the old state of things;

while the stockings of all ages, no regard being paid in them to the toes, pointed in the same direction. But what was of importance was the fact concerning the softness of the goblin feet, which he foresaw might be useful to all miners. What he had to do in the meantime, however, was to discover, if possible, the special evil design the goblins had now in their heads.

Although he knew all the gangs and all the natural galleries with which they communicated in the mined part of the mountain, he had not the least idea where the palace of the king of the gnomes was; otherwise he would have set out at once on the enterprise of discovering what the said design was. He judged, and rightly, that it must lie in a farther part of the mountain, between which and the mine there was as yet no communication. There must be one nearly completed, however; for it could be but a thin partition which now separated them. If only he could get through in time to follow the goblins as they retreated! A few blows would doubtless be sufficient – just where his ear now lay; but if he attempted to strike there with his pickaxe, he would only hasten the departure of the family, put them on their guard, and perhaps lose their involuntary guidance. He therefore began to feel the wall with his hands, and soon found that some of the stones were loose enough to be drawn out with little noise.

Laying hold of a large one with both his hands, he drew it gently out, and let it down softly.

'What was that noise?' said the goblin father.

Curdie blew out his light, lest it should shine through.

'It must be that one miner that stayed behind the rest,' said the mother.

'No; he's been gone a good while. I haven't heard a blow for an hour. Besides, it wasn't like that.'

'Then I suppose it must have been a stone carried down the brook inside.'

'Perhaps. It will have more room by and by.'

Curdie kept quite still. After a little while, hearing nothing but the

sounds of their preparations for departure, mingled with an occasional word of direction, and anxious to know whether the removal of the stone had made an opening into the goblins' house, he put in his hand to feel. It went in a good way, and then came in contact with something soft. He had but a moment to feel it over, it was so quickly withdrawn: it was one of the toeless goblin feet. The owner of it gave a cry of fright.

'What's the matter, Helfer?' asked his mother.

'A beast came out of the wall and licked my foot.'

'Nonsense! There are no wild beasts in our country,' said his father.

'But it was, father. I felt it.'

'Nonsense, I say. Will you malign your native realms and reduce them to a level with the country upstairs? That is swarming with wild beasts of every description.'

'But I did feel it, father.'

'I tell you to hold your tongue. You are no patriot.'

Curdie suppressed his laughter, and lay still as a mouse – but no stiller, for every moment he kept nibbling away with his fingers at the edges of the hole. He was slowly making it bigger, for here the rock had been very much shattered with the blasting.

There seemed to be a good many in the family, to judge from the mass of confused talk which now and then came through the hole; but when all were speaking together, and just as if they had bottle-brushes – each at least one – in their throats, it was not easy to make out much that was said. At length he heard once more what the father goblin was saying.

'Now, then,' he said, 'get your bundles on your backs. Here, Helfer, I'll help you up with your chest.'

'I wish it *was* my chest, father.'

'Your turn will come in good time enough! Make haste. I *must* go to the meeting at the palace tonight. When that's over, we can come back and clear out the last of the things before our enemies return in the morning. Now light your torches, and come along. What a distinction it is to provide our own light, instead of being dependent on a thing hung up in the air – a most disagreeable contrivance – intended no doubt to blind us when we venture out under its baleful influence! Quite glaring and vulgar, I call it, though no doubt useful to poor creatures who haven't the wit to make light for themselves!'

Curdie could hardly keep himself from calling through to know whether they made the fire to light their torches by. But a moment's reflection showed him that they would have said they did, inasmuch as they struck two stones together, and the fire came.

Christina Rossetti

WHAT IS PINK?

Illustrated by Ruth Rivers

What is pink? A rose is pink
By the fountain's brink.
What is red? A poppy's red
In its barley bed.
What is blue? The sky is blue
Where the clouds float through.
What is white? A swan is white
Sailing in the light.
What is yellow? Pears are yellow,
Rich and ripe and mellow.
What is green? The grass is green,
With small flowers between.
What is violet? Clouds are violet
In the summer twilight.
What is orange? Why, an orange,
Just an orange!

As Good as His Word

FROM

AESOP'S FABLES

Illustrated by James Marsh

Aesop was a storyteller in the sixth century BC. *His animal fables have survived the centuries, and many are so well known they have given us phrases we use every day.*

A mouse ran over the body of a sleeping lion. Waking up, the lion seized it and was minded to eat it. But when the mouse begged to be released, promising to repay him if he would spare it, he laughed and let it go. Not long afterwards its gratitude was the means of saving his life. Being captured by hunters, he was tied by a rope to a tree. The mouse heard his groans, and running to the spot freed him by gnawing through the rope. 'You laughed at me the other day,' it said, 'because you did not expect me to repay your kindness. Now you see that even mice are grateful.'

A change of fortune can make the strongest person need a weaker person's help.

Mary Shelley

FROM

FRANKENSTEIN

Illustrated by Richard Jones

It was on a dreary night of November that I beheld the accomplishment of my toils. With an anxiety that almost amounted to agony, I collected the instruments of life around me, that I might infuse a spark of being into the lifeless thing that lay at my feet. It was already one in the morning; the rain pattered dismally against the panes, and my candle was nearly burnt out, when, by the glimmer of the half-extinguished light, I saw the dull yellow eye of the creature open; it breathed hard, and a convulsive motion agitated its limbs.

How can I describe my emotions at this catastrophe, or how delineate the wretch whom with such infinite pains and care I had endeavoured to form? His limbs were in proportion, and I had selected his features as beautiful. Beautiful! Great God! His yellow skin scarcely covered the work of muscles and arteries beneath; his hair was of a lustrous black, and flowing; his teeth of pearly whiteness; but these luxuriances only formed a more horrid contrast with his watery eyes,

238

that seemed almost of the same colour as the dun-white sockets in which they were set, his shrivelled complexion and straight black lips.

The different accidents of life are not so changeable as the feelings of human nature. I had worked hard for nearly two years, for the sole purpose of infusing life into an inanimate body. For this I had deprived myself of rest and health. I had desired it with an ardour that far exceeded moderation; but now that I had finished, the beauty of the dream vanished, and breathless horror and disgust filled my heart. Unable to endure the aspect of the being I had created, I rushed out of the room and continued a long time traversing my bedchamber, unable to compose my mind to sleep. At length lassitude succeeded to the tumult I had before endured, and I threw myself on the bed in my clothes, endeavouring to seek a few moments of forgetfulness. But it was in vain; I slept, indeed, but I was disturbed by the wildest dreams. I thought I saw Elizabeth, in the bloom of health, walking in the streets of Ingolstadt. Delighted and surprised, I embraced her, but as I imprinted the first kiss on her lips, they became livid with the hue of death; her features appeared to change, and I thought that I held the corpse of my dead mother in my arms; a shroud enveloped her form, and I saw the grave-worms crawling in the folds of the flannel. I started from my sleep with horror; a cold dew covered my forehead, my teeth chattered, and every limb became convulsed; when, by the dim and yellow light of the moon, as it forced its way through the window shutters, I beheld the wretch – the miserable monster whom I had created. He held up the curtain of the bed; and his eyes, if eyes they may be called, were fixed on me. His jaws opened, and he muttered some inarticulate sounds, while a grin wrinkled his cheeks. He might have spoken, but I did not hear; one hand was stretched out, seemingly to detain me, but I escaped and rushed downstairs. I took refuge in the courtyard belonging to the house which I inhabited, where I remained during the rest of the night, walking up and down in the greatest agitation, listening attentively, catching and fearing each sound as if it were to announce the approach of the daemoniacal corpse to which I had so miserably given life.

Oh! No mortal could support the horror of that countenance. A mummy again endued with animation could not be so hideous as that wretch. I had gazed on him while unfinished; he was ugly then, but when those muscles and joints were rendered capable of motion, it became a thing such as even Dante could not have conceived.

I passed the night wretchedly. Sometimes my pulse beat so quickly and hardly that I felt the palpitation of every artery; at others, I nearly sank to the ground through languor and extreme weakness. Mingled with this horror, I felt the bitterness of disappointment; dreams that had been my food and pleasant rest for so long a space were now become a hell to me; and the change was so rapid, the overthrow so complete!

Morning, dismal and wet, at length dawned and discovered to my sleepless and aching eyes the church of Ingolstadt, its white steeple and clock, which indicated the sixth hour. The porter opened the gates of the court, which had that night been my asylum, and I issued into the streets, pacing them with quick steps, as if I sought to avoid the wretch

whom I feared every turning of the street would present to my view. I did not dare return to the apartment which I inhabited, but felt impelled to hurry on, although drenched by the rain which poured from a black and comfortless sky.

I continued walking in this manner for some time, endeavouring by bodily exercise to ease the load that weighed upon my mind. I traversed the streets without any clear conception of where I was or what I was doing. My heart palpitated in the sickness of fear, and I hurried on with irregular steps, not daring to look about me:

> Like one, that on a lonesome road
>   Doth walk in fear and dread,
> And having once turned round walks on,
>   And turns no more his head;
> Because he knows, a frightful fiend
>   Doth close behind him tread.

Continuing thus, I came at length opposite to the inn at which the various diligences and carriages usually stopped. Here I paused, I knew not why; but I remained some minutes with my eyes fixed on a coach that was coming towards me from the other end of the street. As it drew nearer I observed that it was the Swiss diligence; it stopped just where I was standing, and on the door being opened, I perceived Henry Clerval, who, on seeing me, instantly sprung out. 'My dear Frankenstein,' exclaimed he, 'how glad I am to see you! How fortunate that you should be here at the very moment of my alighting!'

Nothing could equal my delight on seeing Clerval; his presence brought back to my thoughts my father, Elizabeth, and all those scenes of home so dear to my recollection. I grasped his hand, and in a moment forgot my horror and misfortune; I felt suddenly, and for the first time during many months, calm and serene joy. I welcomed my friend, therefore, in the most cordial manner, and we walked towards my college. Clerval continued talking for some time about our mutual friends and his own good fortune in being permitted to come to Ingolstadt. 'You may easily believe,' said he, 'how great was the difficulty to persuade my father that all necessary knowledge was not comprised in the noble art of bookkeeping; and, indeed, I believe I left him incredulous to the last, for his constant answer to my unwearied intreaties was the same as that to the Dutch schoolmaster in *The Vicar of Wakefield*: "I have ten thousand florins a year without Greek, I eat heartily without Greek." But his affection for me at length overcame his dislike of learning, and he has permitted me to undertake a voyage of discovery to the land of knowledge.'

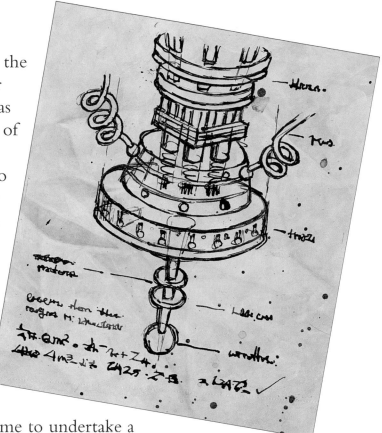

'It gives me the greatest delight to see you; but tell me how you left my father, brothers, and Elizabeth.'

'Very well, and very happy, only a little uneasy that they hear from you so seldom. By the bye, I mean to lecture you a little upon their account myself. But, my dear Frankenstein,' continued he, stopping short and gazing full in my face, 'I did not before remark how very ill you appear; so thin and pale; and look as if you had been watching for several nights.'

'You have guessed right; I have lately been so deeply engaged in one occupation that I have not allowed myself sufficient rest, as you see; but I hope, I sincerely hope, that all these employments are now at an end and that I am at length free.'

I trembled excessively; I could not endure to think of, and far less to allude to, the occurrences of the preceding night. I walked with a quick pace, and we soon arrived at my college. I then reflected, and the thought made me shiver, that the creature whom I had left in my apartment might still be there, alive and walking about. I dreaded to behold this monster, but I feared still more that Henry should see him. Intreating him, therefore, to remain a few minutes at the bottom of the stairs, I darted up towards my own room. My hand was already on the lock of the door before I recollected myself. I then paused, and a cold shivering came over me. I threw the door forcibly open, as children are accustomed to do when they expect a spectre to stand in waiting for them on the other side; but nothing appeared. I stepped fearfully in: the apartment was empty, and my bedroom was also freed from its hideous guest. I could hardly believe that so great a good fortune could have befallen me, but when I became assured that my enemy had indeed fled, I clapped my hands for joy and ran down to Clerval.

We ascended into my room, and the servant presently brought breakfast; but I was unable to contain myself. It was not joy only that possessed me; I felt my flesh tingle with excess of sensitiveness, and my pulse beat rapidly. I was unable to remain for a single instant in the same place; I jumped over the chairs, clapped my hands, and laughed aloud. Clerval at first attributed my unusual spirits to joy on his arrival, but when he observed me more attentively, he saw a wildness in my eyes for which he could not account, and my loud, unrestrained, heartless laughter frightened and astonished him.

'My dear Victor,' cried he, 'what, for God's sake, is the matter? Do not laugh in that manner. How ill you are! What is the cause of all this?'

'Do not ask me,' cried I, putting my hands before my eyes, for I thought I saw the dreaded spectre glide into the room; '*he* can tell. Oh, save me! Save me!' I imagined that the monster seized me; I struggled furiously and fell down in a fit.

Poor Clerval! What must have been his feelings? A meeting, which he anticipated with such joy, so strangely turned to bitterness. But I was not the witness of his grief, for I was lifeless and did not recover my senses for a long, long time.

This was the commencement of a nervous fever which confined me for several months. During all that time Henry was my only nurse. I afterwards learned that, knowing my father's advanced age and unfitness for so long a journey, and how wretched my sickness would make Elizabeth, he spared them this grief by concealing the extent of my disorder. He knew that I could not have a more kind and attentive nurse than himself; and, firm in the hope he felt of my recovery, he did not doubt that, instead of doing harm, he performed the kindest action that he could towards them.

But I was in reality very ill, and surely nothing but the unbounded and unremitting attentions of my friend could have restored me to life. The form of the monster on whom I had bestowed existence was forever before my eyes, and I raved incessantly concerning him. Doubtless my words surprised Henry; he at first believed them to be the wanderings of my disturbed imagination, but the pertinacity with which I continually recurred to the same subject persuaded him that my disorder indeed owed its origin to some uncommon and terrible event.

Daniel Defoe

ROBINSON CRUSOE

Illustrated by Adrian Chesterman

The sole survivor of a shipwreck, Robinson Crusoe has no human contact for over twenty-five years – until one Friday he rescues a prisoner.

About a year and a half after I had entertained these notions, I was surprised one morning early, with seeing no less than five canoes all on shore together on my side of the island; and the people who belonged to them all landed, and out of my sight. The number of them broke all my measures, for seeing so many, and knowing that they always came four or six, or sometimes more in a boat, I could not tell what to think of it, or how to attack twenty or thirty men single-handed; so I lay still in my castle, perplexed and discomforted; however, I put myself into all the same postures for an attack that I had formerly provided, and was just ready for action, if anything had presented. Having waited a good while, listening to hear if they made any noise, at length, being very impatient, I set my guns at the foot of my ladder, and clambered up to the top of the hill; standing so, however, that my head did not appear above the hill, so that they could not perceive me by any means; here I observed, by the help of my perspective-glass, that they were no less

248

than thirty in number, that they had a fire kindled, that they had had meat dressed. How they cooked it, that I knew not, or what it was; but they were all dancing in I know not how many barbarous gestures and figures, their own way, round the fire.

While I was thus looking on them, I perceived two miserable wretches dragged from the boats, where it seems they were laid by, and were now brought out for the slaughter. I perceived one of them immediately fall, being knocked down, I suppose with a club or wooden sword, for that was their way, and two or three others were at work immediately cutting him open for their cookery, while the other victim was left standing by himself, till they should be ready for him. In that very moment this poor wretch seeing himself a little at liberty, nature inspired him with hopes of life, and he started away from them, and ran with incredible swiftness along the sands directly towards me, I mean towards that part of the coast where my habitation was.

I was dreadfully frightened (that I must acknowledge) when I perceived him to run my way, and especially when, as I thought, I saw him pursued by the whole body; and now I expected that part of my dream was coming to pass, and that he would certainly take shelter in my grove; but I could not depend by any means upon my dream for the rest of it – that the other savages would not pursue him thither, and find him there. However, I kept my station, and my spirits began to recover when I found that only three men followed him, and still more was I encouraged when I found that he outstripped them exceedingly in running, and gained ground of them, so that if he could but hold it for half an hour, I saw easily he would fairly get away from them all.

There was between them and my castle the creek which I mentioned at the first part of my story; and this, I saw plainly, he must necessarily swim over, or the poor wretch would be taken there. But when the savage escaping came thither, he made nothing of it, though the tide was then up, but plunging in, swam through in about thirty strokes or thereabouts, landed, and ran on with exceeding strength and swiftness; when the three persons came to the creek, I found that two of them could swim, but the third could not, and that standing on the other side, he looked at the other, but went no further, and soon after went softly back again, which, as it happened, was very well for him in the main.

I observed that the two who swam were yet more than twice as long swimming over the creek as the fellow was that fled from them. It came now very warmly upon my thought, and indeed irresistibly, that now was my time to get me a servant, and perhaps a companion or assistant; and that I was called plainly by Providence to save this poor creature's life; I immediately ran down the ladders with all possible expedition, fetched my two guns, for they were both but at the foot of the ladders, as I observed above; and getting up again, with the same haste, to the top of the hill, I crossed toward the sea; and having a very short cut, and all downhill, thrust myself in the way between the pursuers and the pursued; shouting aloud to him that fled, who looking back, was at first perhaps as much frightened at me as at them; but I beckoned with my hand to him to come back; and in the meantime, I slowly advanced towards the two that followed; then rushing at once upon the foremost, I knocked him down with the stock of my piece; I was loath to fire, because I would not have the rest hear; though at that distance it would not have been easily heard, and being out of sight of the smoke too, they would not have easily known what to make of it. Having knocked this fellow down, the other who pursued with him stopped, as if he had been frighted; and I advanced apace towards him; but as I came nearer, I perceived he had a bow and

arrow, and was fitting it to shoot at me; so I was then necessitated to shoot at him first, which I did, and killed him at the first shot; the poor savage who fled, but had stopped, though he saw both his enemies fallen and killed, as he thought, yet was so frightened with the fire and noise of my piece, that he stood stock still, and neither came forward or went backward, though he seemed rather inclined to fly still than to come on; I called again to him, and made signs to come forward, which he easily understood, and came a little way, then stopped again, and then a little further, and stopped again, and I could then perceive that he stood trembling, as if he had been taken prisoner, and had just been to be killed, as his two enemies were. I beckoned him again to come to me, and gave him all the signs of encouragement that I could think of, and he came nearer and nearer, kneeling down every ten or twelve steps in token of acknowledgement for my saving his life. I smiled at him, and looked pleasantly, and beckoned to him to come still nearer; at length he came close to me, and then he kneeled down again, kissed the ground, and laid his head upon the ground, and taking me by the foot, set my foot upon his head; this it seems was in token of swearing to be my slave for ever; I took him up, and made much of him, and encouraged him all I could. But there was more work to do yet, for I perceived the savage who I knocked down was not killed, but stunned with the blow, and began to come to himself; so I pointed to him, and showing him the savage, that he was not dead; upon this he spoke some words to me, and though I could not understand them, yet I thought they were pleasant to hear, for they were the first sound of a man's voice that I had heard, my own excepted, for above twenty-five years. But there was no time for such reflections now; the savage who was knocked down recovered himself so far as to sit up upon the ground, and I perceived that my savage began to be afraid; but when I saw that, I presented my other piece at the man, as if I would shoot him; upon this my savage, for so I call him now, made a motion to me to lend him my sword, which hung naked in a belt by my side; so I did: he no sooner had it, but he runs to his enemy, and at one blow cut off his head as cleverly, no executioner could have done it sooner or better; which I thought very strange, for one who I had reason to believe never saw a sword in his life before, except their own wooden swords; however, it seems, as I learned afterwards, they make their wooden swords so sharp, so heavy, and the wood is so hard, that they will cut off heads even with them, ay and arms, and that at one blow too; when he had done this, he comes laughing to me in sign of triumph, and brought me the sword again, and with abundance of gestures which I did not understand, laid it down with the head of the savage that he had killed, just before me.

But that which astonished him most, was to know how I had killed the other Indian so far off; so pointing to him, he made signs to me to let him go to him, so I bade him go, as well as I could; when he came to him, he stood like one amazed, looking at him, turned him first on one side, then on t'other, looked at the wound the bullet had made, which it seems was just in his breast, where it had made a hole, and no great quantity of blood had followed, but he had bled inwardly, for he was quite dead. He took up his bow and arrows, and came back, so I turned to go away, and beckoned to him to follow me, making signs to him that more might come after him.

Upon this he signed to me that he should bury them with sand, that they might not be seen by the rest if they followed; and so I made signs again to him to do so; he fell to work, and in an instant he had scraped a hole in the sand with his hands, big enough to bury the first in, and then dragged him into it, and covered him, and did so also by the other; I believe he had buried them both in a quarter of an hour; then calling him away, I took him not to my castle, but quite away to my cave, on the farther part of the island; so I did not let my dream come to pass in that part, that he came into my grove for shelter.

Here I gave him bread, and a bunch of raisins to eat, and a draught of water, which I found he was indeed in great distress for, by his running; and having refreshed him, I made signs for him to go lie down and sleep; pointing to a place where I had laid a great parcel of rice straw, and a blanket upon it, which I used to sleep upon myself sometimes; so the poor creature laid down, and went to sleep.

He was a comely handsome fellow, perfectly well made; with straight, strong limbs, not too large; tall and well shaped, and, as I reckon, about twenty-six years of age. He had a very good countenance, not a fierce and surly aspect; his hair was long and black, not curled like wool; his forehead very high and large, and a great vivacity and sparkling sharpness in his eyes. The colour of his skin was not quite

black, but very tawny; his face was round and plump; his nose small, not flat like the negroes, a very good mouth, thin lips, and his fine teeth well set, and white as ivory. After he had slumbered, rather than slept, about half an hour, he waked again, and comes out of the cave to me; for I had been milking the goats, which I had in the enclosure just by; when he espied me, he came running to me, laying himself down again upon the ground, with all the possible signs of an humble thankful disposition, making many gestures to show it. At last he lays his head flat upon the ground, close to my foot, and sets my other foot upon his head, as he had done before; and after this, made all the signs to me of subjection, servitude, and submission imaginable, to let me know how he would serve me as long as he lived. I understood him in many things, and let him know I was very well pleased with him; in a little time I began to speak to him, and teach him to speak to me; and first, I made him know his name should be Friday, which was the day I saved his life.

Henry Wadsworth Longfellow

HIAWATHA'S CHILDHOOD

FROM

THE SONG OF HIAWATHA

Illustrated by Sue Williams

Then the little Hiawatha
Learned of every bird its language,
Learned their names and all their secrets:
How they built their nests in Summer,
Where they hid themselves in Winter,
Talked with them whene'er he met them,
Called them 'Hiawatha's Chickens'.

Of all the beasts he learned the language,
Learned their names and all their secrets,
How the beavers built their lodges,
How the squirrels hid their acorns,
How the reindeer ran so swiftly,
Why the rabbit was so timid;
Talked with them whene'er he met them,
Called them 'Hiawatha's Brothers'.

Then Iagoo, the great boaster,
He the marvellous story-teller,
He the traveller and the talker,
He the friend of old Nokomis,
Made a bow for Hiawatha:
From a branch of ash he made it,
From an oak-bough made the arrows,
Tipped with flint, and winged with feathers,
And the cord he made of deer-skin.

256

Then he said to Hiawatha:
'Go, my son, into the forest,
Where the red deer herd together,
Kill for us a famous roebuck,
Kill for us a deer with antlers!'

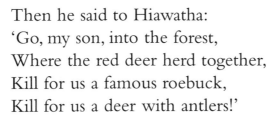

Forth into the forest straightway
All alone walked Hiawatha
Proudly, with his bows and arrows;
And the birds sang round him, o'er him,
'Do not shoot us, Hiawatha!'
Sang the robin, the Opechee,
Sang the bluebird, the Owaissa,
'Do not shoot us, Hiawatha!'

Up the oak-tree, close beside him,
Sprang the squirrel, Adjidaumo,
In and out among the branches,
Coughed and chattered from the oak-tree,
Laughed, and said between his laughing,
'Do not shoot me, Hiawatha!'

And the rabbit from his pathway
Leaped aside, and at a distance
Sat erect upon his haunches,
Half in fear and half in frolic,
Saying to the little hunter,
'Do not shoot me, Hiawatha!'

But he heeded not, nor heard them,
For his thoughts were with the red deer;
On their tracks his eyes were fastened,
Leading downward to the river,
To the ford across the river,
And as one in slumber walked he.

Hidden in the alder-bushes,
There he waited till the deer came,
Till he saw two antlers lifted,
Saw two eyes look from the thicket,
Saw two nostrils point to windward,

And a deer came down the pathway,
Flecked with leafy light and shadow;
And his heart within him fluttered,
Trembled like the leaves above him,
Like the birch-leaf palpitated,
As the deer came down the pathway.

Then, upon one knee uprising,
Hiawatha aimed an arrow;
Scarce a twig moved with his motion,
Scarce a leaf was stirred or rustled,
But the wary roebuck started,
Stamped with all his hoofs together,
Listened with one foot uplifted,
Leaped as if to meet the arrow;
 Ah the singing, fatal arrow,
 Like a wasp it buzzed and stung him.

258

Dead he lay there in the forest
By the ford across the river;
Beat his timid heart no longer;
But the heart of Hiawatha
Throbbed and shouted and exulted,
As he bore the red deer homeward;
But Iagoo and Nokomis
Hailed his coming with applauses.

From the red deer's hide, Nokomis
Made a cloak for Hiawatha;
From the deer's flesh Nokomis
Made a banquet in his honour.
All the village came and feasted,
All the guests praised Hiawatha,
Called him Strong-Heart, Soan-getaha!
Called him Loon-heart, Mahn-go-taysee!

Sir Gawain and the Green Knight

From

King Arthur and His Knights of the Round Table

Illustrated by Greg Becker

King Arthur's adventures did not end when he had defeated the Saxons and brought peace to Britain: for though he had set up the Realm of Logres — the land of true good and piety, nobleness and right living — the evil was always breaking in to attack the good. It would need many books to tell of every adventure that befell during his reign — that brief period of light set like a star of Heaven in the midst of the Dark Ages: and we cannot, for example, tell here how Arthur himself fought with the Giant of St Michael's Mount who carried off helpless wayfarers to his dark and evil castle; nor how he made war against the Emperor Lucius and was received in Rome; nor even of his fight with the dreadful Cat of Losane.

But year by year the fame of his court grew, and spread far and wide, and the bravest and noblest knights in the world came to his court and strove by their deeds of courage and gentleness to win a place at the Round Table.

Many stories are told of these knights also – of Launcelot and Gawain, of Tristram and Gareth, of Percivale, Ywain, Marhaus, Cleges, Agravaine, and many, many others – and more adventures that befell the most famous of these than may possibly be told in one book.

One of the first and bravest of the knights was Sir Gawain – and it was said indeed that only Sir Launcelot, Sir Galahad, and Sir Percivale could surpass him. He had many exciting adventures: but now only one of them can be told.

King Arthur held his Christmas feast at Camelot one year, with all the bravest of his knights about him, and all the fairest ladies of his court – and his chief celebrations fell upon New Year's Day. Queen Guinevere, clad in fair, shining silk, sat beneath an embroidered canopy studded with gems: fair was she to look upon, with her shining eyes of grey, and each knight bent in reverence before her ere he took his place. Beside her sat King Arthur, well pleased to see the noble gathering and the joy that was in the hall: but he would not begin the feast, for such his custom was, until he had been told of some knightly deed, or set before his knights some strange or terrible new quest.

The minstrels had stopped playing and the whole company sat quietly in the great hall, only the roar and crackle of the log fires in the wide hearths breaking the silence – when suddenly there rang out the clash and clang of iron-shod hoofs striking upon stone: the great doors flew open, and into the hall rode a strange and terrible figure.

A great man it was, riding upon a huge horse: a strong-limbed, great-handed man, so tall that an earth-giant almost he seemed. Yet he

261

rode as a knight should, though without armour, and his face, though fierce, was fair to see – but the greatest wonder was that he was green all over. A jerkin and cloak of green he wore above green hose gartered in green, with golden spurs; in the green belt round his waist jewels were set, and his green saddle was inlaid richly, as were also his trappings. But his hair, hanging low to his shoulders, was bright green, and his beard also; green was his face and green his hands; and the horse was also green from head to foot, with gold thread wound and knotted in the mane.

He had no weapons nor shield save for a great axe of green steel and gold, and a bough torn from a holly tree held above his head. He flung the branch upon the inlaid floor of the hall and looked proudly on every side; at the knights seated about the Round Table, and the ladies and squires at the boards on either side, and at Arthur where he sat with Guinevere above the rest. Then he cried in a great voice:

'Where is the governor of this gang? With him would I speak and with none other!'

All sat in amazement gazing at the strange knight: some dire enchantment it must be, they thought – for how else could there be such a man sitting there on his horse, as green as the grass – greener than any grass on this earth?

But at length Arthur, courteous ever, greeted the Green Knight, bade him be welcome and sit down to the feast with them.

'Not so!' cried the stranger in answer. 'I come not to tarry with you: and by the sign of the green bough I come not in war – else had I clothed me in armour and helmet most sure – for such have I richly stored in my castle in the north. But even in that land have I heard of the fame and valour of your court – the bravery of your knights, and their high virtue also.'

'Sir,' replied the King, 'here may you find many to do battle and joust if such be your will.'

'Not so,' cried the Green Knight in his great booming voice. 'Here I see only beardless children whom I could fell with a stroke! Nay, I come rather in this high season of Our Lord's birth to bring Yule-tide

sport, a test of valour to your feast. If any man in this hall is so brave and so courageous as to exchange stroke for stroke, I will give him this noble axe – heavy enough truly to handle as he may desire: yes, and I myself will stand here on the floor and receive the first stroke of the axe wherever he may smite me. Only he must swear, and you, lord king, to give me the right to deal him such another blow, if I may, a twelve-month and a day from now.'

More silent still sat the knights; if they had been surprised before now their amazement was greater still. But none dared answer his challenge, so terrible was the man and so fearsome the great axe which he held in his hand.

Then the Green Knight laughed aloud in mockery: 'Is this indeed the Court of King Arthur?' he cried, 'and are these the far-famed Knights of the Round Table? Now is their glory laid low for ever, since even to hear tell of blows makes them all grow silent in fear!'

King Arthur sprang up at this. 'Fellow,' he cried, 'this foolishness of yours shall have a fitting answer. If none other will take your challenge, give me the axe and make ready for the blow!'

But at this Sir Gawain rose to his feet and said:

'My lord king and noble uncle, grant me a boon! Let this adventure be mine, for still there is my old shame unhealed: still have I to prove my worth as a Knight of your Round Table, still to fit myself to be a champion of Logres.'

'Right happy I am that the quest shall be yours, dear nephew,' answered Arthur. And the Green Knight smiled grimly as he sprang from his horse and met with Gawain in the middle of the hall.

'I too am overjoyed to find one brave man amongst you all,' he said. 'Tell me your name, Sir knight, ere we make our bargain.'

'I am Gawain, son of King Lot of Orkney, and nephew to royal Arthur,' was the answer. 'And here I swear by my knighthood to strike but one blow, and bravely to endure such another if you may

264

strike it me a twelve-month hence.'

'Sir Gawain,' cried the Green Knight, 'overjoyed am I indeed that your hand shall strike this blow. Come now and deal the stroke: thereafter shall I tell you who I am and where you may find me. Take now the axe and let us see how well you can smite.'

'Gladly will I,' said Gawain, taking the axe in his hands and swinging it while the Green Knight made ready by kneeling on the floor and drawing his long hair on to the crown of his head to lay bare his neck for the stroke. Putting all his strength into the blow, Gawain whirled up the axe and struck so hard that the keen blade cut through flesh and bone and set the sparks flying from the stone paving, while the Green Knight's head leapt from his shoulders and went rolling across the floor.

But the knight neither faltered nor fell: swiftly he sprang forward with hands outstretched, caught up his head, and turning with it held in his hand by the hair mounted upon the waiting horse. Then, riding easily as if nothing had happened, he turned his face towards Gawain and said:

'See to it that you keep your oath and seek me out a year hence. I am the Knight of the Green Chapel, and as such men know me in the north. Through Wales shall you seek me, and in the Forest of Wirral: and you will not fail to find me there if you be not a coward and a breaker of your knightly word.'

With that he wheeled his horse and galloped out of the door, the sparks flying up round his horse's hoofs, and away into the distance, his head still held in his hand, swinging easily by the hair.

But all at the feast sat astonished beyond words at this strange adventure, and it was a little while before the hall was filled once more with laughter and the joy of that festal season.

The year went by full swiftly; the trees grew green with spring, the leaves fading through the bright summer days, turned to red and gold in the early autumn; and upon

265

Michaelmas Day King Arthur held a feast at Caerleon with many of his knights, in honour of Sir Gawain who must on the morrow set forth upon his dreadful quest. Ywain and Agravaine and Erec were there; Launcelot and Lionel and Lucan the Good; Sir Bors and Sir Bedivere and Baldwin the lord bishop; Arthur and Guinevere to bless him and wish him God-speed. Gawain donned his armour, curved and shining and inlaid with gold; he girt his sword to his side and took the Green Knight's axe in his hand; then he mounted upon Gringalet his war-horse, and rode into the forests of South Wales, the shield held before him with the device of the Pentangle, the five-pointed Star of Logres, emblazoned in the midst.

So Sir Gawain set out, and rode through the realm of Logres, seeking for no joy but a deadly danger at the end of his quest. After many days he came into the wild lands of North Wales, and fared through lonely valleys and deep forests, forced often to sleep out under the stars by night, and to do battle by day with robbers and wild men.

Grim winter had closed upon him when he came to the northern sea, left the islands of Anglesey upon his left, and came by Clwyd to the Holy Head, near Saint Winifred's Well on the shore of the wide river Dee. Near to the mouth he forded the stream at low tide, and came across the desolate sands into the wild Forest of Wirral. Here were many more robbers and evil men, lying in wait by forest path and lonely stream, by rocky defile and by green valley – and he must fight with all who stayed him.

Everywhere he went he asked tidings of a Green Knight and of a Chapel also of Green near which was his dwelling: but none in the forest could help him in his quest. Only a brave knight could have passed that way, and Gawain endured all foes to overcome, and the bitter weather of mid-winter.

On Christmas Eve he rode upon Gringalet through marsh and mire, and prayed that he might find shelter. And on a sudden he came through open parkland to a fine castle set on a little hill above a deep valley where flowed a wide stream. A fair lawn lay in front of it, and many great oak trees on either side; there was a moat before the castle, and a low palisade of wood.

'Now God be thanked,' said Sir Gawain, 'that I have come to this fair dwelling for Christmas, and may He grant me to find an honourable

welcome herein . . . Good sir!' he cried to the porter who came to the great gate when he knocked, 'Grant me entrance, I pray you, and tell the lord of this castle that I am a knight of King Arthur's court passing this way upon a quest.'

With a kindly smile the porter opened the gate, and Gawain rode over the drawbridge and into the courtyard. And there were squires and serving-men waiting who helped him to alight, led Gringalet away to the stable, and brought Gawain into a goodly hall where a fire burned brightly and the lord of the castle came forth from his chamber to greet his guest, saying:

'Welcome to my dwelling, Sir knight: all that I have is here at your service, and you shall be my honoured guest for as long as it shall please you to remain in this castle.'

'I thank you, noble sir,' said Gawain. 'May God bless you for your hospitality.' With that they clasped hands as good friends should; and Gawain looked upon the knight who greeted him so warmly, and thought what a fine warrior that castle had as its lord. For he was a tall man and broad of shoulder, with an open, honest face tanned red by the sun, with red hair and beard, a firm hand-clasp, a free stride, and a straightforward speech: just such a man as was born to be a leader of valiant men and a lord over wide estates.

The squires led Gawain next to a fair chamber in the keep, where they helped him to lay aside his armour, and clad him in rich, flowing robes lined softly with fur. Then they led him back to the hall and set him in a chair near to the fire, beside the lord of the castle. They brought in the tables then, set them upon trestles, covered them with fair white cloths, set thereon salt cellars and spoons of silver, then brought in the dishes and the goblets of wine. The lord of the castle drank to Sir Gawain, and rejoiced with all his followers that chance had brought so far-famed a knight to his lonely dwelling.

When the meal was ended the two knights went together to the chapel of the castle, where the chaplain celebrated Evensong and the whole service for Christmas Eve.

Then the knight brought Sir Gawain into a comely closet and sat him in a chair by the fire. And there the lady of the castle came to visit him, accompanied by her handmaidens – a very lovely lady, fairer even than Queen Guinevere. So the evening passed in jest and joy, and they brought Gawain to his room with bright tapers, set a goblet of hot spiced wine at his bedside, and left him there to his rest.

Three days were spent in feasting and in Christmas rejoicings – dancing and carol-singing, and much merriment. And even the lady of the castle sat by Gawain, and sang to him and talked with him, and attended to his comfort.

'Tarry with me longer,' said the lord of the castle on the evening of the fourth day. 'For while I live I shall be held the worthier because so brave and courteous a knight as Sir Gawain has been my guest.'

'I thank you, good sir,' answered Gawain, 'but I must away tomorrow on my high quest. For I must be at the Green Chapel upon

the New Year's Day, and I would rather keep mine oath than be ruler of all this land. Moreover as yet I have found none who can instruct me as to where the Green Chapel is.'

The lord of the castle laughed happily. 'This is indeed good news!' he cried. 'Here then you may stay until the very day of your quest's ending. For not two hours' ride from this castle you shall find the Green Chapel – a man of mine shall bring you to it upon the first day of the new year.'

Then Gawain was glad, and he too laughed joyously. 'I thank you, sir, for this news – and greatly also for your kindness. Now that my quest is achieved, I will dwell here in all joy and do what you will.'

'Then these three days,' said the lord of the castle, 'I will ride out hunting in the forest. But you, who have travelled far and endured many things, shall abide in my castle and rest at your ease. And my wife shall attend on you, and entertain you with her company when I am out hunting.'

'I thank you indeed,' said Gawain. 'And in no other wise could I pass with greater joy the three days before my meeting with the Green Knight.'

'Well,' said the lord of the castle, 'so let it be. And as this yet is the festive season of game and jest, let us make a merry bargain together, I vowing each day to give you whatever I may win in the wood, and you giving in exchange anything that may come to you here in the castle. Let us swear to make this exchange, for worse or for better, whatever may happen.'

'With all my heart,' laughed Gawain. And so the oath was sworn.

Next morning the lord of the castle hunted the deer through the forests of Wirral and Delamere; and many a hart and hind fell to his keen arrows.

But Gawain slept long in a soft bed hung about with curtains, and dreamt of many things 'twixt waking and sleeping, until the lady of the castle, stepping silently as a sunbeam, came and sat upon his bed and talked with him merrily. Long they spoke together, and many words of love did the lady utter; but Gawain turned them all with jest and courtesy, as a true knight should who speaks with the lady of his host.

'Now God save you, fair sir,' she said at length, 'and reward you for your merry words. But that you are really Sir Gawain I misdoubt me greatly!'

'Wherefore do you doubt?' asked the knight anxiously, fearing that he had failed in some point of courtesy.

'So true a knight as Gawain,' answered the lady, 'and one so gentle and courteous unto damsels would never have tarried so long with a lady and not begged a kiss of her in parting.'

'Faith, fair lady,' said Gawain, 'and you bid me to it, I will indeed ask a kiss of you: but a true knight asks not otherwise, for fear to displease you.'

So the lady kissed him sweetly, and blessed him and departed; and Gawain rose from his bed and called for the chamberlain to clothe him. And thereafter he ate and drank, and passed his day quietly in the castle until the lord of it came home in the grey evening, bearing the spoils of the chase.

'What think you of this game, Sir knight?' he cried. 'I deserve thanks for my skill as a huntsman, do I not – for all of this is yours, according to our bargain!'

'I thank you,' answered Gawain, 'and I take the gift as we agreed. And I will give to you all that I won within these walls.' And with that he put his hands on the lord of the castle's shoulders and kissed him, saying: 'Take here my spoils, for I have won nothing but this: if more had been mine, as freely would I have given it to you.'

'It is good,' said his host, 'and much do I thank you for it. Yet would I like to know whence came your kiss, and how did you win it?'

'Not so,' answered Gawain, 'that was no part of the bargain!' And thereupon they laughed merrily and sat down to a fine dinner.

Next morning the lord of the castle went forth down the hillside and along the deep valley-bottoms to seek out and slay the wild boar in the marshes.

But Gawain abode in his bed, and the lady came once more to sit by him; and ever she strove to wheedle him into speaking to her words of love unseemly for the lady of a knight. But Gawain the courteous turned all into jest, and defended himself so well by his wit that he won no more than two kisses, given by the lady ere she left him laughing.

'And now, Sir Gawain,' said the lord of the castle when he came home that night and laid the boar's head at his feet. 'Here is my spoil of the day which I give you according to our bargain: now what have you won to give me in exchange?'

'I thank you,' said Gawain, 'for your just dealing in this game. As truly will I give you all that I have gained this day.'

Thereat he took the lord of the castle by the shoulders and gave him two kisses, saying: 'Now are we quits – for this and no more have I got me today.'

'By St Giles!' laughed the lord of the castle, 'you will be rich in a short time if we drive such bargains!' Then they went to the feast, and sat late over their meat and wine, while the lady strove ever to please Gawain, making fair, secret glances at him which, for his honour, he must not return.

The morrow would be the last day of the year. Gawain was eager to ride forth in quest of the Green Knight; but the lord of the castle stayed him with hospitable words:

'I swear by mine honour as a true knight that upon New Year's Day you shall come to the Green Chapel long ere the hour of noon. So stay in your bed tomorrow and rest in my castle. I will up with morning and ride to hunt the fox: so let us make once again our bargain to exchange all the winnings that may be ours tomorrow. For twice have I tried you and found you true; but the next is the third time, and that shall be the best.'

So once more they swore the oath, and while the lord of the castle went forth with his huntsmen and his pack of music-mouthed hounds, Gawain lay asleep, dreaming of the terrible meeting with the Green Knight so close before him. Presently the lady came in, blithe as a bird; she flung up the window so that the clear, frosty sunshine streamed into the room, roused Gawain from his slumbers and claimed of him a kiss.

She was fairer than the sunshine itself that morning, her hair falling each side of her lovely face, and her neck whiter than the snow gleaming between the fur of her gown. Sweetly she kissed Gawain and chid him for a sluggard.

'Surely you are a very man of ice that you take but one kiss! Or is it that you have a lady waiting for you in Camelot?'

'Not so,' answered Gawain gravely, 'no lady yet has my love. But it may not be yours, for you have a lord already – a far nobler knight than ever I shall be!'

'But this one day we may love,' she said. 'Surely it may be so? Then all my life-days I may remember that Gawain held me in his arms.'

'Nay, for the sake of mine oath of knighthood and the glory of Logres, I may not do so – for such were shame indeed.'

Then she blamed him and besought him, but ever he turned aside her words courteously, and ever held true to his honour as a knight of Logres should. At last she sighed sweetly, and kissed him a second time, saying: 'Sir Gawain, you are a true knight, the noblest ever. So give me but a gift whereby to remember you, that by thinking of my knight I may lessen my mourning.'

'Alas,' said Gawain, 'I have nothing to give. For I travel without baggage on this dangerous quest.'

'Then I will give you this green lace from my girdle,' said the lady. 'Wear that for my sake at least.'

'It may not be so,' answered Gawain, 'for I cannot be your knight and wear your favour.'

'It is but a little thing,' she said, 'and you may wear it hidden. Take it, I pray you, for it is a magic lace and while a man wears it he may not be slain, not even by all the magic upon earth. But I charge you to hide it, and tell not my lord.'

This proved too great a temptation for Gawain, and, mindful of his ordeal with the Green Knight next day, he took the lace and promised never to reveal it. Then the lady kissed him for the third time, and went quickly away.

That evening the lord of the castle came home from the hunt bearing with him the skin of one fox. In the bright hall where the fire shone warmly and the tables were all laid richly for dinner, Gawain met him merrily:

'I come with my winnings, and I will be the first giver this night!' he cried gaily; and with that he kissed him solemnly three times.

'By my faith,' cried the lord of the castle, 'you are a good merchant indeed: you give me three such kisses – and I have only a foul fox-skin to give you in return!'

Then with laughter and jests they sat down to the feast, and were merrier that night than on any of the others. But Gawain spoke no word of the green lace which the lady had given him.

The day of the New Year came in with storm: bitterly the winds howled and the sleet lashed against the window pane, and Gawain, who had slept but little, rose at the first light. He clothed himself warmly and buckled on his armour, setting the green lace about his waist in hope that its magic might protect him. Then he went forth into the courtyard, the squires brought out Gringalet, well fed and well groomed, and helped him to mount.

'Farewell,' he said to the lord of the castle. 'I thank you for your hospitality, and pray Heaven to bless you. If I might live a while longer I would reward you for your kindness: but greatly I fear that I shall not see another sun.'

The drawbridge was let down, the gate flung wide, and Gawain rode out of the castle, with a squire to guide him. Through the bitter dawning they rode, beneath trees dripping drearily, and across meadows where the wind moaned as it bit them to the bone, and they came to a great valley with cliffs at one side of it, all filled with mist.

'Sir,' said the squire, 'go no further, I beg of you. Near here dwells the Green Knight, a terrible and a cruel man. There is none so fierce or so strong in this land – and no man may stand against him. Over yonder at the Green Chapel it is ever his custom to stay all who pass by, and fight with them, and kill them – for none can escape him. Flee away now and I will not tell ever that you fled for fear of the terrible Green Knight.'

'I thank you,' said Gawain, 'but I must go forward. I would be a coward and unworthy of knighthood if I fled away now. Therefore, whether I like it or not I must go forward ... And God knows well how to save His servants if so He wills.'

'Well then,' said the squire, 'your death be your own doing. Go down this path by the cliff, into the deep valley, and upon the

276

left hand, beyond the water, you will find the Green Chapel. Now farewell, noble Gawain, for I dare not come with you further.'

Down the path rode Gawain, and came to the bottom of the valley. No chapel could he see, but only the rugged cliff above him, and high, desolate banks in the distance. But at length he saw, under the dripping trees, a low green mound beside the rushing stream; and he heard a sound as of a scythe upon a grindstone coming from a deep hollow in that mound.

'Ah,' said Gawain. 'This must be the Green Chapel! A very devil's oratory it is, and green indeed – a chapel of mischance! And within it I hear the knight himself, sharpening a weapon to smite me this day. Alas that I must perish at his hands in this cursed spot . . . Yet will I go on boldly, for my duty is so to do.'

Gawain sprang from his horse and strode down to the streamside:

'Who waits here,' he cried, 'to keep tryst with me? I am Gawain, who have come to the Green Chapel as I vowed.'

'Wait but a little,' came a mighty voice out of the hollow beneath the mound. 'When my weapon is sharp, you shall have that which I promised you!'

Presently the Green Knight came out with a new, shining axe in his hand. He was as terrible as ever, with his green face and his green hair, as he strode down the bank and leapt over the wide stream.

'You are welcome, Gawain!' he cried in his great voice. 'Now will I repay the stroke you dealt me at Camelot – and none shall come between us in this lonely valley. Now off with your helmet, and make ready for the blow!'

Then Gawain did as he was bidden, bending his head forward, with his neck bare to the stroke.

'Make ready to strike,' he said quietly to the Green Knight, 'for here I shall stand and do naught to stay the blow.'

The Green Knight swung his axe round so that it whistled, and aimed a terrible stroke with the sharp blade of it: and try how he might, Gawain flinched at the sound of it.

'Ha!' grunted the Green Knight, lowering his axe and leaning on the

handle of it: 'You are surely not Gawain the brave, thus to fear even the whistle of the blade! When you struck off my head in King Arthur's hall I never flinched from your blow.'

'I shrank once,' said Gawain, 'but I shall not a second time — even when *my* head falls to the ground, which I cannot replace as you have yours! Come now, strike quickly, I will not stay you again.'

'Have at you then!' cried the Green Knight, whirling his axe. He smote once more, and once more stayed his hand ere the sharp blade drew blood. But Gawain stirred not a jot, nor trembled in any limb. 'Now you are filled with courage once more,' he cried, 'and so I may smite bravely a brave man. Hold aside your hood a little further, I am about to strike my hardest.'

'Strike away,' said Gawain. 'Why do you talk so much? Are you perhaps afraid thus to smite a defenceless man?'

'Then here is the blow I promised!' cried the Green Knight, swinging his axe for the third time. And now he struck truly, yet aimed with such care that the blade only parted the skin at the side of his neck.

But when Gawain had felt the wound and the blood over his shoulders, he sprang away in an instant, put on his helmet, drew his sword, set his shield before him and said to the Green Knight:

'Now I have borne the blow, and if you strike again it is beyond our bargain and I may defend myself, striking stroke for stroke!'

The Green Knight stood leaning on his axe. 'Gawain,' he said, all the fierceness gone out of his voice, 'you have indeed borne the blow – and no other will I strike you. I hold you released of all claims now. If I had wished it, I might have struck you a crueller stroke, and smitten your head off as you smote off mine. The first blow and the second that struck you not – these were for promises truly kept, for the one kiss and the two kisses that my wife gave you in the castle, and you truly rendered to me. But the third time you failed, and therefore had the wound of me: you gave me the three kisses, but not the green lace. Oh, well I know all that passed between you – she tempted you by my will. Gawain, I hold you to be the noblest, the most faultless knight in all the wide world. Had you yielded to dishonour and shamed your knighthood – then would your head be lying now at my feet. As for the lace, you hid it but for love of your life – and that is a little sin, and for it I pardon you.'

'I am ashamed,' said Gawain, handing him the green lace. 'For cowardice and covetousness I betrayed my oath of knighthood. Cut off my head, Sir knight, for I am indeed unworthy of the Round Table.'

'Come now!' cried the Green Knight, laughing merrily, so that Gawain knew him indeed to be the lord of the castle. 'You have borne your penance, and are quite absolved and forgiven. Take and keep this green lace in memory of this adventure; and return to my castle and end the festival in joy.'

'I must back to Camelot,' said Gawain, 'I may not bide longer. But tell me, noble sir, how comes this enchantment? Who are you that ride in Green and die not when beheaded? How come you to dwell, a noble knight in a fine castle, and also to strike axe-blows, the Green Knight of the Green Chapel?'

'My name is Sir Bernlak, the Knight of the Lake,' answered he. 'And the enchantment comes from Nimue, the Lady of the Lake, the favoured of Merlin. She sent me to Camelot, to test the truth of the renown that is spread abroad concerning the valour of the Knights of the Round Table, and the worth of Logres.'

Then the two knights embraced one another and parted with blessings. Gawain rode back swiftly through the Forest of Wirral, and after many more adventures he came to Camelot, where King Arthur welcomed him, marvelled at his tale, and set him with honour in his place at the Round Table. And of all the knights who ever sat there, few indeed were so worthy as Gawain.

Edward Lear

THE JUMBLIES

Illustrated by Paul Birkbeck

I

They went to sea in a Sieve, they did,
　In a Sieve they went to sea:
In spite of all their friends could say,
On a winter's morn, on a stormy day,
　In a Sieve they went to sea!
And when the Sieve turned round and round,
And every one cried, 'You'll all be drowned!'
They called aloud, 'Our Sieve ain't big,
But we don't care a button! we don't care a fig!
　In a Sieve we'll go to sea!'
　Far and few, far and few,
　　Are the lands where the Jumblies live;
　　Their heads are green, and their hands are blue,
　　And they went to sea in a Sieve.

II

They sailed away in a Sieve, they did,
  In a Sieve they sailed so fast,
With only a beautiful pea-green veil
Tied with a riband by way of a sail,
  To a small tobacco-pipe mast;
And every one said, who saw them go,
'O won't they be soon upset, you know!
For the sky is dark, and the voyage is long,
And happen what may, it's extremely wrong
  In a Sieve to sail so fast!'
    Far and few, far and few,
      Are the lands where the Jumblies live;
      Their heads are green, and their hands are blue,
      And they went to sea in a Sieve.

III

The water it soon came in, it did,
  The water it soon came in;
So to keep them dry, they wrapped their feet
In a pinky paper all folded neat,
  And they fastened it down with a pin.
And they passed the night in a crockery-jar,
And each of them said, 'How wise we are!
Though the sky be dark, and the voyage be long,
Yet we never can think we were rash or wrong,
  While round in our Sieve we spin!'
    Far and few, far and few,
      Are the lands where the Jumblies live;
      Their heads are green, and their hands are blue,
      And they went to sea in a Sieve.

IV

And all night long they sailed away;
  And when the sun went down,
They whistled and warbled a moony song
To the echoing sound of a coppery gong,
  In the shade of the mountains brown.
'O Timballo! How happy we are,
When we live in a Sieve and a crockery-jar,
And all night long in the moonlight pale,
We sail away with a pea-green sail,
  In the shade of the mountains brown!'
    Far and few, far and few,
      Are the lands where the Jumblies live;
      Their heads are green, and their hands are blue,
        And they went to sea in a Sieve.

Arthur Ransome

FROM
SWALLOWS AND AMAZONS

Illustrated by Tim Clarey

The children are allowed to use the boat called the Swallow *to go camping on the island, but soon find themselves under attack from the crew of the* Amazon, *who claim the island to be theirs.*

It had been a long wait among the islands, and they were all glad to be moving again at last. In the morning the fair wind had brought them fast from Wild Cat Island down to Rio Bay. They had cruised in and out among the islands, and made sure that the Amazons were not lurking among them, waiting for their chance to capture the island once again. They had made sure that the *Amazon* was still in the Amazon River, so that the plan was working out just as they had hoped, and they would be able to sail in and capture her in the evening. They had anchored close under one of the islands north of Rio to wait till dusk. From there they had been able to look out over the northern part of the lake without being seen themselves, and all day long they had kept a close watch on the promontory behind which, they knew, lay the Amazon River and the stronghold of the Amazon pirates. But the afternoon had been very long, and at one time there had almost been a mutiny.

'Let's go straight on,' Roger had said, and Susan had said, 'Why not?'

Captain John had brought them to reason. Everything had been planned for an attack at dusk. There would be no chance at all of capturing the *Amazon* if they sailed up there in broad daylight. Besides, they had left Able-seaman Titty behind on Wild Cat Island to look after the lights for them so that they could come home in the dark. They could not leave Titty behind and then go and turn the day into an ordinary picnic. Susan had agreed. Roger had suggested swimming instead. The mutiny had thus been suppressed without bloodshed, as they say in the books.

The crew had been rewarded by getting permission from their captain to go ashore. They had landed on the island near which they were anchored. They had bathed from it, and made a fire on the shore, not for cooking, because they had brought no kettle, but because landing on an island without making a fire is waste of an island. They had drunk half their milk and eaten half their rations. Then while John stayed on the island he had sent the mate and the boy to sail in to Rio, to buy stores. They had bought a shilling's worth of the sort of chocolate that has almonds and raisins in it as well as the chocolate, and so is three sorts of food at once. They had come back. They had visited several other islands, and had an unpleasant meeting with some natives on one of them, who pointed to a notice board and said that the island was private, and that no landing was allowed.

Only once Captain John had thought he had seen one of the Amazons moving in the heather on the promontory. But he could not be sure without the telescope. It might have been a sheep. The wait all through the afternoon and early evening had been long and tiring, and though there had been plenty to look at in the steamers and motor boats and

rowing skiffs of the natives, they had seen no sails except those of large yachts far away up the lake. For the first time in their lives all three of them had wished to hurry the sinking sun upon its way.

Now, at last, the sun had set. Twilight was coming on. There was no wind, for the wind had gone with the sun as it so often does, and they were beginning to be afraid that the dark would come too soon for them. All was astir in the *Swallow*.

The mast was unstepped, and laid on the thwarts so that it stuck out over the bows. There was room for it in the ship, for it was a few inches shorter than *Swallow* was long. But to stow it all inside it had to lie straight down the middle, so that it was very uncomfortable for anybody who was rowing.

'Anyway, why shouldn't she have a bowsprit?' said John. 'Besides, it's only for a short time.'

Roger rowed. John was looking at the chart in the guide book. Susan steered.

'Pull with your back,' she said. 'Don't bend your arms till the end of the stroke.'

'I'm pulling with all of me,' said Roger, 'but I've got too many

clothes on.'

'He's making a fair lot of noise and splash,' said the captain.

'He'll be tired before we get near enough for it to matter,' said the mate.

'No I won't,' said Roger.

Slowly they moved across to the western shore. No one could row *Swallow* fast. It was growing dusk. Already the hills were dark, and you could not see the woods on them. It began to seem that after waiting so long because it was too light, they were going to fail after all because it would not be light enough.

'Look here, Susan,' said John, 'I think I'd better row.'

But just then a line of ripples crept over the green and silver surface of the smooth water.

'Thank goodness,' said Captain John. 'Here's the wind again, and it's the same wind. Sometimes it changes after sunset, but this is still from the south.'

The ripples grew as the south wind strengthened.

'It'll be against us on the way home,' said the mate.

'There'll be no hurry then,' said John.

'What about sailing?' said Roger. 'But I'm not tired.'

'It isn't as if *Swallow* had a white sail,' said Captain John. 'They'll never see the brown one in this light, especially if we hug the shore. And we can with this wind. Yes, Mister Mate. Tell the men to bring the sweeps aboard.'

'Easy,' said the mate. 'Bring the sweeps in.'

Roger stopped rowing and lifted first one oar and then the other from the rowlocks and laid them quietly down.

'Keep her heading as she is,' said Captain John.

'As she is, sir,' said the mate. In a calm things go anyway in a sailing ship, but a little wind sharpens them up at once.

John stepped the mast as quietly as he could. He hooked the yard to the traveller and set the sail. There was a little west in the wind and the boom swung out on the starboard side.

'She's moving now like anything,' said the boy.

'I don't want to get there too soon,' said John, 'but I do want to get into the river while it's still light enough to see but late enough for the pirates to be off their guard and feasting in their stronghold.'

'Peggy said they had supper at half-past seven,' said Susan.

'Well, it's ages after that now,' said John. 'I should think we are all right.'

Here and there on the shores of the lake lights twinkled in the houses of the natives. Astern of them, over the tops of the islands, there was a huge cluster of lights in Rio Bay. But it was not quite dark yet, though the first stars were showing.

Swallow was sailing fast and in a very little time they were abreast of the promontory, and could see its great dark lump close to them.

'We must lower sail now,' said the captain.

He lowered the sail himself. He could not trust even Susan to lower it without making a noise. Then he wetted the rowlocks so that they would not squeak.

The *Swallow* drifted on past the point. Beyond the promontory was a wide bay with deep beds of rushes on either side of it. Somewhere at the head of the bay was a house with lights in its windows. The lights, reflected in the water, showed exactly where was the opening of

the river mouth between the reeds. A moment later they lost sight of the reflections and knew that they had drifted too far.

'Now, Mister Mate,' whispered John. 'Will you row, as quietly as ever you can? Roger goes forward to keep a look-out. Don't shout if you see anything. Just tell the mate under your breath.'

'What about the mast?' asked the mate.

'If they're watching, they'll see the ship and know her, anyhow,' said Captain John. 'If they're not watching, the mast doesn't matter. If they are in the house in those lighted rooms, they won't be able to see anything at all out here. I'm sure we've done them, if we can find the boathouse. They'd have challenged us long before this if they'd seen us.'

The mate rowed with slow, steady strokes. Her oars made no noise at all. They slipped in and out of the water without a splash. *Swallow* was in smooth water now, sheltered by the high ground of the promontory. John steered till he could see the lights of the house reflected in the river. That was the opening in the reeds. He steered towards it. Presently there were tall reeds on either side of them. They were in the Amazon River. 'The boathouse is somewhere on the right bank,' whispered John. 'That's our left. Tell Roger to keep a look-out to port.'

Suddenly there was a splash in the reed beds, followed by a loud quack.

'What's that?' said Susan, startled.

'Duck,' said the captain.

Susan rowed on.

There was a whisper from the look-out. 'There it is. I see it.'

'Where?' whispered the mate looking over her shoulder.

'There,' said the boy.

High above the reeds, not far ahead of them, on the right bank of the river rose the black square shape of a large building.

'That's it,' whispered the captain.

'The boathouse,' said the mate.

'Quiet.'

'Sh.'

The boathouse stood deep in an inlet among the reeds. Captain John steered towards it.

'Easy all!' he whispered. There was a dead silence on the river as the *Swallow* drifted on. There was a noise of music in the house with the lights in it.

'Captain Nancy said the boathouse had a skull and cross-bones on it,' whispered Captain John.

'I see it. I see it,' cried Roger.

'Shut up. Be quiet,' hissed the mate.

'That's it, all right,' whispered Captain John.

On the front of the big open boathouse, high up over the entrance, cut out of wood and painted staring white were a huge skull and cross-bones big enough to have belonged to an elephant.

'Can you see in?' asked Captain John.

'There's a big boat in there,' said Roger.

'They said there would be. That'll be the launch that belongs to the natives. Will our mast clear that beam? Gently now, gently.'

Swallow slid into the big dark boathouse as Susan brought her oars in.

'There's a rowing boat,' whispered Roger loudly.

'Look out. Don't bump the launch,' whispered Susan.

'There's nothing else,' said Roger. 'The *Amazon* isn't here.'

John was standing in the stern of the *Swallow*, holding on to the gunwale of the launch. He pulled out his pocket torch. 'They won't be able to see the light from the house,' he said, and pressed down the button.

The bright light wavered round the boathouse. It showed a rowing skiff and the big launch and an empty space on the further side. It was clear that a boat was usually moored there. Pinned to the wooden stage that ran along that wall of the boathouse there was a big envelope, white in the light of the torch.

Captain John pushed at the launch and *Swallow* moved across towards the wall. Roger grabbed the envelope.

'Give it to me,' said the mate, and the boy obediently gave it.

The captain and the mate examined the envelope by the light of the torch. There was a skull and cross-bones on it, done in red pencil. Under that, in blue pencil, was written, 'To the Swallows.' John tore the envelope open. Inside there was a sheet of paper with another skull and cross-bones, done in blue. Under them in red were the words 'Ha! Ha!' written very large, and under them were the words, 'The Amazon Pirates,' and two names, 'Nancy Blackett, Captain' and 'Peggy Blackett, Mate' also written in red.

Captain John thought for a moment.

'It's quite simple,' he said. 'They've hidden her up the river. It's an old pirate trick. We know they haven't put to sea, for we've been watching all day. Come on.' He shut off the torch.

They pushed out.

Out of doors it seemed quite light after the darkness of the big boathouse.

'Now, Mister Mate, lay to your oars,' said Captain John. 'There's still light enough to find her if we're quick.'

Mate Susan bent to her oars and *Swallow* moved fast up the river. John, staring as hard as he could into the dusk, kept her clear of the reeds. In another minute they were round a bend in the river.

Again there was a splash in the deep reed beds at the river's mouth. Again a duck quacked loudly. It quacked two or three times, until a voice said sternly, 'Stow it, you goat. Don't overdo things.'

The nose of a boat pushed its way out from among the reeds. Just above the nose of the boat was the head of Captain Nancy Blackett. She watched for a moment and listened.

'All clear,' she said. 'They've gone up river. That'll give us a bit more start. Come on.'

There was more splashing in the reeds as Peggy Blackett poled over the stern. The boat came out of the reeds into the mouth of the river and drifted out towards the lake. Captain Nancy took the oars. She rowed hard for a minute or two.

'Safe enough now,' she said. 'I'm going to step the mast. Lucky we thought of taking it down or they'd have seen it over the reeds. Hang on to the main-sheet, you son of a seacook,' she said with great good temper and satisfaction. She hoisted the sail.

'Now then, my hearties,' she said as she clambered aft. 'Wild Cat Island and Amazons for ever! We've done them fairly brown.'

Hilaire Belloc

Jim Who Ran Away from his Nurse, and was Eaten by a Lion

Illustrated by Raymond Briggs

There was a boy whose name was Jim;
His friends were very good to him.
They gave him tea, and cakes, and jam,
And slices of delicious ham,
And chocolate with pink inside,
And little tricycles to ride,
And read him stories through and through,
And even took him to the Zoo –
But there it was the dreadful fate
Befell him, which I now relate.

You know – at least you *ought* to know,
For I have often told you so –
That children never are allowed
To leave their nurses in a crowd;
Now this was Jim's especial foible,
He ran away when he was able,
And on this inauspicious day
He slipped his hand and ran away!
He hadn't gone a yard when – Bang!
With open jaws, a lion sprang,
And hungrily began to eat
The boy: beginning at his feet.

Now, just imagine how it feels
When first your toes and then your heels,
And then by gradual degrees,
Your shins and ankles, calves and knees,
Are slowly eaten, bit by bit.
No wonder Jim detested it!
No wonder that he shouted 'Hi!'
The honest keeper heard his cry,
Though very fat he almost ran
To help the little gentleman.
'Ponto!' he ordered as he came
(For Ponto was the lion's name),
'Ponto!' he cried, with angry frown
'Let go, Sir! Down, Sir! Put it down!'

PONTO!

HI!

The lion made a sudden stop,
He let the dainty morsel drop,
And slunk reluctant to his cage,
Snarling with disappointed rage.
But when he bent him over Jim,
The honest keeper's eyes were dim.
The lion having reached his head,
The miserable boy was dead!

When Nurse informed his parents, they
Were more concerned than I can say: –
His Mother, as she dried her eyes,
Said, 'Well – it gives me no surprise,
He would not do as he was told!'
His Father, who was self-controlled,
Bade all the children round attend
To James's miserable end,
And always keep a-hold of Nurse
For fear of finding something worse.

Washington Irving

FROM

RIP VAN WINKLE

Illustrated by Mark Edwards

*A very strange thing happens when lazy but good-natured Rip
falls asleep on a grassy knoll in the Kaatskill Mountains.*

In a long ramble of the kind of a fine autumnal day, Rip had unconsciously scrambled to one of the highest parts of the Kaatskill Mountains. He was after his favourite sport of squirrel shooting, and the still solitudes had echoed and re-echoed with the reports of his gun. Panting and fatigued, he threw himself, late in the afternoon, on a green knoll, covered with mountain herbage, that crowned the brow of a precipice. From an opening between the trees he could overlook all the lower country for many a mile of rich woodland. He saw at a distance the lordly Hudson far, far below him, moving on its silent but majestic course, with the reflection of a purple cloud or the sail of a lagging bark here and there sleeping on its glassy bosom, and at last losing itself in the blue highlands.

On the other side he looked down into a deep mountain glen, wild, lonely, and shagged, the bottom filled with fragments from the impending cliffs, and scarcely lighted by the reflected rays of the setting sun. For some time Rip lay musing on this scene. Evening was gradually advancing; the mountains began to throw their long blue shadows over the valleys. He saw that it would be dark long before he could reach the village, and he heaved a heavy sigh when he thought of encountering the terrors of Dame Van Winkle.

As he was about to descend, he heard a voice from a distance, hallooing, 'Rip Van Winkle! Rip Van Winkle!' He looked around, but could see nothing but a crow winging its solitary flight across the mountain. He thought his fancy must have deceived him, and turned again to descend, when he heard the same cry ring through the still evening air, 'Rip Van Winkle! Rip Van Winkle!' At the same time Wolf bristled up his back and, giving a low growl, skulked to his master's side, looking fearfully down into the glen. Rip now felt a vague apprehension stealing over him; he looked anxiously in the same direction and perceived a strange figure slowly toiling up the rocks, and bending ·under the weight of something he carried on his back. He was surprised to see any human being in this lonely and unfrequented place, but supposing it to be someone of the neighbourhood in need of his assistance, he hastened down to yield it.

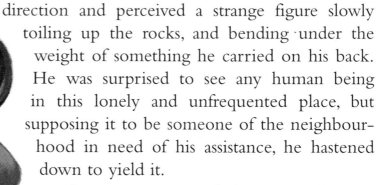

On nearer approach he was still more surprised at the singularity of the stranger's appearance. He was a short, square-built old fellow, with thick, bushy hair and a grizzled beard. His dress was of the antique Dutch fashion – a cloth jerkin strapped around the waist and several pairs of breeches, the outer one of ample volume, decorated with rows of buttons down the sides and bunches at the knees. He bore on his shoulder a stout keg that seemed full of liquor, and made signs for Rip to approach and assist him with the load. Though rather shy and distrustful of this new acquaintance, Rip complied with his usual alacrity, and mutually relieving one another, they clambered up a narrow gully, apparently the dry bed of a mountain torrent. As they ascended, Rip every now and then heard long rolling peals, like distant thunder, that seemed to issue out of a deep ravine, or rather cleft, between lofty rocks, toward which their rugged path conducted. He paused for an instant, but supposing it to be the muttering of one of those transient thunder showers which often take place in mountain heights, he proceeded. Passing through the ravine, they came to a hollow, like a small amphitheatre, surrounded by perpendicular precipices, over the brinks of which impending trees shot their branches, so that you only caught glimpses of the azure sky and the bright evening cloud. During the whole time, Rip and his companion had laboured on in silence, for though the former marvelled greatly what could be the object of carrying a keg of liquor up this wild mountain, yet there was something strange and incomprehensible about the unknown that inspired awe and checked familiarity.

On entering the amphitheatre, new objects of wonder were to be seen. On a level spot in the centre was a company of odd-looking personages playing at ninepins. They were dressed in a quaint, outlandish fashion; some wore short doublets, others jerkins, with long knives in their belts, and most of them had enormous breeches, of similar style with that of the guide's. Their visages, too, were peculiar; one had a large beard, broad face, and small piggish eyes, the face of another seemed to consist entirely of nose and was surmounted by a white sugar-loaf hat set off with a little red cock's tail. They all had beards, of various shapes and colours. There was one who seemed to be the commander. He was a stout old gentleman, with a weather-beaten countenance; he wore a laced doublet, broad belt and hanger, high-crowned hat and feather, red stockings, and high-heeled shoes, with roses in them. The whole group reminded Rip of the figures in an old Flemish painting, in the parlour of Dominie Van Shaick, the village parson, and which had been brought over from Holland at the time of the settlement.

What seemed particularly odd to Rip was that though these folks were evidently amusing themselves, yet they maintained the gravest faces, the most mysterious silence, and were, withal, the most melancholy party of pleasure he had ever witnessed. Nothing interrupted the stillness of the scene but the noise of the balls, which, whenever they were rolled, echoed along the mountains like rumbling peals of thunder.

As Rip and his companion approached them, they suddenly desisted from their play and stared at him with such fixed, statuelike gaze and such strange, uncouth, lacklustre countenances that his heart turned within him and his knees smote together. His companion now emptied the contents of the keg into large flagons and made signs to him to wait upon the company. He obeyed with fear and trembling; they quaffed the liquor in profound silence and then returned to their game.

By degrees Rip's awe and apprehension subsided. He even ventured, when no eye was fixed upon him, to taste the beverage, which he found had much of the flavour of excellent Hollands. He was naturally a thirsty soul and was soon tempted to repeat the draught. One taste provoked another; and he reiterated his visits to the flagon so often that at length his senses were overpowered, his eyes swam in his head, his head gradually declined, and he fell into a deep sleep.

On waking, he found himself on the green knoll whence he had first seen the old man of the glen. He rubbed his eyes – it was a bright, sunny morning. The birds were hopping and twittering among the bushes, and the eagle was wheeling aloft and breasting the pure mountain breeze. 'Surely,' thought Rip, 'I have not slept here all night.' He recalled the occurrences before he fell asleep. The strange man with a keg of liquor – the mountain ravine – the wild retreat among the rocks – the woebegone party at ninepins – the flagon – 'Oh! That flagon! That wicked flagon!' thought Rip. 'What excuse shall I make to Dame Van Winkle?'

He looked around for his gun, but in place of the clean, well-oiled

fowling piece he found an old firelock lying by him, the barrel encrusted with rust, the lock falling off, and the stock worm-eaten. He now suspected that the grave roysters of the mountain had put a trick upon him, and, having dosed him with liquor, had robbed him of his gun. Wolf, too, had disappeared, but he might have strayed away after a squirrel or partridge. He whistled after him and shouted his name, but all in vain; the echoes repeated his whistle and shout, but no dog was to be seen.

He determined to revisit the scene of the last evening's gambol, and if he met with any of the party, to demand his dog and gun. As he rose to walk, he found himself stiff in the joints and wanting in his usual activity. 'These mountain beds do not agree with me,' thought Rip, 'and if this frolic should lay me up with a fit of the rheumatism, I shall have a blessed time with Dame Van Winkle.' With some difficulty he got down into the glen; he found the gully up which he and his companion had ascended the preceding evening, but to his astonishment a mountain stream was now foaming down it, leaping from rock to rock and filling the glen with babbling murmurs. He, however, made shift to scramble up its sides, working his toilsome way through thickets of birch, sassafras, and witch hazel, and sometimes tripped up or entangled by the wild grapevines that twisted their coils or tendrils from tree to tree and spread a kind of network in his path.

At length he reached to where the ravine had opened through the cliffs to the amphitheatre, but no traces of such opening remained. The rocks presented a high, impenetrable wall over which the torrent came tumbling in a sheet of feathery foam and fell into a broad, deep basin, black from the shadows of the surrounding forest. Here, then, poor Rip was brought to a stand. He again called and whistled after his dog;

he was only answered by the cawing of a flock of idle crows, sporting high in air about a dry tree that overhung a sunny precipice, and who, secure in their elevation, seemed to look down and scoff at the poor man's perplexities. What was to be done? The morning was passing away, and Rip felt famished for want of his breakfast. He grieved to give up his dog and gun, and he dreaded to meet his wife, but it would not do to starve among the mountains. He shook his head, shouldered the rusty firelock, and, with a heart full of trouble and anxiety, turned his steps homeward.

As he approached the village he met a number of people, but none whom he knew, which somewhat surprised him, for he had thought himself acquainted with everyone in the country around. Their dress, too, was of a different fashion from that to which he was accustomed. They all stared at him with equal marks of surprise, and whenever they cast their eyes upon him invariably stroked their chins. The constant recurrence of this gesture induced Rip, involuntarily, to do the same, when, to his astonishment, he found his beard had grown a foot long!

He had now entered the skirts of the village. A troop of strange children ran at his heels, hooting after him and pointing at his grey beard. The dogs, too, not one of which he recognized for an old acquaintance, barked at him as he passed. The very village was altered; it was larger and more populous. There were rows of houses which he had never seen before, and those which had been his familiar haunts had disappeared. Strange names were over the doors – strange faces at the windows – everything was strange. His mind now misgave him; he began to doubt whether both he and the world around him were not bewitched. Surely this was his native village, which he had left but the day before. There stood the Kaatskill Mountains – there ran the silver Hudson at a distance – there was every hill and dale precisely as it had always been. Rip was sorely perplexed. 'That flagon last night,' thought he, 'has addled my poor head sadly!'

It was with some difficulty that he found the way to his own house, which he approached with silent awe, expecting every moment to hear the shrill voice of Dame Van Winkle. He found the house gone

to decay – the roof fallen in, the windows shattered, and the doors off
the hinges. A half-starved dog that looked like Wolf was skulking about
it. Rip called him by name, but the cur snarled, showed his teeth, and
passed on. This was an unkind cut indeed. 'My very dog,' sighed poor
Rip, 'has forgotten me!'

He entered the house, which, to tell the truth, Dame Van Winkle
had always kept in neat order. It was empty, forlorn, and apparently
abandoned. This desolateness overcame all his connubial fears – he
called loudly for his wife and children; the lonely chambers rang for a
moment with his voice, and then all again was silence.

He now hurried forth and hastened to his old resort, the village inn
– but it too was gone. A large, rickety, wooden building stood in its
place, with great gaping windows, some of them broken and mended
with old hats and petticoats, and over the door was painted, 'the Union
Hotel, by Jonathan Doolittle'. Instead of the great tree that used
to shelter the quiet little Dutch inn of yore, there now was reared
a tall, naked pole, with something on the top that looked like a
red nightcap, and from it was fluttering a flag, on which was
a singular assemblage of stars and stripes – all this was strange and
incomprehensible. He recognized on the sign, however, the ruby face
of King George, under which he had smoked so many a peaceful pipe;

but even this was singularly metamorphosed. The red coat was changed for one of blue and buff, a sword was held in the hand instead of a sceptre, the head was decorated with a cocked hat, and underneath was painted in large characters, GENERAL WASHINGTON.

There was, as usual, a crowd of folk about the door, but none that Rip recollected. The very character of the people seemed changed. There was a busy, bustling, disputatious tone about it, instead of the accustomed phlegm and drowsy tranquillity. He looked in vain for the sage Nicholas Vedder, with his broad face, double chin, and fair long pipe, uttering clouds of tobacco smoke instead of idle speeches; or Van Bummel, the schoolmaster, doling forth the contents of an ancient newspaper. In place of these, a lean, bilious-looking fellow, with his pockets full of handbills, was haranguing vehemently about rights of citizens – elections – members of congress – liberty – Bunker's Hill – heroes of Seventy-six – and other words, which were a perfect Babylonish jargon to the bewildered Van Winkle.

The appearance of Rip, with his long, grizzled beard, his rusty fowling piece, his uncouth dress, and an army of women and children at his heels, soon attracted the attention of the tavern politicians. They crowded around him, eyeing him from head to foot with great curiosity. The orator bustled up to him and, drawing him partly aside, inquired 'on which side he voted?' Rip stared in vacant stupidity. Another short but busy little fellow pulled him by the arm, and, rising on tiptoe, inquired in his ear, 'whether he was Federal or Democrat?' Rip was equally at a loss to comprehend the question; when a knowing, self-important old gentleman in a sharp cocked hat made his way through the crowd, putting them to the right and left with his elbows as he passed, and, planting himself before Van Winkle, with one arm akimbo, the other resting on his cane, his keen eyes and sharp hat penetrating, as it were, into his very soul, demanded in an austere tone, 'what brought him to the election with a gun on his shoulder, and a mob at his heels, and whether he meant to breed a riot in the village?' 'Alas! Gentlemen,' cried Rip, somewhat dismayed, 'I am a poor, quiet man, a native of the place, and a loyal subject of the king, God bless him!'

Here a general shout burst from the bystanders. 'A tory! A tory! A spy! A refugee! Hustle him! Away with him!' It was with great difficulty that the self-important man in the cocked hat restored order; and, having assumed a tenfold austerity of brow, demanded again of the unknown culprit what he came there for and whom he was seeking. The poor man humbly assured him that he meant no harm, but merely came there in search of some of his neighbours, who used to keep about the tavern.

'Well — who are they? Name them.'

Rip bethought himself a moment, and inquired, 'Where's Nicholas Vedder?'

There was a silence for a little while, then an old man replied, in a thin, piping voice, 'Nicholas Vedder! Why, he is dead and gone these eighteen years! There was a wooden tombstone in the churchyard that used to tell about him, but that's rotten and gone too.'

'Where's Brom Dutcher?'

'Oh, he went off to the army in the beginning of the war; some say he was killed at the storming of Stony Point – others say he was drowned in a squall at the foot of Antony's Nose. I don't know – he never came back again.'

'Where's Van Bummel, the schoolmaster?'

'He went off to the wars, too, was a great militia general, and is now in Congress.'

Rip's heart died away at hearing of these sad changes in his home and friends, and finding himself thus alone in the world. Every answer puzzled him, too, by treating of such enormous lapses of time and of matters which he could not understand: war – Congress – Stony Point. He had no courage to ask after any more friends, but cried out in despair, 'Does nobody here know Rip Van Winkle?'

'Oh, Rip Van Winkle!' exclaimed two or three. 'Oh, to be sure! That's Rip Van Winkle yonder, leaning against the tree.'

Rip looked, and beheld a precise counterpart of himself as he went up the mountain: apparently as lazy, and certainly as ragged. The poor fellow was now completely confounded. He doubted his own identity, and whether he was himself or another man. In the midst of his bewilderment, the man in the cocked hat demanded who he was, and what was his name?

'God knows,' exclaimed he, at his wit's end. 'I'm not myself – I'm somebody else – that's me yonder – no – that's somebody else got into my shoes – I was myself last night, but I fell asleep on the mountain, and they've changed my gun, and everything's changed, and I'm changed, and I can't tell what's my name, or who I am!'

The bystanders began now to look at each other, nod, wink

significantly, and tap their fingers against their foreheads. There was a whisper also about securing the gun and keeping the old fellow from doing mischief, at the very suggestion of which the self-important man in the cocked hat retired with some precipitation. At this critical moment a fresh, comely woman pressed through the throng to get a peep at the grey-bearded man. She had a chubby child in her arms, which, frightened at his looks, began to cry. 'Hush, Rip,' cried she, 'hush, you little fool; the old man won't hurt you.' The name of the child, the air of the mother, the tone of her voice, all awakened a train of recollections in his mind. 'What is your name, my good woman?' asked he.

'Judith Gardenier.'

'And your father's name?'

'Ah, poor man, Rip Van Winkle was his name, but it's twenty years since he went away from home with his gun, and never has been heard of since — his dog came home without him; but whether he shot himself, or was carried away by the Indians, nobody can tell. I was then but a little girl.'

Rip had but one question more to ask; but he put it with a faltering voice:

'Where's your mother?'

'Oh, she too had died but a short time since; she broke a blood vessel in a fit of passion, at a New England pedlar.'

There was a drop of comfort, at least, in this intelligence. The honest man could contain himself no longer. He caught his daughter and her child in his arms. 'I am your father!' cried he. 'Young Rip Van Winkle once — old Rip Van Winkle now! Does nobody know poor Rip Van Winkle?'

All stood amazed, until an old woman, tottering out from among the crowd, put her hand to her brow and, peering under it in his face for a moment, exclaimed, 'Sure enough! It is Rip Van Winkle – it is himself! Welcome home again, old neighbour. Why, where have you been these twenty long years?'

Rip's story was soon told, for the whole twenty years had been to him but as one night. The neighbours stared when they heard it; some were seen to wink at each other and put their tongues in their cheeks, and the self-important man in the cocked hat, who, when the alarm was over, had returned to the field, screwed down the corners of his mouth and shook his head – upon which there was a general shaking of the head throughout the assemblage.

It was determined, however, to take the opinion of old Peter Vanderdonk, who was seen slowly advancing up the road. He was a descendant of the historian of that name, who wrote one of the earliest accounts of the province. Peter was the most ancient inhabitant of the village, and well versed in all the wonderful events and traditions of the neighbourhood. He recollected Rip at once and corroborated his story in the most satisfactory manner. He assured the company that it was a fact, handed down from his ancestor the historian, that the Kaatskill Mountains had always been haunted by strange beings. That it was affirmed that the great Hendrick Hudson, the first discoverer of the river and country, kept a kind of vigil there every twenty years, with his crew of the *Half Moon*, being permitted in this way to revisit the scenes of his enterprise and keep a guardian eye upon the river and the great city called by his name. That his father had once seen them in their old Dutch dresses playing at ninepins in a hollow of the mountain, and that he himself had heard, one summer afternoon, the sound of their balls, like distant peals of thunder.

To make a long story short, the company broke up and returned to the more important concerns of the election. Rip's daughter took him home to live with her; she had a snug, well-furnished house, and a stout, cheery farmer for a husband, whom Rip recollected for one of the urchins that used to climb upon his back. As to Rip's son, and heir, who was the ditto of himself, seen leaning against the tree, he was employed to work on the farm, but evinced a hereditary disposition to attend to anything else but his business.

Rip now resumed his old walk and habits; he soon found many of his former cronies, though all rather the worse for the wear and tear of time, and preferred making friends among the rising generation, with whom he soon grew into great favour.

Having nothing to do at home, and being arrived at that happy age when a man can be idle with impunity, he took his place once more on the bench at the inn door and was reverenced as one of the patriarchs of the village, and a chronicle of the old times 'before the war'. It was some time before he could get into the regular track of gossip, or could be made to comprehend the strange events that had taken place during his torpor. How that there had been a revolutionary war – that the country had thrown off the yoke of old England – and that, instead of being a subject of his Majesty George the Third, he was now a free citizen of the United States. Rip, in fact, was no politician – the changes of states and empires made but little impression on him; but there was one species of despotism under which he had long groaned, and that was – petticoat government. Happily that was at an end; he had got his neck out of the yoke of matrimony and could go in and out whenever he pleased, without dreading the tyranny of Dame Van Winkle. Whenever her name was mentioned, however, he shook his head, shrugged his shoulders, and cast up his eyes, which might pass either for an expression of resignation to his fate or joy at his deliverance.

He used to tell his story to every stranger that arrived at Mr Doolittle's hotel. He was observed, at first, to vary on some points every time he told it, which was, doubtless, owing to his having so recently awaked. It at last settled down precisely to the tale I have related, and not a man, woman, or child in the neighbourhood but knew it by heart. Some always pretended to doubt the reality of it, and insisted that Rip had been out of his head, and that this was one point on which he always remained flighty. The old Dutch inhabitants, however, almost universally gave it full credit. Even to this day they never hear a thunderstorm of a summer afternoon about the Kaatskill but they say Hendrick Hudson and his crew are at their game of ninepins; and it is a common wish of all henpecked husbands in the neighbourhood, when life hangs heavy on their hands, that they might have a quieting draught out of Rip Van Winkle's flagon.

Clement Clarke Moore

A VISIT FROM ST NICHOLAS

Illustrated by Alison Jay

'Twas the night before Christmas, when all through the house
Not a creature was stirring, not even a mouse;
The stockings were hung by the chimney with care,
In hopes that St Nicholas soon would be there;
The children were nestled all snug in their beds,
While visions of sugar-plums danced in their heads;
And Mamma in her kerchief, and I in my cap,
Had just settled our brains for a long winter's nap –
When out on the lawn there arose such a clatter,
I sprang from my bed to see what was the matter.
Away to the window I flew like a flash,
Tore open the shutters and threw up the sash.
The moon, on the breast of the new-fallen snow,
Gave a lustre of mid-day to objects below;
When, what to my wondering eyes should appear,
But a miniature sleigh, and eight tiny reindeer,
With a little old driver, so lively and quick,
I knew in a moment it must be St Nick.
More rapid than eagles his coursers they came,
And he whistled, and shouted, and called them by name;
'Now, Dasher! now, Dancer! now, Prancer and Vixen!
On! Comet, on! Cupid, on! Donder and Blitzen –
To the top of the porch, to the top of the wall!
Now, dash away, dash away, dash away all!'
As dry leaves that before the wild hurricane fly,

When they meet with an obstacle, mount to the sky,
So, up to the house-top the coursers they flew,
With the sleigh full of toys – and St Nicholas too.
And then in a twinkling I heard on the roof
The prancing and pawing of each little hoof.
As I drew in my head, and was turning around,
Down the chimney St Nicholas came with a bound.

He was dressed all in fur from his head to his foot,
And his clothes were all tarnished with ashes and soot;
A bundle of toys he had flung on his back,
And he looked like a pedlar just opening his pack.
His eyes how they twinkled! his dimples how merry!
His cheeks were like roses, his nose like a cherry;
His droll little mouth was drawn up like a bow,
And the beard on his chin was as white as the snow.
The stump of a pipe he held tight in his teeth,
And the smoke, it encircled his head like a wreath.
He had a broad face and a little round belly
That shook, when he laughed, like a bowl full of jelly.
He was chubby and plump – a right jolly old elf;
And I laughed when I saw him, in spite of myself.
A wink of his eye, and a twist of his head,

Soon gave me to know I had nothing to dread.
He spoke not a word, but went straight to his work,
And filled all the stockings; then turned with a jerk,
And laying his finger aside of his nose,
And giving a nod, up the chimney he rose.
He sprang to his sleigh, to his team gave a whistle,
And away they all flew like the down of a thistle;
But I heard him exclaim, ere he drove out of sight,
'Happy Christmas to all, and to all a good-night!'

Captain Marryat

FROM

THE CHILDREN OF THE NEW FOREST

Illustrated by Paul Young

During the English Civil War between the Cavaliers and the Roundheads, the four Beverley children are forced to live in hiding in the forest. Living off the land, they face many dangerous challenges – but they are not completely without friends.

'A narrow escape, Humphrey!' said Edward, as he held his brother's hand.

'Yes, indeed; we may thank Heaven for our preservation,' replied Humphrey. 'And poor Smoker! Let us see if he is much hurt.'

'I trust not,' said Edward, going up to the dog, who remained quite still on the ground, with his tongue out, and panting violently.

They examined poor Smoker all over very carefully, and found that there was no external wound; but on Edward pressing his side, the animal gave a low howl.

'It is there where the horn of the bull took him,' observed Humphrey.

'Yes,' said Edward, pressing and feeling softly; 'and he has two of his ribs broken. Humphrey, see if you can get him a little water; that will

314

recover him more than anything else. The bull has knocked the breath out of his body. I think he will soon be well again, poor fellow.'

Humphrey soon returned with some water from a neighbouring pool. He brought it in his hat, and gave it to the dog, who lapped it slowly at first, but afterwards much faster, and wagging his tail.

'He will do now,' said Edward; 'we must give him time to recover himself. Now then, let us examine our quarry. Why, Humphrey, what a quantity of meat we have here! It will take three journeys to Lymington at least.'

'Yes, and no time to lose, for the weather is getting warm already, Edward. Now, what to do? Will you remain while I go home for the cart?'

'Yes, it's no use both going. I will stay here and watch poor Smoker, and take off the skins ready by the time you are back again. Leave me your knife as well as my own, for one will soon be blunt.'

Humphrey gave his knife to Edward, and taking up his gun, set off for the cottage. Edward had skinned two of the bulls before Humphrey's return; and Smoker, although he evidently was in great pain, was on his legs again. As soon as they had finished and quartered the beasts, the cart was loaded, and they returned home; they had to return a second time, and both the pony and they were very tired before they sat down to supper. They found the gipsy boy very much recovered, and in good spirits. Alice said that he had been amusing Edith and her by tossing up three potatoes at a time, and playing them like balls; and that he had spun a platter upon an iron skewer and balanced it on his chin. They gave him some supper, which he ate in the chimney-corner, looking up and staring every now and then at Edith, to whom he appeared very much attached already.

'Is it good?' said Humphrey to the boy, giving him another venison steak.

'Yes; not have so good supper in pit-hole,' replied Pablo, laughing.

Early on the following morning Edward and Humphrey set off to Lymington with the cart laden with meat. Edward showed Humphrey all the shops and the streets they were in where the purchases were to be made – introduced him to the landlord of the hostelrie – and having sold their meat, they returned home. The rest of the meat was taken to Lymington and disposed of by Humphrey on the following day; and the day after that the three skins were carried to the town and disposed of.

'We made a good day's work, Edward,' said Humphrey, as he reckoned up the money they had made.

'We earned it with some risk, at all events,' replied Edward; 'and now, Humphrey, I think it is time that I keep my promise to Oswald, and go over to the Intendant's house, and pay my visit to the young lady, as I presume she is – and certainly she has every appearance of being one. I want the visit to be over, as I want to be doing.'

'How do you mean, Edward?'

'I mean that I want to go out and kill some deer; but I will not do it till after I have seen her. When my visit is over, I intend to defy the Intendant and all his verderers.'

'But why should this visit prevent you going out this very day, if so inclined?'

'I don't know, but she may ask me if I have done so, and I do not want to tell her that I have; neither do I want to say that I have not if I have; and therefore I shall not commence till after I have seen her.'

'When will you set off?'

'Tomorrow morning; and I shall take my gun, although Oswald desired me not; but, after the fight we had with the wild cattle the other day, I don't think it prudent to be unarmed; indeed, I do not feel comfortable without I have my gun at any time.'

'Well, I shall have plenty to do when you are away – the potatoes must be hoed up, and I shall see what I can make of Master Pablo. He appears well enough, and he has played quite long enough, so I shall take him with me to the garden tomorrow, and set him to work. What a quantity of fruit there is a promise of in the orchard this year! And, Edward, if this boy turns out of any use, and is a help to me, I think that I shall take all the orchard into garden, and then enclose another piece of ground, and see if we cannot grow some corn for ourselves. It is the greatest expense that we have at present, and I should like to take my own corn to the mill to be ground.'

'But will not growing corn require plough and horses?' said Edward.

'No; we will till it by hand: two of us can dig a great deal at odd times, and we shall have a better crop with the spade than with the plough. We have now so much manure that we can afford it.'

'Well, if it is to be done, it should be done at once, Humphrey, before the people from the other side of the forest come and find us out, or they will dispute our right to the enclosure.'

'The forest belongs to the King, brother, and not to the Parliament; and we are the King's liege men, and only look to him for permission,' replied Humphrey. 'But what you say is true: the sooner it is done the better, and I will about it at once.'

'How much do you propose fencing in?'

'About two or three acres.'

'But that is more than you can dig this year or the next.'

'I know that; but I will manure it without digging, and the grass will grow so rich to what it will outside of the enclosure, that they will suppose it has been enclosed a long while.'

'That's not a bad idea, Humphrey; but I advise you to look well after that boy, for he is of a bad race, and has not been brought up, I am afraid, with too strict notions of honesty. Be careful, and tell your sisters also to be cautious not to let him suppose that we have any money in the old chest, till we find out whether he is to be trusted or not.'

'Better not let him know it under any circumstances,' replied Humphrey. 'He may continue honest if not tempted by the knowledge that there is anything worth stealing.'

'You are right, Humphrey. Well, I will be off tomorrow morning and get this visit over. I hope to be able to get all the news from her, now that her father is away.'

'I hope to get some work out of this Master Pablo,' replied Humphrey. 'How many things I could do, if he would only work! Now, I'll tell you one thing. I will dig a sawpit and get a saw, and then I can cut out boards, and build anything we want. The first time I go to Lymington I will buy a saw − I can afford it now; and I'll make a carpenter's bench for the first thing, and then, with some more tools, I shall get on; and then, Edward, I'll tell you what else I will do.'

'Then, Humphrey,' replied Edward, laughing, 'you must tell me some other time, for it is now very late, and I must go to bed, as I have to rise early. I know you have so many projects in your mind that it would take half the night to listen to them.'

'Well, I believe what you say is true,' replied Humphrey, 'and it will be better to do one thing at a time than to talk about doing a hundred; so we will, as you say, to bed.'

At sunrise Edward and Humphrey were both up. Alice came out when they tapped at her door, as she would not let Edward go without his breakfast. Edith joined them, and they went to prayers. While they were so employed, Pablo came out and listened to what was said. When prayers were over, Humphrey asked Pablo if he knew what they had been doing.

'No, not much; suppose you pray sun to shine.'

'No, Pablo,' said Edith; 'pray to God to make us good.'

'You bad then?' said Pablo. 'Me not bad.'

'Yes, Pablo, everybody very bad,' said Alice; 'but if we try to be good, God forgives us.'

The conversation was then dropped, and as soon as Edward had made his breakfast he kissed his sisters, and wished Humphrey farewell.

Edward threw his gun over his arm, and calling his puppy which he had named Holdfast, bade Humphrey and his sisters farewell, and set off on his journey across the forest.

Holdfast, as well as Humphrey's puppy, which had been named Watch, had grown very fine young animals. The first had been named Holdfast, because it would seize the pigs by the ears and lead them into the sty; and the other, because it was so alert at the least noise; but, as Humphrey said, Watch ought to have learnt to lead the pigs, it being more in his line of business than Holdfast's, which was to be brought up for hunting in the forest, while Watch was being educated as a house and farmyard dog.

Edward had refused to take the pony, as Humphrey required it for the farm work, and the weather was so fine that he preferred walking – the more so as it would enable him on his return across the forest to try for some venison, which he could not have done if he had been mounted on Billy's back. Edward walked quick, followed by his dog, which he had taught to keep to heel. He felt happy, as people do who have no cares, from the fine weather – the deep green of the verdure chequered by the flowers in bloom, and the majestic scenery which met his eye on every side. His heart was as buoyant as his steps, as he walked along, the light summer breeze fanning his face. His thoughts, however, which had been more of the chase than anything else, suddenly changed, and he became serious. For some time he had heard no political news of consequence, or what the Commons were doing with the King. This reverie naturally brought to his mind his father's death, the burning of his property, and its sequestration. His cheeks coloured with indignation, and his brow was moody. Then he built castles for the future. He imagined the King released from his prison, and leading an army against his oppressors; he fancied himself at the head of a troop of cavalry, charging the Parliamentary horse. Victory was on his side. The King was again on his throne, and he was again in possession of the family estate. He was rebuilding the hall, and somehow or another it appeared to him that Patience was standing by his side, as he gave directions to the artificers, when his reverie was suddenly disturbed by Holdfast barking and springing forward in advance.

Edward, who had by this time got over more than half his journey, looked up, and perceived himself confronted by a powerful man, apparently about forty years of age, and dressed as a verderer of the forest. He thought at the time that he had seldom seen a person with a more sinister and forbidding countenance.

'How now, young fellow, what are you doing here?' said the man, walking up to him, and cocking the gun which he held in his hand as he advanced.

Edward quietly cocked his own gun, which was loaded, when he perceived that hostile preparation on the part of the other person, and then replied, 'I am walking across the forest, as you may perceive.'

'Yes, I perceive you are walking, and you are walking with a dog and a gun; you will now be pleased to walk with me. Deer-stalkers are not any longer permitted to range this forest.'

'I am no deer-stalker,' replied Edward. 'It will be quite sufficient to give me that title when you find me with venison in my possession; and as for going with you, that I certainly shall not. Sheer off, or you may meet with harm.'

'Why, you young good-for-nothing, if you have not venison, it is not from any will not to take it; you are out in pursuit of it, that is clear. Come, come, you've the wrong person to deal with: my orders are to take up all poachers, and take you I will.'

'If you can,' replied Edward. 'But you must first prove that you are able to so do. My gun is as good and my aim is as sure as yours, whoever you may be. I tell you again I am no poacher, nor have I come out to take the deer, but to cross over to the Intendant's cottage, whither I am now going. I tell you thus much, that you may not do anything foolish; and having said this, I advise you to think twice before you act once. Let me proceed in peace, or you may lose your place, if you do not, by your own rashness, lose your life.'

There was something so cool and so determined in Edward's quiet manner that the verderer hesitated. He perceived that any attempt to take Edward would be at the risk of his own life; and he knew that his orders were to apprehend all poachers, but not to shoot people. It was true that resistance with firearms would warrant his acting in self-defence; but admitting that he should succeed, which was doubtful, still Edward had not been caught in the act of killing venison, and he had no witnesses to prove what had occurred. He also knew that the Intendant had given very strict orders as to the shedding of blood, which he was most averse to, under any circumstances; and there was something in Edward's appearance and manner so different from a common person that he was puzzled. Moreover, Edward had stated that he was going to the Intendant's house. All things considered, as he found that bullying would not succeed, he thought it advisable to change his tone, and therefore said, –

'You tell me that you are going to the Intendant's house; you have business there, I presume? If I took you prisoner, it is there I should have conducted you; so, young man, you may now walk on before me.'

'I thank you,' replied Edward, 'but walk on before you I will not; but if you choose to half-cock your gun again, and walk by my side, I will do the same. Those are my terms, and I will listen to no other; so be pleased to make up your mind, as I am in haste.'

The verderer appeared very indignant at this reply, but after a time said, 'Be it so.'

Edward then uncocked his gun, with his eyes fixed upon the man, and the verderer did the same; and then they walked side by side, Edward keeping at the distance of three yards from him, in case of treachery.

After a few moments' silence the verderer said, –

'You tell me you are going to the Intendant's house: he is not at home.'

'But young Mistress Patience is, I presume,' said Edward.

'Yes,' replied the man, who, finding that Edward appeared to know so much about the Intendant's family, began to be more civil – 'yes, she is at home, for I saw her in the garden this morning.'

'And Oswald, is he at home?' rejoined Edward.

'Yes, he is. You appear to know our people, young man. Who may you be, if it is a fair question?'

'It would have been a fair question had you treated me fairly,' replied Edward; 'but as it is no concern of yours, I shall leave you to find it out.'

This reply puzzled the man still more, and he now, from the tone of authority assumed by Edward, began to imagine that he had made some mistake, and that he was speaking to a superior, although clad in a forester's dress. He therefore answered humbly, observing that he had only been doing his duty.

Edward walked on without making any reply.

As they arrived within a hundred yards of the Intendant's house, Edward said, –

'I have now arrived at my destination, and am going into that house, as I told you. Do you choose to enter it with me, or will you go to Oswald Partridge and tell him that you have met with Edward Armitage in the forest, and that I should be glad to see him? I believe you are under his orders, are you not?'

'Yes, I am,' replied the verderer, 'and as I suppose that all's right, I shall go and deliver your message.'

Edward then turned away from the man, and went into the wicket-gate of the garden, and knocked at the door of the house. The door was opened by Patience Heatherstone herself, who said, 'Oh, how glad I am to see you! Come in.' Edward took off his hat and bowed. Patience led the way into her father's study, where Edward had been first received.

'And now,' said Patience, extending her hand to Edward, 'thanks, many thanks, for your preserving me from so dreadful a death. You don't know how unhappy I have been at not being able to give you my poor thanks for your courageous behaviour.'

Her hand still remained in Edward's while she said this.

'You rate what I did too highly,' replied Edward; 'I would have done the same for any one in such distress: it was my duty as a − man' − cavalier he was about to say, but he checked himself.

'Sit down,' said Patience, taking a chair; 'nay, no ceremony. I cannot treat as an inferior one to whom I owe such a debt of gratitude.'

Edward smiled as he took his seat.

'My father is as grateful to you as I am − I'm sure that he is; for I heard him when at prayer call down blessings on your head. What can he do for you? I begged Oswald Partridge to bring you here, that I might find out. O sir, do pray let me know how we can show our gratitude by something more than words.'

'You have shown it already, Mistress Patience,' replied Edward. 'Have you not honoured a poor forester with your hand in friendship, and even admitted him to sit down before you?'

'He who has preserved my life at the risk of his own becomes to me as a brother − at least I feel as a sister towards him. A debt is still a debt, whether indebted to a king or to a −'

'Forester, Mistress Patience − that is the real word that you should not have hesitated to have used. Do you imagine that I am ashamed of my calling?'

'To tell you candidly the truth, then,' replied Patience, 'I cannot believe that you are what you profess to be. I mean to say that, although a forester now, you were never brought up as such. My father has an opinion allied to mine.'

'I thank you both for your good opinion of me, but I fear that I cannot raise myself above the condition of a forester; nay, from your father's coming down here, and the new regulations, I have every chance of sinking down to the lower grade of a deer-stalker and poacher. Indeed, had it not been that I had my gun with me, I should have been seized as such this very day as I came over.'

'But you were not shooting the deer, were you, sir?' inquired Patience.

'No, I was not; nor have I killed any since I saw you.'

'I am glad that I can say that to my father,' replied Patience; 'it

will much please him. He said to me that he thought you capable of much higher employment than any that could be offered here, and only wished to know what you would accept. He has interest – great interest – although just now at variance with the rulers of this country, on account of the –'

'Murder of the King you would or should have said, Mistress Patience. I have heard how much he was opposed to that foul deed, and I honour him for it.'

'How kind, how truly kind you are to say so!' said Patience, the tears starting in her eyes. 'What pleasure to hear my father's conduct praised by you!'

'Why, of course, Mistress Patience, all of my way of thinking must praise him. Your father is in London, I hear?'

'Yes, he is; and that reminds me that you must want some refreshment after your walk. I will call Phoebe.' So saying, Patience left the room.

The fact was, Mistress Patience was reminded that she had been sitting with a young man some time, and alone with him – which was not quite proper in those times – and when Phoebe appeared with the

'Indeed! Then you are of gentle blood?'

'I believe so,' replied Patience, with surprise.

'Thank you for your condescension, Mistress Patience. And now, if you will permit me, I will take my leave.'

'Before you go, let me once more thank you for saving a worthless life,' said Patience. 'Well, you must come again when my father is here. He will be but too glad to have an opportunity of thanking one who has preserved his only child. Indeed, if you knew my father, you would feel as much regard for him as I do. He is very good, although he looks so stern and melancholy; but he has seldom smiled since my poor mother's death.'

'As to your father, Mistress Patience, I will think as well as I can of one who is joined to a party which I hold in detestation. I can say no more.'

'I must not say all that I know, or you would perhaps find out that he is not quite so wedded to that party as you suppose. Neither his brother-in-law nor he are great friends of Cromwell's, I can assure you; but this in confidence.'

'That raises him in my estimation. But why, then, does he hold office?'

'He did not ask it – it was given to him, I really believe, because they wished him out of the way; and he accepted it because he was opposed to what was going on, and wished himself to be away. At least I infer so much from what I have learnt. It is not an office of power or trust which leagues him with the present Government.'

'No; only one which opposes him to me and my malpractices,' replied Edward, laughing. 'Well, Mistress Patience, you have shown great condescension to a poor forester, and I return you many thanks for your kindness towards me. I will now take my leave.'

'And when will you come and see my father?'

'I cannot say. I fear that I shall not be able very soon to look in his injured face, and it will not be well for a poacher to come near him,' replied Edward. 'However, some day I may be taken and brought before you as a prisoner, you know, and then he is certain to see me.'

'I will not tell you to kill deer,' replied Patience; 'but if you do kill them, no one shall harm you — or I know little of my power or my father's. Farewell, then, sir; and once more gratitude and thanks.'

Patience held out her hand again to Edward, who this time, like a true Cavalier, raised it respectfully to his lips. Patience coloured a little, but did not attempt to withdraw it; and Edward, with a low obeisance, quitted the room.

Edward Lear

THE OWL AND THE PUSSY-CAT

Illustrated by Paul Birkbeck

The Owl and the Pussy-Cat went to sea
  In a beautiful pea-green boat,
They took some honey, and plenty of money,
  Wrapped up in a five-pound note.
The Owl looked up to the stars above,
  And sang to a small guitar,
'O lovely Pussy! O Pussy, my love,
  What a beautiful Pussy you are,
    You are,
    You are!
  What a beautiful Pussy you are!'

Pussy said to the Owl, 'You elegant fowl!
  How charmingly sweet you sing!
O let us be married! too long we have tarried
  But what shall we do for a ring?'
They sailed away for a year and a day,
  To the land where the Bong-tree grows,
And there in a wood a Piggy-wig stood,
  With a ring at the end of his nose,
    His nose,
    His nose,
  With a ring at the end of his nose.

'Dear Pig, are you willing to sell for one shilling
  Your ring?' Said the Piggy, 'I will.'
So they took it away, and were married next day
  By the Turkey who lives on the hill.
They dined on mince, and slices of quince,
  Which they ate with a runcible spoon;
And hand in hand, on the edge of the sand,
  They danced by the light of the moon,
    The moon,
    The moon,
  They danced by the light of the moon.

Oscar Wilde

THE SELFISH GIANT

FROM
THE HAPPY PRINCE AND OTHER STORIES

Illustrated by Greg Becker

Every afternoon, as they were coming from school, the children used to go and play in the Giant's garden.

It was a large lovely garden, with soft green grass. Here and there over the grass stood beautiful flowers like stars, and there were twelve peach-trees that in the spring-time broke out into delicate blossoms of pink and pearl, and in the autumn bore rich fruit. The birds sat on the trees and sang so sweetly that the children used to stop their games in order to listen to them. 'How happy we are here!' they cried to each other.

One day the Giant came back. He had been to visit his friend the Cornish ogre, and had stayed with him for seven years. After the seven years were over he had said all that he had to say, for his conversation was limited, and he determined to return to his own castle. When he arrived he saw the children playing in the garden.

'What are you doing here?' he cried in a very gruff voice, and the children ran away.

'My own garden is my own garden,' said the Giant; 'anyone can understand that, and I will allow nobody to play in it but myself.' So he built a high wall all round it, and put up a notice-board.

> ## TRESPASSERS
> WILL BE
> ## PROSECUTED

He was a very selfish Giant.

The poor children had now nowhere to play. They tried to play on the road, but the road was very dusty and full of hard stones, and they did not like it. They used to wander round the high walls when their lessons were over, and talk about the beautiful garden inside. 'How happy we were there!' they said to each other.

Then the Spring came, and all over the country there were little blossoms and little birds. Only in the garden of the Selfish Giant it was still winter. The birds did not care to sing in it as there were no children, and the trees forgot to blossom. Once a beautiful flower put its head out from the grass, but when it saw the notice-board it was so sorry for the children that it slipped back into the ground again, and went off to sleep. The only people who were pleased were the Snow and the Frost. 'Spring has forgotten this garden,' they cried, 'so we will live here all the year round.' The Snow covered up the grass with her great white cloak, and the Frost painted all the trees silver. Then they invited the North Wind to stay with them, and he came. He was wrapped in furs, and he roared all day about the garden, and blew the chimney pots down. 'This is a delightful spot,' he said, 'we must ask the Hail on a visit.' So the Hail came. Every day for three hours he rattled on the roof of the castle till he broke most of the slates, and then he ran round and round the garden as fast as he could go. He was dressed in grey, and his breath was like ice.

'I cannot understand why the Spring

is so late in coming,' said the Selfish Giant, as he sat at the window and looked out at his cold, white garden; 'I hope there will be a change in the weather.'

But the Spring never came, nor the Summer. The Autumn gave golden fruit to every garden, but to the Giant's garden she gave none. 'He is too selfish,' she said. So it was always winter there, and the North Wind and the Hail, and the Frost, and the Snow danced about through the trees.

One morning the Giant was lying awake in bed when he heard some lovely music. It sounded so sweet to his ears that he thought it must be the King's musicians passing by. It was really only a little linnet singing outside his window, but it was so long since he had heard a bird sing in his garden that it seemed to him to be the most beautiful music in the world. Then the Hail stopped dancing over his head, and the North Wind ceased roaring, and a delicious perfume came to him through the open casement. 'I believe the Spring has come at last,' said the Giant; and he jumped out of bed and looked out.

What did he see?

He saw a most wonderful sight. Through a little hole in the wall the children had crept in, and they were sitting in the branches of the trees. In every tree that he could see there was a little child. And the trees were so glad to have the children back again that they had covered themselves with blossoms, and were waving their arms gently above the children's heads. The birds were flying about and twittering with delight, and the flowers were looking up through the green grass and laughing. It was a lovely scene, only in one corner it was still winter. It was the farthest corner of the garden, and in it was standing a little boy. He was so small that he could not reach up to the branches of the tree, and he was wandering all round it, crying bitterly. The poor tree was still covered with frost and snow, and the North Wind was blowing and roaring above it. 'Climb up! little boy,' said the Tree, and it bent its branches down as low as it could but the boy was too tiny.

And the Giant's heart melted as he looked out. 'How selfish I have been!' he said: 'now I know why the Spring would not come here. I

will put that poor little boy on the top of the tree, and then I will knock down the wall, and my garden shall be the children's playground for ever and ever.' He was really very sorry for what he had done.

So he crept downstairs and opened the front door quite softly, and went out into the garden. But when the children saw him they were so frightened that they all ran away, and the garden became winter again. Only the little boy did not run for his eyes were so full of tears that he did not see the Giant coming. And the Giant stole up behind him and took him gently in his hand, and put him up into the tree. And the tree broke at once into blossom, and the birds came and sang on it, and the little boy stretched out his two arms and flung them round the Giant's neck, and kissed him. And the other children when they saw that the Giant was not wicked any longer, came running back, and with them came the Spring. 'It is your garden now, little children,' said the Giant, and he took a great axe and knocked down the wall. And when the people were going to market at twelve o'clock they found the Giant playing with the children in the most beautiful garden they had ever seen.

All day long they played, and in the evening they came to the Giant to bid him good-bye.

'But where is your little companion?' he said: 'the boy I put into the tree.' The Giant loved him the best because he had kissed him.

'We don't know,' answered the children: 'he has gone away.'

'You must tell him to be sure and come tomorrow,' said the Giant. But the children said that they did not know where he lived and had never seen him before; and the Giant felt very sad.

Every afternoon, when school was over, the children came and played with the Giant. But the little boy whom the Giant loved was never seen again. The Giant was very kind to all the children, yet he longed for his first little friend, and often spoke of him. 'How

I would like to see him!' he used to say.

Years went over, and the Giant grew very old and feeble. He could not play about any more, so he sat in a huge armchair, and watched the children at their games, and admired his garden. 'I have many beautiful flowers,' he said; 'but the children are the most beautiful flowers of all.'

One winter morning he looked out of his window as he was dressing. He did not hate the Winter now, for he knew that it was merely the Spring asleep, and that the flowers were resting.

Suddenly he rubbed his eyes in wonder and looked and looked. It certainly was a marvellous sight. In the farthest corner of the garden was a tree quite covered with lovely white blossoms. Its branches were golden, and silver fruit hung down from them, and underneath it stood the little boy he had loved.

Downstairs ran the Giant in great joy, and out into the garden. He hastened across the grass, and came near to the child. And when he came quite close his face grew red with anger, and he said, 'Who hath dared to wound thee?' For on the palms of the child's hands were the prints of two nails, and the prints of two nails were on the little feet.

'Who hath dared to wound thee?' cried the Giant, 'tell me, that I may take my big sword and slay him.'

'Nay,' answered the child: 'but these are the wounds of Love.'

'Who art thou?' said the Giant, and a strange awe fell on him, and he knelt before the little child.

And the child smiled on the Giant, and said to him, 'You let me play once in your garden, today you shall come with me to my garden, which is Paradise.'

And when the children ran in that afternoon, they found the Giant lying dead under the tree, all covered with white blossoms.

Kenneth Grahame

DUCKS' DITTY

Illustrated by E. H. Shepard

All along the backwater,
Through the rushes tall,
Ducks are a-dabbling,
Up tails all!

Ducks' tails, drakes' tails,
Yellow feet a-quiver,
Yellow bills all out of sight
Busy in the river!

Slushy green undergrowth
Where the roach swim –
Here we keep our larder,
Cool and full and dim.

Everyone for what he likes!
We like to be
Heads down, tails up,
Dabbling free!

High in the blue above
Swifts whirl and call –
We are down a-dabbling,
Up tails all!

Alfred, Lord Tennyson

FROM

THE LADY OF SHALOTT

Illustrated by Alison Jay

On either side the river lie
Long fields of barley and of rye,
That clothe the wold and meet the sky;
And thro' the field the road runs by
   To many-tower'd Camelot;
And up and down the people go,
Gazing where the lilies blow
Round an island there below,
   The island of Shalott.

Willows whiten, aspens quiver,
Little breezes dusk and sliver
Thro' the wave that runs for ever
By the island in the river
   Flowing down to Camelot.
Four grey walls, and four grey towers,
Overlook a space of flowers,
And the silent isle embowers
   The Lady of Shalott.

By the margin, willow-veil'd,
Slide the heavy barges trail'd
By slow horses; and unhail'd
The shallop flitteth, silken-sail'd
   Skimming down to Camelot:
But who hath seen her wave her hand?
Or at the casement seen her stand?
Or is she known in all the land,
   The Lady of Shalott?

Only reapers, reaping early
In among the bearded barley,
Hear a song that echoes cheerly
From the river winding clearly,.
   Down to tower'd Camelot:
And by the moon the reaper weary,
Piling sheaves in uplands airy,
Listening, whispers, ''Tis the fairy
   Lady of Shalott.'

Henry Williamson

FROM

TARKA THE OTTER

Illustrated by Patrick Benson

*The young otter cub has his first taste of life
outside of the holt in which he was born.*

In mid–May the buds of the fallen oak began to open hopefully and to show their ruddy leaves. Seven small kingfishers perched on an alder branch outside the entrance of their tunnel, while the wind stirred the fledgeling down between their feathers, and they waited for loach or beetle or shrimp or elver or troutling. At sunset seven beaks were laid on shoulders, sometimes to lift at a whistle shriller and louder than the whistle of their parents; but the night was to other hunters.

While the moon was full and bright the otters went to hunt the fish lying in the Tunnel Pool below Halfpenny Bridge – bass, grey mullet, and flukes, or flatfish. The cubs were two months old and they had learned to squeeze through the inner opening of the holt and run along the root, in order to play on the grassy bank. One night as they were playing rough-and-tumble round the base of an ash tree, they heard their mother's whistle. This cry was not as piercing as the dog's call to his mate, but like wet fingers drawn down a pane of glass.

Immediately Tarka stopped biting the tail of his younger sister, and the third cub ceased to gnaw his neck. As fast as they could they ran across the root and into the holt. The bitch was waiting for them, with a trout in her mouth. Tarka sniffed at it as she was breaking it up, then turned away, for he did not like the smell of it. The cubs struggled for their own food, so the bitch lay down and fed them with her milk until she grew tired of them. Shaking them off, she went away with the dog, who had swum upriver with her.

When next she returned, she brought two skinned frogs, which she had caught in the reed-grown, marshy bed of the old canal. She dropped them in the holt and slid back into the river, heedless of the cubs' cries. Tarka licked a frog and liked the taste of it; he bared his milk teeth at his sisters, but he did not eat it. They rolled and snarled and played until their mother's return, when they ran to her. She had brought an eel, which she bit into pieces, beginning near the tail, but leaving the head above the paired fins. Tarka swallowed little pieces of the fish and licked his small sister's head afterwards, because it tasted nice. Then he licked his own paws. He was cleaning himself for the first time.

The new food changed them almost at once. They grew swift and fierce. Their frolics on the bank often ceased at the cry of a night-bird, or the distant bark of a cattle dog in the village. They started whenever their mother started. They began to fear. Sometimes at sunset, when their mother left the holt, they ran on the bank and mewed to her as she hunted upstream. She would leave the water and chase them back again to the holt. Her smooth movements near them on land were often broken; she would stand still and uncertain, or run on, jerky with fear. Many times she stood upright and listened, her nose towards the village. People occasionally walked over Canal Bridge, which now carried a drive to a house near the weir; and whenever she heard voices she ceased to hunt, and swam down the river to be near the cubs. Human voices frightened her; but the thunderous noise of trains in the valley and the long, whisking lights of motor-cars on the road beyond the railway were ignored because she was used to them, and knew them to be harmless.

The buds of the ash, sullen for so long in their coverings shaped like the black hooves of cattle, broke into browny-green sprays. The cuckoo sang all night. Reed-buntings chattered among the rising green, water-holding stems of balsam; soon Antares would burn dull red in the low southern night sky.

One warm evening when the river was low, the mother swam down to the holt and called the cubs into the water, and although they were ravening, she did not climb up, but waited for them with a fish below the tree. They whimpered and peered, moving their heads sideways and telling her that below was fearful. She lay on her back in the water and let the fish go, in order to catch it, and rise with it gleaming again. The two youngest cubs ran back over the damp, trodden couch to get through the tunnel, but they were too fat to squeeze through. Perhaps Tarka would have gone with them, if he had not wanted the fish so much. His eyes were on it, he smelled it, his mouth filled with eat-water. He mewed, he yikkered, he tissed, but there was no fish. The otter swam on her back and called him into the water.

Tarka watched her. He wanted the fish, but he dared not let go with

his feet. The fish came no nearer, so he dropped down into the black, star-shivery water. He was clutched in a cold and terrible embrace, so that he could neither see nor breathe, and although he tried to walk, it smothered him, choked him, roared in his ears, and stifled every mew for help, until his mother swam under him, pressing pads and tail against her back. Tarka was carried to the stony margin of an islet, where the closed flowers of the water-crowsfoot were floating among their leaves. He spluttered and sneezed and shook water out of his eyes, and saw the stars above him, and felt his mother's tongue on his head.

When he had eaten the fish, Tarka began to enjoy the strangeness. He was playing with the fish-tail when he heard the whistle so often listened to from the holt. When he saw the animal with the wide flat head and great bristling whiskers that had loomed over his head once before, Tarka tissed and snarled at it and ran for his mother. He snapped at the nose sniffing at him. The dog turned on his back and tried to touch Tarka with his paws, in play. Tarka watched him and wanted to roll as well, but he was awed by the stranger's size.

An hour later, the three cubs had eaten their fish happily on the stones. The bitch had grown tired of coaxing the other cubs to enter the water and had dragged them by their scruffs out of the holt and dropped them into the river.

The first otter to go into deep water had felt the same fear that Tarka felt that night; for his ancestors, thousands of years ago, had been hunters in woods and along the banks of rivers, running the scent of blooded creatures on the earth, like all the members of the weasel race to which they belonged. This race had several tribes in the country of the Two Rivers. Biggest were the brocks, a tribe of badgers who lived in holts scratched among the roots of trees and bushes, and rarely went to water except to drink. They were related to the fitches or stoats, who chased rabbits and jumped upon birds on the earth; and to the vairs or weasels, who sucked the blood of mice and dragged fledgelings from the nest; and to the grey fitches or polecats, so rare in the forests; and to the pine-martens, a tribe so harried by men that one only remained, and he had found sanctuary in a wood where a gin was never tilled and a gun was never fired, where the red deer was never roused and the fox never chased. He was old; his canine teeth worn down. Otters knew the ponds in this wood and they played in them by day, while herons stalked in the shallows and nothing feared the old lady who sometimes sat on the bank, watching the wild creatures which she thought of as the small and persecuted kinsfolk of man.

Long ago, when moose roared in the forest at the mouth of the Two Rivers, otters had followed eels migrating in autumn from ponds and swamps to the seas. They had followed them into shallow water; and one fierce old dog had run through the water so often that he swam, and later, in his great hunger, had put under his head to seize them so often that he dived. Other otters had imitated him. There was a web of skin between the toes, as in the feet of wolves and dogs, and generations of swimming otters had caused the spread of the toes to increase and the web of skin to widen between them. Claws grew shorter. Tails used as rudders became longer, thicker, and powerful with muscles. Otters became hunters under water.

The moose are gone, and their bones lie under the sand in the soft coal which was the forest by the estuary, thousands of years ago. Yet otters have not been hunters in water long enough for the habit to become an instinct. And so the original water-fear was born with Tarka, whose mind had to overlay a weak instinct with habit, just as his ancestor had done when he was hungry.

When he went into the water the next night and tried to walk towards his mother, he floated. He was so pleased that he set out across the river by himself, finding that he could turn easily towards his mother by swinging his hindquarters and rudder. He turned and turned many times in his happiness; east towards Willow Island and the water-song, west towards the kingfisher's nest, and Peal Rock below Canal Bridge, and the otter-path crossing the big bend. North again and then south-west, where the gales came from, up and down, backwards and forwards, sometimes swallowing water, at other times sniffing it up his nose, sneezing, spitting, coughing, but always swimming. He learned to hold his nose above the ream, or ripple, pushed in front of it.

While swimming in this happy way, he noticed the moon. It danced on the water just before his nose. Often he had seen the moon, just outside the hollow tree, and had tried to touch it with a paw. Now he tried to bite it, but it swam away from him. He chased it. It wriggled like a silver fish and he followed to the sedges on the far bank of the river, but it no longer wriggled. It was waiting to play with him. Across the river Tarka could hear the mewing of his sisters, but he set off after the moon over the meadow. He ran among buttercups and cuckoo-flowers and grasses bending with bright points. Farther and farther from the river he ran, the moonlight gleaming on his coat. Really it was brown like the dust in an October puff-ball, but the water sleeked the hair.

As he stopped to listen to the bleat of lambs, a moth whirred by his head and tickled him. While he was scratching, a bird flying with irregular wingbeats and sudden hawk-like glidings took the moth in its wide gape and flew out of his sight. Tarka forgot the moon-play. He crouched in the grasses, which rose above his head like the trees of a forest, some with tops like his rudder, others like his whiskers, and all whispering as they swayed. The nightjar returned, clapping its wings over its head with the noise of a dry stick cracking. Tarka was glad to hear his mother calling him. He mewed. He listened and her whistle was nearer, so he ran away in the wet grasses. The cub did not know how alarmed his mother was nor did he know that less than fifty flaps away a bird with great eyes and wings spanning a yard was flying upon him. The nightjar had seen the bird, too, and had clapped its wings as a danger signal to its mate whose two eggs were laid among ferns in the woods.

The nightjar twirled and planed away; Tarka scampered on. The great bird, who had raised two tufts of feathers on its head, dropped with taloned feet spread for a clutch. The otter saw it drop and ran forwards so swiftly that the sound of her going through the grasses was like the first wind which uncoils as it runs before the south-westerly gale. The bird, which was a short-eared owl, thought that Tarka was a small rabbit, and fanned above him while it considered whether or not he was small enough to be attacked. It did not hesitate longer than the time of six flaps, but stopped, while screaking to terrify and subdue its prey. But Tarka came of a family fiercer and quicker in movement than the owl. Tissing with rage, he jumped and bit his assailant as a foot grasped his back and four talons pierced his skin. The other foot of the bird grasped grasses and it had turned with clacking beak to peck the base of the cub's skull when the paw-stroke of the bitch tore half the feathers from its breast. She stood on it, bit once, twice, thrice, in a second of time, and so the owl died.

Tarka was nipped in the neck, shaken, picked up, bumped all the way back to the bank, scraped over the stones, and dropped into the water. Obediently he followed his mother across the river, to where the dog was lying on his back and gravely watching two cubs playing with the tip of his rudder.

Fish were brought alive to the cubs when they had been swimming about a fortnight, and dropped in the shallowest water. And when they were nearly three months old their mother took them downstream, past Leaning Willow Island, and across the bend, to where the banks were glidden into mud smothered by the sea. The tide had lapsed from the mud, leaving fresh water to tear the rocky bed below.

Tarka galloped through the tall green reeds to the river, stopping by a gut to sniff at the tracks of a curlew, which had been feeding there during the ebb-tide. Near the water he found another track, of five toes well spread, and the prick of five claws. The dog had walked there. Just above Halfpenny Bridge they saw him, half out of the water, and chewing a fish which he did not trouble to hold in his paws. He crunched it from the head downwards, gulping his bites quickly, and as soon as the tail was swallowed, he turned and went underwater for more.

The bitch took her cubs to a pool below the bridge and walked with them across a shallow tail of water. She stared at the stones, brown and slippery with seaweed, and the cubs stared also. They watched the glimmers in the claws of water, sometimes trying to bite them. While

they were watching the mother ran along the bank to the top of the pool and slid into the water. More often than usual her head looked up as she swam from bank to bank, for she was not hunting, but driving the fish down to the cubs. Tarka became excited and, seeing a fish, he swam after it and went underwater to get it. In order to travel faster, he struck out with all four webs together, and lo! Tarka was swimming like an otter near a fish. It was the biggest fish he had seen, and although he kicked after it at the rate of nearly two hundred kicks a minute, he lost it after a yard. He yikkered in his anger, and oh! Tarka was no longer swimming like an otter, but gasping and coughing on the surface, a poor little sick-feeling cub mewing for his mother.

He felt better when he had eaten a mullet caught by his mother. The fish had come up with the tide and remained in the still pool. Later in the night Tarka caught a pollywiggle, or tadpole, in a watery hoof-hole and thought himself a real hunter as he played with it, passing it from paw to paw and rolling on his back in the mud. He was quite selfish over his prey when his mother went to see what he was doing, and cried, *Iss-iss-ic-yang!* an old weasel threat, which being interpreted, means, Go away, or I will drink your blood!

Old Nog, the heron, beating his loose grey wings over Leaning Willow Island as the sun was making yellow the top of the tall tree, saw five brown heads in the salmon-pool. Three small heads and a larger head turned to the left by the fallen tree, and the largest head went on upriver alone. The cubs were tired and did not like being washed when they were in the holt. Afterwards Tarka pushed his sister from his mother's neck, the most comfortable place in the holt, and immediately fell asleep. Sometimes his hindlegs kicked, gently. He was trying to catch a shining fish that wriggled just before his nose, when he was abruptly flung awake. He yawned, but his mother, tissing through her teeth, frightened him into silence. The day was bright outside the hole.

Halcyon the kingfisher sped down the river, crying a short, shrill *peet!* as it passed the holt. The otter got on her forelegs and started towards the opening. Soon after the kingfisher had gone, a turtle dove alighted on the ash tree above the holt and looked about her; she had just flown off her two eggs, nearly dropping through a loose raft-like nest in a hawthorn by the weir. The bird held out a wing and began to straighten the filaments of a flight-quill which had struck a twig during her sudden flight out of the bush-top. She drew the feather through her beak thrice, shook her wings, listened, and went on preening.

Tarka closed his eyes again, breathed deeply and settled to sleep on the youngest cub's neck. He looked up when his mother ran to the opening. The otter was listening to a sound like the high, thin twang of a mosquito. Hair bristled on her neck. From far away there came a deep rolling sound, and a screaming cheer. The otter instantly returned to her cubs and stood over them in a protective attitude, for she knew that hounds were hunting the water.

Tarka crouched down, listening to the cries. They became more distinct. Always a deeper, gruffer note was heard among them. The sounds, almost continuous, became louder and louder. Nearer came another sound – the wings of the dove striking against twigs as it flew away.

A minute later the pair of cole-tits that had a nest in a hole of the ash tree began to make their small, wheezy notes of alarm. The white owl had flown from the bridge and was perched against the ivy of the trunk, turning its head from side to side and blinking. One cole-tit, about as long as a man's finger, flittered with rage on the twigs a few inches from the gold-grey head. The owl blinked slowly; the baying swelled under the bridge; it swung its head round without moving its body and stared straight behind it. *Chizzy-chizzy-chizzy-te!* wheezed the cole-tit as the owl floated away. Tarka was used to this sound, for usually it greeted him whenever he looked out of the holt in daylight.

Chizzy-chizzy-chizzy-te! the bird wheezed again, and then Tarka saw the big head of the dog-otter by the opening, and his wet paws on the bark. The bitch tissed at him, her teeth snapped at his head, and the dog was gone.

The cries were now very loud. Tarka heard thuds in the wood all around him. The cubs crouched in the darkest corner. Nearer came the shouts of men, until the thuds of running feet ceased on the bank. The water began to wash against and lap the half-drowned trunk, claws scraped the wood, the opening grew dark and the tongue he had heard above the others boomed in the hollow. The otter crouched back, larger than usual, for her body was rigid and all the hair of her back stood straight. Swish, swish swept her rudder. She recognized another sound and tissed every time it cried the names of hounds, in a voice thin and high as though it were trying to become as the horn which so often took its rightful breath. The voice ceased. The horn sang its plain note. Whips cracked.

By their big feet hounds pulled themselves out of the water, except the one who threw his deep tongue at the holt opening. He was all black-and-white, with great flews, and the biggest stallion-hound in the pack. He was black from nose to neck except for the pallid nicks of old quarrel scars on his muzzle and head. No hound quarrelled with him now, for Deadlock was master of all. In his veins ran the blood of the Talbots, and one of his bloodhound ancestors had eaten man. He had mastiff in him. His dam and sire had pulled down many a deer at bay in the waters of the moor, and died fireside deaths after faithful service to red coats. A pink weal ran down his belly, for in his second stag-hunting season the great pied hound had been ripped open by the brow-point of a stag; and his pace had gone from him afterwards. The otter-hunters bought him for a guinea, liking his long legs, and now Deadlock was the truest marking hound in the country of the Two Rivers.

He held by his paws, and his teeth tore at the sodden tinderwood. He could thrust in only his head. While he was kicking the water for a foothold, the otter ran forward and bit him through the ear, piercing the earmark where the blue initial letters of his original pack were tattooed. Deadlock yarred through his bared teeth. Three small mouths

at the other end of the holt opened and tissed in immense fright.

Then Tarka heard a cry which he was to hear often in his wanderings; a cry which to many otters of the Two Rivers had meant that the longest swimmings, the fastest land-looping, the quietest slipping from drain or holt were unavailing.

Tally Ho!

The cry came from down the river, just above Leaning Willow Island, from the throat of an old man in a blue coat and white breeches, who had been leaning his bearded chin on hands clasping a ground-ash pole nearly as long and as old as himself. From his look-out place he had seen something moving down like brown thong-weed just under the clear and shallow water. Off came the hat, grey as lichen, to be held while he cried again.

Tally Ho!

The horn of the huntsman sang short and urgent notes; the air by the holt was scored by the names of hounds as he ran with them to where, amidst purple-streaked stems of hemlock, the old man was standing on the shillets.

Soon afterwards the horn sounded again near the holt and the baying of hounds grew louder. Footfalls banged the wood above Tarka's head, as a man climbed along the trunk. The water began to lap: hound-taint from a high-yelping throat came into the holt: the bitch grew larger along her back when, above her head, a man's voice cried snarlingly, *Go'rn leave it, Captain! Go'rn leave it!* A thong swished, a lash cracked. *Go'rn leave it, Captain!*

The high yelping lessened with the taint of breath. The cries went up the river. The rudder of the bitch twitched. The hair on her back fell slanting; but it rose when something scratched above. Her nose pointed, she breathed through her mouth. She moved away uneasily. Tarka sneezed. Tobacco smoke. A man was sitting in the branches over them.

After half an hour the cries came down to the holt again. They passed, and then Tarka heard a new and terrible noise – the noise as of mammoth iron-toed centipedes crossing on the stones, or shillets, at the tail of the pool.

Tally Ho! Look out, he's coming down!

Iron toes scraped the shillets faster. Here, across the shallow, a dozen men and women stood almost leg-to-leg in the water, stirring the stream with their ironshod poles to stop the dog-otter passing down to the next pool.

Tarka and the cubs breathed fast again. Deadlock's great bellow swam nearer, with the high yelping of Captain. Many wavelets slapped against the tree. A dozen hounds were giving tongue between Canal Bridge and the stickle above Leaning Willow Island. A shaggy face looked into the holt and a voice cried just over Tarka's head, *Go'rn leave it, Dewdrop! Go'rn leave it!* Boots knocked on the trunk. *Is-isss-iss! Go'rn leave it!* And Dewdrop left it, bitten in the nose.

Unable to break the stickle, the dog-otter

went back under the bridge. Baying became fainter. The notes of the cole-tits in the ash tree were heard again.

In the quiet hollow the otter unstiffened and scratched for ticks as though the hunt had never come there. Hounds and men were above the bridge, where another stickle was standing. The water flowed with small murmurs. She heard the rustling clicks of dragon-flies' wings over the sun-splashy ripples. Silence, the tranquil *chee-chee* of a cole-tit seeking a grub in an oak-apple, and the sunbeam through the wood-pecker hole roving over the damp wood dust on the floor. The otter lay down, she dozed, she jumped up when sudden cries of *Tally Ho!* and a confused clamour arose beyond the bridge. Now all the sounds of the past hours were increasing together, of tongues, and horns, and cheers; and very soon they were overborne by a deep new noise like the rumbling of the mill when the water-wheel was turning. Then with the deep rumbling came the prolonged thin rattle of the horn, and the triumphant whooping of whips and huntsmen. The sounds slowed and ceased, except for the lone baying of a hound; they broke out again, and slowed away into silence; but long afterwards the strange blowing noises made by their mother frightened the huddled cubs.

Sometimes the slits of the owl's lids opened, and dark eyes would watch a drop of water falling from one of the thin horns of lime hanging from crevices between stones of the arch. Yellow ripple-light no longer passed across the stonework of Canal Bridge. The sun made shadows on the meadow slightly longer than the trees were tall. For more than an hour the water had been peaceful. A blackbird sang in the sycamore growing by the bridge. The otter looked out of the holt and listened. She feared sunlight on the field less than the taint of hounds still coming down on the water, and, calling her cubs, she slid into the river and ran out under the bank, and to the grass. *Iss-iss-iss!* The ground in patches was damp with the water run off hounds' flews, flanks, and sterns. Only a carrion-crow saw them hastening across the meadow to the leat, and its croaks followed them into the wood where bees were burring round purple spires of foxgloves, and chiffchaffs flitted through honeysuckle bines. Otter and cubs passed low and swift among the green seedheads of the bluebells; and uphill over blackening leaves, until they saw the river again below them, where the sun-points glittered, and a young kingfisher, one of the sons of Halcyon, drew a blue line in the shade of oak trees.

Christina Rossetti

WHO HAS SEEN THE WIND?

Illustrated by Ruth Rivers

Who has seen the wind?
Neither I nor you:
But when the leaves hang trembling,
The wind is passing through.

Who has seen the wind?
Neither you nor I:
But when the trees bow down their heads,
The wind is passing by.

Alfred, Lord Tennyson

THE CHARGE OF THE LIGHT BRIGADE

Illustrated by Gino D'Achille

I

Half a league, half a league,
  Half a league onward,
All in the valley of Death
  Rode the six hundred.
'Forward, the Light Brigade!
Charge for the guns!' he said;
Into the valley of Death
  Rode the six hundred.

II

'Forward, the Light Brigade!'
Was there a man dismay'd?
Not tho' the soldier knew
  Some one had blunder'd:
Their's not to make reply,
Their's not to reason why,
Their's but to do and die:
Into the valley of Death
  Rode the six hundred.

III

Cannon to right of them,
Cannon to left of them,
Cannon in front of them
  Volley'd and thunder'd;
Storm'd at with shot and shell,
Boldly they rode and well,
Into the jaws of Death,
Into the mouth of Hell
  Rode the six hundred.

IV

Flash'd all their sabres bare,
Flash'd as they turn'd in air,
Sabring the gunners there,
Charging an army, while
  All the world wonder'd:
Plunged in the battery-smoke
Right thro' the line they broke;
Cossack and Russian
Reel'd from the sabre-stroke
  Shatter'd and sunder'd.
Then they rode back, but not,
  Not the six hundred.

V

Cannon to right of them,
Cannon to left of them,
Cannon behind them
  Volley'd and thunder'd;
Storm'd at with shot and shell,
While horse and hero fell,
They that had fought so well
Came thro' the jaws of Death
Back from the mouth of Hell,
All that was left of them,
  Left of six hundred.

VI

When can their glory fade?
O the wild charge they made!
  All the world wonder'd.
Honour the charge they made!
Honour the Light Brigade,
  Noble six hundred!

I give you the end of a golden string,
Only wind it into a ball,
It will lead you in at Heaven's gate
Built in Jerusalem's wall.

WILLIAM BLAKE

INDEX OF AUTHORS

BIOGRAPHICAL NOTES

AESOP was said by Herodotus to have been a slave on the island of Samos, off Greece, in the sixth century BC. Legend describes him as an ugly man, and audiences were said to laugh at his grotesque appearance as well as his brilliant storytelling. It is likely that he did exist, and compose many of the tales, or fables, associated with him.

WILLIAM ALLINGHAM (1824–89) was a contemporary and friend of the Pre-Raphaelites, including CHRISTINA ROSSETTI. His most famous and popular work, 'The Fairies', has been a favourite inclusion in anthologies since it was first published in 1850.

HANS CHRISTIAN ANDERSEN (1805–75) was born in Odense, Denmark, the son of a shoemaker. His father doted on him, reading stories from *The Arabian Nights* and other dramatic works and taking him to the theatre, but he died when Hans was only eleven. At fourteen he made his way to Copenhagen and worked in the theatre before embarking on a literary career that was to make him famous the world over.

J(AMES) M(ATTHEW) BARRIE (1860–1937) was born in Scotland, the son of a weaver. Many of the children in *Peter Pan* were inspired by real children he knew and loved. When he died he left all the royalties from this book to the Great Ormond Street Hospital for Children.

HILAIRE BELLOC (1870–1953) was born in St Cloud, near Paris, and became a British citizen in 1902. He led a distinguished journalistic and teaching career, editing many journals on literature and writing a column for the *Sunday Times*, as well as teaching English in London and at Glasgow University. He was knighted in 1934.

WILLIAM BLAKE (1757–1827) was the son of a London hosier. He did not go to school, but was instead apprenticed to an engraver to the Society of Antiquaries. His first poem was published in 1783, which he engraved with his own illustrations. His work was often extremely satirical and even revolutionary for the time.

ROBERT BROWNING (1812–89) was born in Camberwell (now part of London), the son of a clerk in the Bank of England. In 1846, by which time he was a moderately famous poet, he eloped with the poetess Elizabeth Barrett to Italy, where he lived until she died in 1861. He returned to find enormous fame in London; the Browning Society was formed in 1881, during his lifetime!

FRANCES HODGSON BURNETT (1849–1924) was a Lancashire ironmonger's daughter who was taken to America in her teens. She married an American and became a successful writer of stories for magazines. *Little Lord Fauntleroy* was based on her son Vivian, who had long ringlets and wore a velvet knickerbocker suit. *The Secret Garden* was partly drawn from her memories of a back garden in her Manchester childhood.

LEWIS CARROLL was the pen-name of CHARLES LUTWIDGE DODGSON (1832–98), the third of eleven children born to a priest in Derbyshire. He taught mathematics at Christ Church, Oxford, and made up the first 'Alice' story after he had met Alice Liddell and her sisters, the daughters of the Dean of Christ Church.

SAMUEL TAYLOR COLERIDGE (1772–1834) was born in Devon, the youngest son of a vicar. He was a brilliant classical scholar, but his first love was the life of the imagination, and he devoted himself to poetry and the ideals of fellow Romantics such as WILLIAM WORDSWORTH and Robert Southey.

CARLO COLLODI is the pen-name of CARLO LORENZINI (1826–90). He worked as a journalist and began writing for children under this alias. His first published short story was about a little wooden puppet. Adults and children loved it, and the adventures of Pinocchio were serialized in an Italian newspaper in 1881–2 before being published in book form in 1883 and then in English in 1892.

N. J. DAWOOD is one of this century's pre-eminent Arabic scholars. As well as translating two volumes of *The Arabian Nights* he has worked on *The Koran*. In 1959 he founded The Arabic Advertising and Publishing Co. Ltd, London, one of the major producers of Arabic translations outside the Middle East.

DANIEL DEFOE (*c.* 1660–1731) was born in London, the son of a butcher. He was a supporter of the Duke of Monmouth's uprising in 1685 and became a friend of King William III. This led to his employment as a writer for the Government. A real-life incident fired his imagination to write *Robinson Crusoe*, and in all he wrote over 250 works.

WALTER DE LA MARE (1873–1956) was born near Woolwich on the outskirts of London. His father worked in the Bank of England and he himself worked in the City for eighteen years. He was desperate for literary success, however, and in 1902 his first collection of poems was published. He was then able to give up his profession and devote himself to writing for the rest of his life.

CHARLES DICKENS (1812–70) was the son of a government clerk. His family were poor and he had no education. He gained work, however, as a journalist reporting debates in the House of Commons. His first novel, *The Pickwick Papers*, was serialized in a magazine from April 1836. He wrote many other books and is considered by many to be the most famous and successful of all British novelists.

SIR ARTHUR CONAN DOYLE (1859–1930) was born in Edinburgh and studied medicine, then set up practice as an oculist. He had few patients, however, and turned to writing instead. Sherlock Holmes first appeared in 1887 in *A Study in Scarlet*. He is perhaps the best-known detective in literature, with characteristics immediately recognizable by everyone.

KENNETH GRAHAME (1859–1932) was born in Edinburgh, but brought up by relations in England after his mother died when he was five. After school he worked for the Bank of England and began to write. He achieved considerable critical approval and success, but stopped writing in his later years to enable him to travel extensively.

ROGER LANCELYN GREEN (1918–87) was born in Norwich. At Oxford University he became especially interested in the Arthurian tales, which he rewrote for children. He wrote many other books based on famous myths and legends, in his manor in Cheshire, where his family had lived for more than 900 years.

FELICIA DOROTHEA HEMANS (1793–1835) was born Dorothea Brown and married Captain Hemans in 1812. She was hugely popular in the United States and is chiefly remembered for her poetry, including 'Casabianca', printed here.

JAMES HOGG (1770–1835) was born in Ettrick Forest in Scotland, and became a shepherd. He was discovered by Sir Walter Scott, and published his first collection of poems in 1807, only to retire to farming. However, he lost what money he had made and returned to Edinburgh in 1810 to renew writing.

MARY HOWITT (1799–1888) was born into a Quaker family. She married her husband, William, in 1821 and settled in Nottingham, where he owned a chemist's shop. From 1836, however, they lived off their writing, between them penning more than 180 books of verse, short stories and fairy tales.

WASHINGTON IRVING (1783–1859) was born in New York and travelled widely, including a period in England when young. He made his fame with books of European folk tales retold with American settings. He was later appointed a diplomatic attaché in Spain. This led to the writing of *Alhambra*, which mixed stories of Spanish life with Moorish tales.

RUDYARD KIPLING (1865–1936) was born in India, educated in England, and returned to India to become a journalist. He began writing short stories and verse and became hugely popular for his children's novels. The majority of his adult life was spent in England. He was awarded the Nobel Prize for Literature in 1907 and is buried in Poet's Corner in Westminster Abbey.

ERIC KNIGHT (1897–1943) was born in Yorkshire, but became an American citizen and died in action as a Major in the United States Army during the Second World War. He is one of a number of authors who wrote prolifically for all ages, but is best remembered as a children's author for his standard version of the story of Lassie.

EDWARD LEAR (1812–88) was born in London, the twentieth child of a stockbroker! He was a talented artist and was commissioned by Lord Stanley to produce a set of animal drawings at his home. Lord Stanley (later the Earl of Derby) became his patron, supporting him while he collected and illustrated his first collection of limericks, the *Book of Nonsense*. He also published books of landscape pictures and, later in his life, longer poems for children.

LADY (ANNE) LINDSAY (1750–1825) was the daughter of the Fifth Earl of Balcarres. She wrote poetry in her twenties and is chiefly remembered for 'Auld Robin Gray', a ballad published in 1771. After marrying she and her husband lived in South Africa.

JACK LONDON (1876–1916) was brought up among the poor of San Francisco in the last century. He became a sailor and gold prospector before starting to write books about his experiences. His two most popular books, *The Call of the Wild* and *White Fang*, both feature dogs as their central figures.

HENRY WADSWORTH LONGFELLOW (1807–82) was born in Portland, Maine. He travelled extensively in Europe and was fluent in several modern languages, which he taught, chiefly at the famous Harvard University, for many years. Even during his time as a professor, however, he was writing poetry, and for much of his life he was the best-loved poet in the United States.

GEORGE MACDONALD (1824–1905) was born in Aberdeenshire, where his family farmed and ran a bleaching service. He became a Congregationalist minister, but lost his job after writing some strange ideas about his religion. He wrote weird, fantastic novels for adults as well as children. The castles that appear in many of them are of a kind found all over his home country.

CAPTAIN FREDERICK MARRYAT (1792–1848) first went to sea as a midshipman at the age of thirteen during the Napoleonic War. He rose rapidly to the rank of Commander by the time war ended in 1815. He resigned his command in 1830 and turned to writing. Many of his books are salty yarns of the sea, but the excerpt printed here is from one of his most famous works.

JOHN MASEFIELD (1878–1967) was born in Herefordshire. His father was a solicitor, but his mother died when he was young and the children were put in the charge of a governess. The children hated her, and he himself said he once stabbed her with a fork! He wrote poetry as a boy and eventually became a journalist,

but only after the First World War did he achieve fame. He became Poet Laureate in 1930.

JOHN MILTON (1608–74) was born in Cheapside, London. His father was a scrivener and composer of music. John was educated at Cambridge, where he began writing poetry. From 1649 until the Restoration in 1660, he held the post of Latin secretary to the Council of State. He later returned to poetry and wrote his most famous work, *Paradise Lost*.

CLEMENT CLARKE MOORE (1779–1863) was born in New York, the son of a bishop of the city. Both his father and he were noted Hebrew scholars, and he himself became a professor. His poem 'A Visit from St Nicholas', printed here, was first published in 1823 and helped to establish the modern image of Father Christmas.

E(DITH) NESBIT (1858–1924) was born in Kennington, London. Her father was a chemist, but died when she was only three. For a time her mother took her to live in France, but they settled in Kent when Edith was thirteen. Unfortunately her mother ran out of money, a fact Edith remembered all her life – she would say she had to continue to write for money even after she became famous and successful.

EDGAR ALLAN POE (1809–49) was born in Boston, Massachusetts, and became an orphan in early childhood. He was brought to England and sent to school in Stoke Newington, London, before returning to the United States. He wrote poetry from an early age, but success came slowly: he enlisted in the US Army and turned to journalism before achieving wide popularity.

ARTHUR RANSOME (1884–1967) was born in Leeds. His father was Professor of History at Yorkshire College (now Leeds University) and a keen fisherman, who took his family to the Lake District each summer holiday, where his experiences influenced his most famous book. Eleven more titles in the *Swallows and Amazons* sequence were to follow.

CHRISTINA ROSSETTI (1830–94) was the daughter of Gabriele Rossetti, an Italian patriot, who came to England in 1824. Theirs was a prodigiously gifted family – one brother was Dante Gabriel Rossetti, the Pre-Raphaelite painter; another, William, was a famous art critic. Christina wrote spiritual and melancholic poetry for all ages, with a high degree of technical perfection.

WILLIAM SHAKESPEARE (1564–1616) was born in Stratford-upon-Avon. His father was a husband-man and held various municipal offices. William was educated in the free grammar school in Stratford, married Anne Hathaway in 1582, and left Stratford for London in about 1585. By 1592 he was an actor and playwright, writing some of the most famous plays ever performed.

MARY SHELLEY (1797–1851) was born in London, the daughter of the philosopher William Godwin. She met PERCY BYSSHE SHELLEY in 1813 while he was still married and they eloped to the Continent the following year. Her married life was surrounded by tragedy – three of her four children died young, and her husband drowned. Mary returned to England for the last thirty years of her life.

PERCY BYSSHE SHELLEY (1792–1822) was born in Sussex and educated at Eton and Oxford University. He was extremely gifted and had his first poems published while a student. But he also led a tragic and short life. His first wife drowned herself in the Serpentine, in London's Hyde Park, in 1816, and he himself accidentally drowned off Greece in 1822, his thirtieth year.

JOHANNA SPYRI (1827–1901) was born in a village near Zurich. Her father was a doctor. She started to write to earn money to help refugees of the Franco-Prussian war. *Heidi* was her first full-length story and she wrote many other books for children, some of which have been translated into English.

ROBERT LOUIS STEVENSON (1850–94) was born in Edinburgh. His parents wanted him to become a lawyer, but he had already decided to devote himself to writing. He is as famous for his novels as he is for his poetry.

JONATHAN SWIFT (1667–1745) was born in Dublin and ordained in 1694, later becoming a dean. He was an ardent pacifist and wrote many pamphlets on religion and war. His most famous work, *Gulliver's Travels*, was, and still is, a controversial and powerful satire on man and human institutions. It is also one that appeals to adults and children alike.

ALFRED, LORD TENNYSON (1809–92) was the third son of the rector of Somersby, Lincolnshire. He began to have poetry published while he was a student at Cambridge University, and soon became the most popular poet of his time. He was made Poet Laureate in 1850 and the first Baron Tennyson in 1884.

P(AMELA) L(YNDON) TRAVERS (1906–96) was born in Australia and came to England when she was seventeen, working as a dancer and actress. She was recovering from an illness when she started work on the first book about Mary Poppins, which was published in 1934 and was an immediate success.

MARK TWAIN was the pen-name of SAMUEL LANGHORNE CLEMENS (1835–1910). He spent most of his childhood living in the town of Hannibal on the Mississippi river. His father died when he was twelve, so he had to work for his living. He started as a printer, working his way to New York and, after a period of time as a river-pilot on the Mississippi, he became a very successful journalist.

OSCAR WILDE (1856–1900) was born in Dublin, where he attended Trinity College, and he later went to Magdalen College, Oxford. While in Oxford he cultivated his long hair and unusual mode of dress. His intelligence and wit were famous. In addition to the stories he wrote for his sons, he also wrote several plays, of which the best known is *The Importance of Being Earnest*.

HENRY WILLIAMSON (1895–1977) was born in Blackheath, London. He was seriously wounded during the First World War and his experiences cast a shadow over the rest of his life. He always had a passion for wildlife, however, and this feeling led him to write the books about animals for which he is famous worldwide.

WILLIAM WORDSWORTH (1770–1850) was the son of an attorney and was educated at grammar school and Cambridge University. He is remembered as much for his love of the Lake District as for his poetry, for which he was justly famous, becoming Poet Laureate in 1843. Together with SAMUEL TAYLOR COLERIDGE he was responsible for a revival in the art of the English poem. They published *Lyrical Ballads* together in 1798.

ACKNOWLEDGEMENTS

The publishers gratefully acknowledge the following for permission to reproduce copyright material in this book.

The Royal Mail for the use of the illustration accompanying 'The Fairies' by William Allingham; from 'The Snow Queen' from *Hans Andersen's Fairy Tales*, retold by Naomi Lewis, published in Puffin Books 1981, copyright © Naomi Lewis, 1981, reprinted by kind permission of Naomi Lewis; from *Peter Pan* by J. M. Barrie, first published by Hodder & Stoughton 1911, copyright © the Great Ormond Street Hospital for Children, 1911, revived 1988, reprinted by permission of the Great Ormond Street Hospital for Children; 'Jim Who Ran Away from his Nurse' by Hilaire Belloc from *Cautionary Verse*, first published by Random House UK Ltd 1940, copyright © the Estate of Hilaire Belloc, 1964, reprinted by permission of the Peters Fraser & Dunlop Group Ltd; 'Ali Baba and the Forty Thieves' from *Sindbad the Sailor and Other Tales from the Arabian Nights* retold by N. J. Dawood, first published in the USA by Doubleday & Company Inc. 1978, published in Great Britain in Puffin Books 1989, copyright © N. J. Dawood, 1978, reprinted by kind permission of N. J. Dawood; 'The Listeners' and 'Tartary' by Walter de la Mare from *The Complete Poems of Walter de la Mare*, reprinted by permission of the Literary Trustees of Walter de la Mare, and The Society of Authors as their representative; from 'The Priory School' by Sir Arthur Conan Doyle, first published in *The Return of Sherlock Holmes*, copyright © Sheldon Reynolds, 1996, reprinted by permission of Jonathan Clowes Ltd, London, on behalf of Sheldon Reynolds, published in *The Great Adventures of Sherlock Holmes* in Puffin Books 1990; 'Ducks' Ditty' and 'The River Bank' by Kenneth Grahame from *The Wind in the Willows*, first published by Methuen 1908, copyright © The University Chest, Oxford, 1908, reprinted by permission of Curtis Brown, London, line illustrations copyright © E. H. Shepard under the Berne Convention, colouring copyright © E.H. Shepard and Methuen Children's Books Ltd, 1970, 1971, reproduced by permission of Curtis Brown, London; 'Robin Hood and the Butcher' from *The Adventures of Robin Hood* retold by Roger Lancelyn Green, published in Puffin Books 1956, copyright © Roger Lancelyn Green, 1956, reprinted by kind permission of The Literary Estate of Roger Lancelyn Green; 'Sir Gawain and the Green Knight' by Roger Lancelyn Green from *King Arthur and his Knights of the Round Table*, published in Puffin Books 1953, copyright © Roger Lancelyn Green, 1953, reprinted by kind permission of The Literary Estate of Roger Lancelyn Green; from 'Tiger! Tiger!' from *The Jungle Book*, first published 1894, 'If' and 'A Smugglers' Song' by Rudyard Kipling, all reprinted by permission of A. P. Watt Ltd on behalf of The National Trust for Places of Historic Interest and Natural Beauty; 'Sea Fever' by John Masefield from *Salt Water Ballads*, reprinted by kind permission of the Estate of John Masefield; from *Swallows and Amazons* by Arthur Ransome, first published by Jonathan Cape 1930, copyright © the Estate of Arthur Ransome, 1930, reprinted by kind permission of the Estate of Arthur Ransome and by permission of Random House UK Ltd.

Every effort has been made to trace the copyright holders. The publishers would like to hear from any copyright holder not acknowledged.